A step-by-step guide to surviving a haunted house

Addison Acres

Addison Acres

A step-by-step guide to surviving a haunted house

ISBN: 978-1-923410-05-3

Edited by SJ Buckley

Cover Art by Addison Acres

Cover Photography from Canva Pro

Notes and Warnings

This book contains mature themes, including a romantic relationship between two stepbrothers, with low heat sex scenes. There are also horror themes, including violent attacks by ghosts, blood, and some graphic descriptions consistent with the genre. There is a very brief, on-page sexual assault by a ghostly entity via possession. Mentions and depictions of anxiety attacks and side effects from medications are made throughout the story. There is also a brief, historical mention of the death of an animal.

Readers are cautioned to use their discretion when deciding to read. Your mental health is of the utmost importance.

Please note that as this book is set in Australia, Australian English and Australian lingo is used throughout.

CHAPTER 1

Dawson

"Hey everyone!" Dawson Miller said into his phone camera after hitting *Go Live* on his Vewz social media account. "Wow, you guys are *keen!* It's just gone seven a.m. and I didn't expect so many of you to be online this early!"

Numerous comments were already flooding in, most with more than one exclamation mark.

I love you Dawson!!

Hi from Clarkson!

You said you'd be live, so of course I'm gonna wake up just for you.

Seeing your face first thing in the morning is better than coffee!!!

I love you!!!

Hi from Melbourne.

It's late afternoon here in LA.

When are we gonna get married?!?

He scrolled the comments coming in, picking out a couple to respond to. "Hi, over in Clarkson. We drove past that way about an hour ago. Aww,

it's so sweet you got up just for me. G'day LA! Good to see you online."
He gave the camera his most winning smile. "You guys make getting up
early so worth it. I gotta admit, when the alarm on my Quest smartwatch
went off this morning, I almost cried, but you guys have made the morning
better already." Dawson mentally ticked off one mention of a sponsor. He
tried to mention all his major sponsors in his Live videos, and even if it was
sometimes hard to make it seem natural, he did his best, as he found his
fans were more responsive when it just felt like part of the conversation. His
sponsors didn't seem to care too much, though, as long as he plugged them
the contracted number of times a week, but it was a matter of principle for
him. "Is it too early for a fit check?" he asked, but did it anyway, holding
the phone out a little farther to show off more of his outfit. "It's moving
day so I'm dressed for comfort, and I gotta say, this shirt from TK Lane is
killing it. And what do we think of the bucket hat from Kozi? You likey?"

His screen lit up with more comments, as well as a flurry of gift icons.

It looks great but it covers your gorgeous curls.

The colour matches your eyes!

ILY Dawson!

U look tired. U ok babe?

Nice hat.

Dawson tipped the brim of the hat at the camera. "Why thank you,
I'm rather fond of the colour myself. Kozi Hats have the best range of
colours and this blue is stunning." He fluttered his lashes outrageously,
which caused another rush of icons for gifts and heart emojis. "But yeah, I
am tired. It is *way* too early and I need coffee."

"Don't believe a word he says," Chip called from the driver's seat. "We
stopped at the roadhouse thirty k's back and he got sufficiently caffeinated
there."

Dawson pouted at the camera. "Judas!" he cried, and then turned the camera so Chip was in the shot. "Say hi to Chip, everyone!"

The comments went wild.

Chip!!!

OMG, I love you Chip!

When is Chip gonna get his own account?

You two are the best. I love u both!

Morning Chip.

Fuck Chip, I wanna have your babies so bad.

**swoon* Love you boys.*

Chip waved dutifully and Dawson let the camera linger on him to give the fans a chance to ogle him properly. His stepbrother was a regular in his videos and his fans absolutely loved him. They were the complete opposites of each other—if Dawson was the white swan with his pale skin, head of crazy blond curls, and bright blue eyes, then Chip was most definitely the black swan. His bronze skin seemed to glint with health in the early morning sunshine, and the light turned his hazel eyes an almost amaretto colour under his thick dark brows. His shoulder-length black hair was pushed back from his face by a backwards-facing baseball cap, and his square jaw was covered in a day's worth of stubble. Fine lines appeared around his eyes as he glanced briefly at the camera again and smiled, which set off his dimples, and even more heart emojis filled the screen.

Dawson grinned at Chip over the back of the phone and then turned it back to point at himself. He caught Chip's good-natured eye roll as he turned his attention back to the road. "Well, today is the day!" he told his viewers. "As you all know, Grandpa Miller died last year, and he left me and Chip his place in Brockman. We weren't sure if we should just sell it or not, but we decided that given the shitty rental market right now and the sky-high cost of living, we'd make the move to the country instead."

More comments appeared, commiserating about how hard it was to find somewhere to live and how lucky he was to be moving into a place with his brother, with others expressing their heartbreak that he was moving away from the city.

"We haven't been there in years so we're not sure what to expect. Grandpa Miller was sick for a few years so I have a feeling the place might be a little run-down. The cottage is like, a hundred and fifty years old or something, so I reckon we'll have a bit of work ahead of us, but you know how handy Chip is so I think we'll manage." He chatted a little more about how they were going to try and do as much of the work as they could themselves but then started to wind up the Live. "Okay, guys, thanks so much for joining me today. I'll post later today to give you a tour of the place but for now I'm gonna get going. Much love. Dawson out."

He hit *end* and then reached over to grab his coffee that was still in the cup holder. He noticed that Chip was frowning a little. "What?" he asked.

"Daw," Chip said in a low voice. "Was all of that really necessary?"

Dawson avoided his stepbrother's gaze. "What do you mean?" he asked, but he already knew exactly what Chip was alluding to.

"Perth might be small, but at least it was large enough your more stalkery followers couldn't pinpoint your exact location. Brockman is tiny. I'm not comfortable with you telling people exactly which small town we're moving to."

"None of my followers are stalkers," he asserted.

"Seriously, dude? *That's* the part you're stuck on?" Chip's voice was incredulous and he looked away from the road to narrow those hazel eyes at him. "Are we forgetting about that Sasha chick? You know, the one who found out where you went to the gym, followed you there every day for three weeks, and then finally stole your sweat towel? Or the guy who keyed a love heart into your car when he saw you at the shops? Or how about the chick who made *thirteen* different Vewz accounts so she could spam every one of your videos with comments telling you how good she is at sucking cock?"

Dawson flushed a little but couldn't help jumping to their defence. "They're just fans, man. They can't help but be excited. I know they get a little intense, but without them I wouldn't have the sponsors I have. I'd have to —" He shuddered a little. "—urgh, get a *job*."

"Hey, we both know you work hard at this and it's not as easy as it looks. You put in longer hours than me." Chip reached over and clapped him on the shoulder. "Just because influencers weren't a thing twenty years ago, doesn't mean it's not a legitimate career now."

A wave of warmth flooded him at Chip's unrelenting support. It had always been that way, from the very first time he met Tate "Chip" George on his first day of kindy. Attached at the hip and instant best friends, they'd almost been an extension of each other. When Chip's mum had passed away from an aneurysm when they were only seven, Dawson's mum, Carolyn, had stepped in to help out. She made sure that Chip and his Dad, Harry, ate regular meals, she catered for the wake, and she made sure that Chip had everything he needed for school. Even when the worst of Harry's grief passed, she kept it up, looking after all three of her "boys". A few years later, when Carolyn and Harry sat them both down to explain they'd fallen in love and were going to get married, Dawson and Chip had been over the moon, they'd officially be brothers.

"You know Mum and Harry don't exactly see it that way."

Chip shrugged. "They might not understand but they can't deny your success." He flicked on the indicator and then pulled out to overtake the roadtrain they had come up behind.

Dawson let his eyes close briefly until he felt the car move back into the left hand lane. He had never been a confident driver and was grateful Chip had volunteered to drive them the two hours to Brockman. The larger trucks made him nervous, and if he'd been the one driving, the trip would have taken twice as long as he would have stayed behind the first road train they'd gotten stuck behind. He'd left his car at their parents' place for now, not sure whether he'd bother to bring it up.

"They'd still be happier if I had a *real* job."

"I think they're just worried about longevity," Chip said. "But once your music career takes off, I think they'll feel better about it all."

Dawson snorted. It was a sad state of affairs when a career as a musician was considered a more stable career than what he was currently doing. "Maybe."

They fell into a comfortable silence for the remainder of the drive. Dawson grabbed a little footage of the rolling paddocks, bright yellow with flowering canola as far as the eye could see. The drive was vaguely familiar from when he'd last visited, but it had been at least five years since he'd been up this way so enough had changed to make it all new and fresh. When his grandpa had fallen sick, he'd made the trip into Perth for treatment so often that Dawson and Chip had visited with him at their parents' place instead of making the drive to Brockman. It had just seemed easier at the time, with both of them studying and working, but now Dawson just felt regret he'd not made more of an effort.

They were soon entering the small town of Brockman and driving through the sleepy streets. The highway branched off and bypassed the place five kilometres out of town, so the heavy trucks were absent from the main street. A few early-morning commuters were out and about but at this time of the morning, what passed for peak-hour traffic wouldn't hit for another half an hour or so.

The main drag in town was the commercial centre and consisted of an IGA, a branch of the community bank, the Brockman Arms—the one and only pub in town—and a dozen other small businesses that rounded out the not-so-bustling main street. They drove past all that Brockman had to offer until Chip made a left turn off the main road and headed towards the outskirts of town. They passed a small stone church and ancient cemetery, a few houses on quarter acre blocks, then crossed over a bridge where the river was flowing freely after the late winter rains. Chip slowed the car a couple of kilometres further down the road and turned right into a burnt-orange gravel driveway.

Dawson jumped out of the car to open the gate, and got straight back in, not bothering to close it afterwards. He knew by the time they unpacked and settled in, they'd have a list of things they'd forgotten to bring with them and would need to head into town to do a shop. They meandered up the long, winding drive until they came to a stop in front of the small stone farmhouse from their childhood.

Chip turned off the engine and they were both quiet as they stayed in the car, just looking at the house, lost in thought.

"I guess this is home now," Chip finally said, breaking the silence.

Dawson nodded and looked over at him, giving him a smile. "It is."

"How long until you reckon you'll be sick of me?" Chip joked. "It's been a while since we lived together."

It was true. They'd chosen separate paths after high school—Dawson went to uni at Curtin where he'd done his Bachelor of Arts, majoring in Digital and Social Media, and Chip had gone straight into the workforce, getting a tech-support position with a startup company. The company had grown in leaps and bounds and he still worked for them, but now in a management position, leading the support team he had started on. He'd worked in the northern suburbs, whereas Dawson was at uni south of the river, which meant they'd both moved out of home and into their own places with various housemates. They'd remained close, visiting each other several times a week and hanging out on weekends, but they'd not actually lived together since they'd been at their parents' place. During COVID, Chip's job had transformed into a remote position, which meant he'd be working from home as well. They'd be spending a hell of a lot of time together, without the freedom of the city and metro areas close by to escape to.

Some would find it suffocating, but not Dawson. First and foremost, Chip was his best friend and his favourite person in the entire world. He wasn't at all worried that they'd get on each other's nerves. "I'm not gonna get sick of you," he assured him. "I reckon I'm the luckiest guy on the planet, to get to set up house with you."

An odd expression flickered over Chip's face, but before Dawson could analyse it further, Chip was giving him his wide smile and unbuckling his belt. "Let's check this place out then."

CHAPTER 2

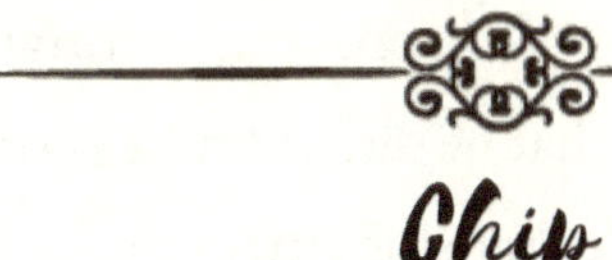

Chip

Urgh, why the hell did Dawson have to go and say that? *I reckon I'm the luckiest guy on the planet to be setting up house with you.* It would be so easy to take it out of context, to assign it meaning it didn't have, and dammit, Chip's heart wished more than anything that Dawson *had* meant it in a romantic way. But of course, he didn't. He couldn't. Because they were brothers. Maybe brothers by marriage, but brothers nonetheless.

But oh how Chip wanted more.

He'd been in love with Dawson for as long as he could remember. Even before puberty he was more attached than other kids to their best friends. He remembered telling his mum he was going to marry Dawson. She'd hugged him tightly and told him she would be blessed to have Dawson as a son-in-law as he was a great kid and she was sure he'd grow into an even greater man. She'd died a week later, standing at the sink washing dishes when the undiagnosed aneurysm burst, and she never got to see Dawson grow up. Never got to see how right she was, how great Dawson turned out to be. But at least she never lived to see Chip pining over his best friend with no hope in hell of his dreams ever coming true.

Dawson had never shown any interest in guys, let alone in Chip. He was a staunch ally of the LGBTQI+ community, but that seemed to be the extent of it. When they were fourteen, Dawson had been gushing to Chip over how much he liked Katie Atkinson and asked Chip if there was anyone in their class that he liked. He'd not specifically asked if there was a girl he liked, but instead had kept it pronoun neutral, like he already had an idea. Chip had confessed that he didn't find *any* of their classmates attractive, girls or boys. He didn't share his attraction for Dawson because he wasn't that brave, but it had been scary enough admitting how different he was.

Dawson hadn't even blinked. He'd pulled out his laptop and done a Google search, and asked Chip what felt like a hundred different questions. He'd stumbled his way through the answers, skirting the truth when they would give away his feelings for his stepbrother, but he must have given enough information for Dawson to come to a conclusion.

"So I think you probably identify as demisexual *and* pansexual," Dawson had said with all the confidence only a fourteen year old boy could manifest.

"What does that mean?" Chip had asked, terrified it meant he was attracted to someone who was kind of related to him. He knew that was definitely frowned upon.

"It means you need an emotional connection to someone *before* you get any other feelings for them," Dawson had explained. "That's the demi part. Pansexual means you like hearts not parts."

"What now?"

"You know, like, it doesn't matter what gender someone is, it's who they are as a person that matters."

For someone who had been relying on a ten minute Google search for information, Dawson had gotten it pretty spot on. To this day, Chip still identified as both demi and pan. Not that having a designation helped him any. He'd never had any sort of physical relationship other than with his hand, and the only emotional relationship he'd had was his one-sided love affair with his stepbrother.

He was absolutely pathetic.

He sighed as he crossed the overgrown expanse of front lawn that was drowning in winter grass, and jogged up the three steps to the front door. A wide tin-roofed verandah circled the cottage, the old-fashioned, red-painted concrete faded and dusty.

"You okay?" Dawson asked from behind his right shoulder.

"Yeah, all good, man," he lied.

Chip didn't have to turn to see that Dawson was frowning. He'd always been good at telling when Chip was full of shit but he was also good at not pushing. Dawson always respected when he didn't want to talk.

"You mind if I get some footage?" Dawson asked instead.

Chip turned and saw that he had pulled out his GoPro. Dawson preferred to use his phone for Lives but his GoPro for capturing other footage, and it was almost an extension of his body, he used it so often. "Yeah, no worries."

Chip had been rather camera shy when Dawson had started his journey on social media but he'd soon gotten accustomed to being filmed. His old housemates used to tease him over how many thirsty comments he got from Dawson's followers, telling him he could get laid anytime he wanted thanks to his secondhand Vewz fame. They even insinuated that was the reason he so willingly went along with every silly trend and viral video that Dawson made. He'd never bothered sharing his sexuality with them and would just laugh off the comments. He certainly wasn't going to tell them he did it just to make Dawson happy. Just to see that blinding smile on his angelic face.

Dawson began to film, narrating everything they were doing, and Chip stayed quiet so as not to ruin the sound. He slipped the key into the lock and it turned with a soft click. He glanced over at Dawson, unable to help the grin as he pushed open the door to their new house. Their new *home*.

The door opened into a hallway that ran the length of the house. To the right was a small loungeroom. Despite the wide verandah and the grimy windows, enough sunlight filtered into the room to send dust motes dancing. A thick layer of dust lay over the floor and spider webs hung from every corner. The room was high ceilinged but still cosy, with exposed beams and an open fireplace on the far side.

To the left of the hall was a combined kitchen and dining area. It had last been renovated in the seventies and had mustard yellow benchtops, orange patterned tiles on the wall behind the stove, and cupboards that were painted with fading mint-green paint.

They both grimaced a little at the sight.

"Wow, I do *not* remember it being this hideous," Dawson said as he panned the camera around.

"Neither do I," Chip agreed.

"I'm so sorry for your retinas, guys," Dawson said to the camera, speaking to his viewers. "Here, this will make up for it a bit." He grinned as he swung the camera around to face Chip and then panned up and down his body. "I know a lot of you are big fans of these shorts."

Chip groaned and rolled his eyes but didn't move away as Dawson filmed him. He wasn't a huge fan of being considered a heart-throb by his stepbrother's fans, but he *did* kind of like the way Dawson played it up. It almost felt like he agreed with them. Almost. He'd chosen his clothes that morning for ease of movement and comfort. The running shorts brushed the tops of his thighs and his tank top was cut low at the sides, which showed off his biceps. He wasn't hugely muscular by any means but he was solid, with great arms—even if he did say so himself—and powerful thighs. He didn't have rock-hard abs and his stomach was a little soft, but he was fit enough to send half of Dawson's fan's frothing at the mouth. He just wished it was Dawson drooling over him instead.

Dawson finally moved the camera away, but not before giving Chip a cheeky wink that went straight to his cock. He hurried from the room so as not to get his semi caught on film—something he had no doubt Dawson would pick up on during the editing process.

He headed down the hall and opened doors as he went. There were two bedrooms opposite each other halfway down the hall, then a bathroom at the end on one side and a linen closet on the other. A door at the very end of the hall opened up into a sunroom, and he could just make out through the windows the old laundry off to the side of the house and the small wooden hut that housed an outdoor toilet.

"Oh man, I forgot we had a genuine outback dunny!" Dawson exclaimed from behind, then rushed past him to fumble with the lock on the back door. Once he got it open, he hurried outside to film the small wooden hut that was probably infested with red backs.

Chip left him to it and meandered back down the hall to check out the bedrooms more closely. They were both large and roomy and almost identical to one another. One faced east and still bore the imprints in the carpet from where Grandpa Miller's bed had once sat. Their parents had made the trip up after the funeral and had packed up the personal belongings that Carolyn had wanted to keep, and then had arranged for everything else to be donated to the op shop in town. They were lucky they didn't have to worry about moving everything out before moving their own stuff in.

The other bedroom faced west and Chip earmarked that for Dawson. He tended to stay up later at night to edit and catch up on social media trends whereas Chip went to bed earlier as he had to be awake to start work at eight a.m.. He wouldn't mind the morning sun streaming in his window but it would disrupt Dawson's sleep. He headed back through to the room he'd claim as his own and dropped his backpack inside the door.

Dawson came back inside, his GoPro turned off, and leaned up against the doorway to Chip's room. He was five inches taller than Chip, and he was lithe and lanky. His face was round, almost cherubic, which was only accentuated by the mass of blond curls that stuck out in every direction from under his bucket hat. He grinned at Chip with genuine excitement and happiness, which was all for Chip and not the fans who would eventually watch his videos. It never failed to make his heart stutter. "I can't believe we have our own place, man!"

Chip grinned back. "I know. It's kinda crazy. I didn't think I'd ever own a place of my own, ya know?"

"Seriously, I'm so glad we get to do this together," Dawson told him earnestly. "I don't think I could have made the move to a small town by myself. I would never survive without you."

"Same," was all that Chip could manage.

"What time's the truck coming?" Dawson asked.

Chip glanced at his watch. "Shit, soon. We'd better get a move on if we want to be ready for them."

The removalists were scheduled for ten a.m. so they hurried to the car to grab out the vacuum and the cleaning supplies that Carolyn had insisted they bring with them. The old house was filthy, and Chip really did not want to have to move their furniture more than once if they didn't get the carpets cleaned before the truck arrived.

They worked quickly, divvying up the tasks between them. Chip took the floors while Dawson put his height to good use and attacked the cobwebs. They didn't have time to do much more than that, but it was at least a start. Chip figured they'd be painting soon enough anyway so there was no need to clean the walls, and the windows could wait until they were moved in properly. He was giving the bathroom a quick scrubbing when he heard the sound of a horn beeping at the front of the house.

"Tate George?" the driver of the truck asked as he and Dawson headed outside to greet the removalists.

"That's me," Chip said, extending his hand for a shake. Dawson had given him the nickname of Chip on the first day they met, after he shared his bag of chips with him at recess. It had started off as Tater Chip, but he soon shortened it to Chip and that had stuck for good. Even his parents, as well as Carolyn, had called him that. He used Tate for work, to keep his professional and private life somewhat separated, but the only other time he heard the name was in an official capacity. "This is Dawson," he said, making the introductions.

"Graham," the driver said. "The young bloke with me is Aiden. Did you want to do a walk-through with us to give us an idea where you want everything?"

Chip agreed and then he and Dawson helped the removalists empty the truck. At one point he was helping Aiden with a heavy bookcase when he looked up to find Dawson filming them. "Really?" he asked, trying to sound exasperated but sounding more amused than anything.

"What?" Dawson asked innocently. "I'm just giving your fans what they want." He held up his free arm and flexed his much smaller bicep.

"Firstly, they're *your* fans not mine, and secondly, maybe you could help with this instead before we drop it?"

It took most of the day to get themselves sorted. Graham and Aiden were nice enough to help them carry their gym equipment out to one of the sheds, which took a few trips. After the removalists left, they got the fridge turned on so they could unpack the eskies they'd brought with them, and they demolished a couple of vegemite sandwiches each for lunch. Then they got their beds assembled and made so they'd at least have somewhere to sleep that night before they decided where the rest of the furniture should go.

They decided to turn the sunroom into their office and they each claimed a corner for their workspaces—Chip with his work computer and Dawson with his editing suite. The loungeroom had their large screen TV and gaming systems, and the kitchen became a dumping ground for the random boxes full of cutlery and dishes, small appliances, and the pantry staples they'd brought with them.

"I'm knackered," Dawson complained, stretching his arms above his head, his spine popping audibly.

Chip steadfastly refused to look at the pale stretch of stomach that was now on display, and instead put his hands on his aching lower back and tried to stretch out himself. "I feel fucking fifty," he whined. He looked wistfully through the doorway across the hall to the loungeroom and their extremely comfortable couch before dismissing the idea. If he sat down, he was never going to get back up. "Should we take a proper look outside and see what we're dealing with?" he suggested.

Dawson grimaced but nodded. "Sure. It just occurred to me we don't have mains water out here, do we?"

Chip shook his head. "Nope. There's two tanks and I *think* a bore, but don't quote me on that."

They meandered outside, shoulders brushing as they walked companionably side by side. The property was one of the original farms from when Brockman had been established by European settlers, but over the years it had been subdivided off until only eighteen acres remained. The stone cottage was the original homestead, built in 1864. They were lucky the house wasn't heritage listed, so they could make some modifications to it, though neither of them wanted to change it too much. Just add a few modern conveniences, like air-conditioning and surround sound for the entertainment system.

There were two large sheds about fifty metres away from the house, side by side, with a smaller wood shed a short distance away. The largest of the sheds was the one they'd earmarked as their gym and they stepped inside to better inspect the space.

Dawson pivoted on his feet, surveying the area. "You know, this could be a really sweet entertaining space as well as the gym," he suggested. He held out his hands, as if framing one corner. "A bar over there, pool table there, and some comfy couches."

Chip raised a brow at him. "Sure," he drawled. "An entertaining space for all the *entertaining* you'll want to do here."

The pink flush on Dawson's cheeks was adorable. "You never know," he protested.

Chip crossed to him and slung an arm around his shoulder, pulling him against him in a one-armed hug. "Daw, I love you, man, but you are one of the most introverted people I know. You're not gonna want people round here, like, ever."

Dawson huffed and crossed his arms over his chest, but he did lean into the hug. "I have over eight hundred thousand followers I'll have you know. I don't think that makes me an introvert."

"That's your *job*," Chip argued. "When you switch off from that, you don't like to do anything but chill on the couch. You hate partying and you hate socialising."

"I don't see *you* out clubbing or partying either," he retorted with a pout.

Chip shrugged. "Maybe not, but I like hanging out with other people as well. We'll be a lot more isolated out here so it's important to get to know people around town."

Dawson snorted. "You thinking of joining the old blokes down at the Men's Shed?"

Chip twisted around until he had Dawson in a headlock and he knuckled the top of his head. "Fuck off," he laughed.

"Let me go, you bastard," Dawson cried, squirming around until he hooked an ankle around the back of Chip's knee and took them both to the hard concrete in an ungainly heap. "Ow," he whined, as Chip's elbow connected with his sternum and then the rest of his weight landed on top of him. "Get off me."

"Nah, I'm pretty comfy here, man," Chip declared and settled himself down so he was crushing his stepbrother beneath him. "I think I might take a nap."

"You weigh a fucking tonne!" Dawson huffed, trying unsuccessfully to push Chip off him.

"I'm only eighty-three kilos, fuck you very much."

"Are you sure?"

Just for that, Chip wriggled a little, pushing his knee painfully against Dawson's thigh. "Sorry, what was that?" he sing-songed as Dawson grunted in pain.

"I hate you," Dawson wheezed.

"Nah you don't. You love me." He smacked a wet kiss to Dawson's cheek, and was sure to leave behind a heap of spit.

"You're so fucking gross," Dawson complained, reaching up to wipe at his cheek.

"You know it." Chip finally took pity on him and leapt to his feet, then held out a hand to haul Dawson up as well. "Come on. Let's go check out the other shed."

"So, what did you mean before?" Dawson asked as Chip wriggled the rusty padbolt on the door. "How are you gonna meet people?"

"Cricket season starts soon. There should be a local team so I figured I'd join up," Chip said, and then grunted in triumph as the padbolt finally gave way and he could slide it free. He pushed open the door and grinned as he walked inside. It must have been Grandpa Miller's woodworking shed as it was still full of workbenches and tools, and the smell of cut wood lingered in the air. In one corner near the roller door was a dusty ride-on mower. "Sweet." He picked up a plane from the bench and examined it, and said over his shoulder, "You should join up too."

"I haven't played in years, man," Dawson said with a shake of his head.

"You might be a little rusty but this isn't International Test Cricket. It's just for fun."

"I dunno . . ."

"Think about it?"

He finally nodded and they left the shed to continue to explore.

The side of the house was a mess, stacked high with bits and pieces of junk that Grandpa Miller had probably thought would come in handy one day. There were rusty forty-gallon drums, rolls of ringlock fencing, planks of wood, pieces of tin, a wire cage, a rickety wooden ladder, a rusted wheelbarrow, and piles and piles of old bricks and pavers. Since nothing on the property was made from bricks, and there were no paved areas, Chip could only guess their grandpa had gotten them off someone "just in case".

"Let's leave this for later," Dawson said, eying the pile dubiously.

Chip nodded. "Just know that 'later' may in fact be 'never'."

"I'm okay with that," Dawson said.

They inspected the tanks—one fed off the house roof and the smaller tank off the sheds. They were both full after the winter rains and Chip was grateful. He knew in dry summers, Grandpa Miller had had to get water trucked in and that negated any savings made from being off the grid for their water. If he had a choice, Chip would have preferred to pay yearly water rates and then monthly bills to be guaranteed a water supply but he wasn't in the city anymore so he'd have to get used to doing a lot of things the hard way.

There was a large citrus orchard beyond the house yard, but the trees were getting too old to produce fruit regularly now. The original farm had been used for wheat and other crops, as well as sheep, but in the early eighties the family had subdivided for the first time and had branched out into citrus farming. This was the only remaining orchard from that time and Chip had fond memories of playing there as a kid. He was pretty sure if they looked hard enough, they might even find the remains of the cubby house they'd built over the Christmas holidays when they'd been eleven.

Beyond the orchard was a dam, the water dark and still in the fading light. Chip remembered swimming in it when they were kids under the watchful eyes of their parents, and he knew it was much deeper than it looked. Beyond the dam was thick, dense bush, and the mixture of weeds and native grass around the dam was littered with roo droppings. "We'll have to be careful of ticks," he noted, nodding towards the poo.

Dawson shuddered and began to scratch absently at the back of his neck. "Christ, I didn't even think of that."

"I'm sure the chemist will have some of that freeze spray for them. It's too late to head into town now but we can go tomorrow and grab some."

"Sounds good. Let's go and make something for dinner," Dawson said, turning back towards the house. "I'm fucking starving."

"Same. Food and couch sound really good right now."

"Yes they do." Dawson turned to Chip with a cheeky grin and said, "Race ya?" And then he was off, darting away into the orchard.

Chip gave a challenging shout and took off after him, leaving his laughter floating behind him on the breeze.

CHAPTER 3

Dawson

They'd crashed relatively early that night, both exhausted from the day. Dawson had quickly edited a video to post while Chip made them an easy dinner of pasta and sauce, which they ate standing at the kitchen bench.

There was no moon, and the night was the sort of dark you simply didn't get in the suburbs. Before he'd gone to bed, Dawson had stepped outside to get his phone charger from the car and he'd been amazed at how bright the stars were. Above him, the Milky Way was resplendent in all her glory and he'd stood, awestruck, for a long minute, just craning his neck to take it all in. He didn't have his phone on him, and he didn't bother going to get it. He knew that footage of the sky wouldn't hold a candle to reality, but deep down, he selfishly just wanted the moment for himself. He didn't want to share it with his hundreds of thousands of fans. He didn't even want to share it with Chip. He just wanted to be alone, with the vastness of space above him shining brilliantly from a million miles away.

He'd fallen into bed soon after and was asleep almost as soon as his head hit the pillow—a deep, dreamless sleep.

It was the cold that woke him.

He jolted awake to find he was absolutely freezing. No matter how tightly he clutched the blankets to him, his entire body was shivering uncontrollably. It was the sort of bone-aching cold he had rarely experienced. The day had been mild and he'd not expected it to get so cold overnight. As he sat up in bed to check the time on his phone, he saw his breath misting in the air, and realised it had surpassed chilly and was almost freezing.

Dawson had no idea if the spare blankets had been unpacked yet or which box they were in. He'd not unpacked the majority of his clothing yet either so he didn't know where his jumpers were. As his teeth chattered noisily in the dark, he knew he wasn't going to get any more sleep when he was this cold. Slipping out of bed, he darted from his room and across the hall.

Chip's room was cold but much warmer than Dawson's had been. From the light of his phone screen, he could just make out the lump under the covers that was Chip. Dawson pulled the blanket up and slipped underneath, scooching across the mattress until he was pressed as close against Chip's warm body as he could get.

The minute Dawson's cold hand made contact with Chip's bare back, his stepbrother jerked awake with a gasp. "Jesus fucking Christ," he swore, flinching away. "What the hell?"

"S-sorry," Dawson managed from between his chattering teeth. "It's s-s-so c-cold in my room."

Chip rolled over. "What do you mean?" he asked, even as he reached out a hand. "It's not that—holy fuck, you're freezing!" he exclaimed as he felt the chill of Dawson's skin. Without another word, he pulled Dawson into his arms and surrounded him with his warmth.

Dawson couldn't stop shivering and he wanted to simply climb inside Chip and stay there forever. Chip had always run warmer than him and he was never more grateful for that than now. Dawson had to ball his hands into fists against his stomach to resist the urge to reach out and press his frigid palms against Chip's warm skin.

Of course, Chip knew him better than anyone. He chuckled—a low, throaty noise due to sleep—and he grabbed one of Dawson's hands and pressed it flat against his belly. "It's fine," he said. "You can leech all my warmth."

"Why i-i-s it so c-c-cold?" Dawson stuttered, his jaw beginning to ache from his chattering teeth. He unfurled his other hand and pressed it flat against his other on Chip's stomach. He looked so solid, built from pure muscle, but his stomach was a little soft and the skin was velvety smooth and radiating heat like a roaring fire. Would it be weird if Dawson scooted down and buried his cold nose against his stomach?

Yeah . . . yeah, that would probably be weird.

"Do you think you're coming down with something?" Chip asked. "It's really not that cold tonight, Daw. Maybe you're getting sick?"

"I d-d-on't f-f-feel sick," he chattered.

"Well, *something* is making you shiver worse than Ed Sheeran." Chip's body twisted as he reached behind himself to grab his phone off the bedside table. Dawson could feel the ripple of muscles and the protrusion of his hip bone as he moved, and he pressed even closer to chase the warmth that was moving away from him.

"Are you sure you're not part reptile?" Chip teased, as he settled down on his back with Dawson plastered to his side. With one hand, he clumsily unlocked his phone screen while the other rubbed warmth into Dawson's back. "According to this, it's eleven degrees." He didn't state the obvious, that it wasn't anywhere near cold enough to warrant this reaction, and for that, Dawson was grateful. He just put his phone down and wrapped his other arm over Dawson's shoulder. "You warming up any?"

His teeth were no longer trying to clatter their way out of his jaw and he could feel warmth finally seeping back into his extremities. He nodded against Chip's shoulder. "Yeah. Thanks, man."

"Anytime. Try and get some sleep, yeah?"

He nodded again, letting his eyes close. Chip was so warm and cosy that it didn't take long for the pull of sleep to drag him under. Just before he passed into oblivion, he felt the gentle pressure of lips against his temple.

Chip was gone when Dawson woke the next morning, but he had found the spare blankets and had piled another two on top of Dawson to keep him warm. It worked a little too well as he was a sweaty, sweltering mess under the heavy weight of the blankets. He pushed them off, exposing his overheated body to the cool air of the morning, and he lay there, listening to the unfamiliar sounds of their new home.

He could hear the happy warbling of magpies outside competing with the screech of the pink and greys and the caw of a raven. From down the hall there was the sound of a box shifting and then the clinking of glassware. Then the creak of floorboards, and a moment later a pipe squealed as the kitchen tap turned on.

Deciding it was time to get his arse out of bed, Dawson climbed out and headed straight for the bathroom. His curls were plastered to his face with sweat and he wondered if it was simply because Chip had gone overboard with the blankets or if he *was* coming down with something. The last thing he wanted was to get sick when they had so much to do so he'd just have to keep his fingers crossed.

After showering, he wrapped a towel around his waist and headed through to his own bedroom. He threw his sleep shorts and tee onto the bed and grabbed his phone from where it was charging on the bedside table. He flipped the camera to forward facing and hit record, lifting a hand to wave at the camera and flexing his muscles a little as he did so. He was lean and toned, and he always got an influx of new subscribers when he posted thirst traps. That kept his sponsors happy, so even though it made him feel like an idiot, he buried his insecurities and got on with the job.

"Morning, sunshines," he said into the camera. "It's the first full day at our new place and I can't wait to share it with you all!".

He ended the recording, added a quick filter, some hashtags, and then posted it. He tossed his phone on the bed and crossed to his dresser, pausing as he caught sight of his reflection in the mirror. Yeah, the filter had definitely been needed that morning. He had dark bags under his eyes and he looked utterly exhausted. In the fickle world of social media, it didn't take much to lose momentum and he knew he constantly had to be on his game. He really could not afford to get sick right now.

He grabbed some jeans and a tee out of the drawers and got dressed, took his anti-anxiety meds, then ran a hand through his still-damp curls. There was no point trying to wrangle them into any semblance of order as they had a mind of their own. He'd shaved his head once, sick of trying to tame the curls, but he'd ended up looking like a sad nineties punk rocker and had worn a hat for three months solid until he had some length back. He'd only trimmed his hair since then and the curls touched his shoulders now.

Giving up on his hair, Dawson ran through a mental checklist of things he had to get done today. He was expecting a contract extension to come through from Rivalry Shades, a fairly newish sponsor for him. They didn't have mail delivery this far out of town so he needed to hit the post office to arrange a PO box and then update his mailing address with all his sponsors.

Then, he needed to check out the latest viral videos for new trends, and depending on what was out there, create new content to release. He also wanted to spend some time working on a new song. That was all on top of the unpacking and organising from the move, and figuring out what repairs and minor renovations were the priority.

Dawson took a deep breath and decided that first of all, he needed coffee. So he headed out into the hall, and then doubled back to grab his phone. He frowned as he searched the bed, sure that's where he'd put it, but there was nothing there apart from his sleep clothes. After scanning the room he spotted the phone on top of the dresser and figured he must have taken it with him when he got dressed. He shrugged and grabbed it, before heading through to the kitchen.

Chip had obviously been busy. There was an empty cardboard box by the door that was filled with the broken-down remnants of other packing boxes. On the kitchen counter was the kettle, toaster, and blender. Their crockery was stacked neatly on the bench, sorted into piles.

"Hey." Dawson greeted him as he entered, rubbing at his eyes.

"Morning," Chip replied, his lips tugging down into a frown as he took in his appearance. He crossed to him and laid the back of his hand against Dawson's forehead. "You feeling okay?"

Shrugging, he said, "Eh. I think so. Just tired."

"Do you still have chills?"

"Nah, man, I woke up so fucking hot. I'll need to wash your sheets since I sweated all over them."

Concern flooded Chip's features. "You've got a fever?" he asked.

Dawson rolled his eyes. "Nope. *Someone* tried to suffocate me with blankets which made me overheat."

Chip didn't look at all abashed by that. "As soon as I got up, you started shivering again. I didn't want you getting cold."

"Why were you up so early anyway?" Dawson asked, ignoring the flush of warmth he felt, knowing how much Chip cared about him. He was so damn lucky to have him, not just as a stepbrother but a best friend.

"I wanted to get in a workout this morning," he said. "And get a start on unpacking." He gestured at the cupboards. "I've got all the cutlery away, and the pots and pans. I've put everything above the cupboards that I think they should go in but have a look and move them if you prefer somewhere else."

Dawson snorted. "Dude, I don't really care where the mugs live."

"Some people have very strong opinions about where the mugs live!" Chip protested.

"Like who?"

"Dave used to have an absolute conniption if they weren't in the cupboard closest to his fancy coffee machine," Chip explained, talking about one of his old housemates.

"Well, I'm not Dave and we don't have a fancy coffee machine, so I'm sure wherever you've chosen for the mugs to live will be fine." He nodded at the kettle. "Speaking of, you want a cuppa?"

"Nah, I've had one. Kettle just boiled though."

"Cheers." He opened the pantry and found the jar of Moccona easily enough and set about making a coffee. He liked a coffee from a café as much as the next person but he preferred to drink instant when he was at home. His mum had a Nespresso machine, and when he stayed there for a week while his place was having some wiring fixed, he'd put on two kilos just from drinking so much milk. It hadn't been disastrous, since he could afford to put the weight on, but a pair of boardies from one of his sponsors had been a bit snug afterwards so he'd been sure to go back to his instant coffee with just a splash of milk.

Once he had his coffee, he sank into a chair at their small dining table and watched absently as Chip began putting away the dishes into the cupboards he'd allocated them. He was wearing another pair of running shorts today, this time navy blue, and a plain white tee. The bronze skin of his biceps was dark against the pale material of the shirt, and when he dropped into a crouch to slot a serving dish onto the bottom shelf of a cupboard, the short shorts rode up to show off how his thigh muscles bunched and bulged. His legs were hairy, something Dawson had teased him mercilessly about when they were younger, and his bare feet were a shade lighter thanks to his sock tan.

It took a long moment for his brain to kick in and realise he was ogling his stepbrother, and he jerked his eyes away and down to his coffee cup instead. He was just tired and was zoning out. He did that sometimes. Caffeine would help. He took a long gulp as Chip stood up, nodding happily at the now empty bench space.

"The mugs have a new home?" he asked.

"The mugs have a new home," Chip confirmed. "And I think that's the kitchen sorted."

Dawson drained the rest of his coffee and stood to place the mug in the sink. "Awesome. So, what's next?"

CHAPTER 4

Chip

Chip had way too much energy to burn and his entire body was thrumming with it. He'd woken up hard and aching, with Dawson clinging to him, and it had taken everything he possessed to not stay in bed and rut against him. Instead, he'd gotten up and punished himself in the gym, then had the coldest shower he could stand. His cock had been begging for release all morning, and even after the exercise and the cold shower, it had refused to flag. He'd finally relented, jerking himself off hard and fast in the bathroom, trying not to think about Dawson's hands on him the night before.

It hadn't done much to ease his restlessness and he needed to move, to burn it off before it came bursting out of him in the form of him throwing himself onto his knees and begging to suck Dawson until he exploded over his tongue. He was almost relieved when Dawson had asked him to learn one of the viral dances that had just started doing the rounds on Vewz.

"If I get in now, I'll be ahead of the curve," Dawson said, handing over his phone so he could watch the couple on-screen dance.

The steps looked simple enough, similar to a few other dances they'd done. It seemed to be more about jumping on the popularity of the song than anything else. Considering it was an absolute banger, he could see why. He watched it a few times and then walked through the steps. "Okay, I think I got it," he said.

"You always pick it up so quickly," Dawson said, giving him a grateful smile.

It took a couple of takes, but overall, it was one of the quicker videos they'd made. The activity helped burn off his energy somewhat and it always made him feel good to be helping Dawson. Chip was by far the more outgoing of the two of them, though no one ever guessed that right away. Dawson just wanted to make music, but to do that, he needed a brand. He needed to have a following to even get noticed by a label, but building that following took a lot of effort. It was almost a catch-22 situation. Spend the time to make content to gain followers, but then not have the time to spend creating the music he loved. If Chip had to do silly dances, mime along to movie quotes and song lyrics, and recreate funny memes just to give Dawson a leg up, then that's what he was going to do. He was happy to make a fool of himself if it served Dawson's cause.

Once that was done, they headed into town to get everything on the shopping list they'd compiled. While Dawson went to get a post office box sorted, Chip went to the chemist to pick up the few things they needed in their first aid kit. He was done first so he sat on a wooden bench out the front of the chemist and opened his phone, bringing up his Vewz account.

It was as anonymous as he could make it and he wasn't even sure if Dawson knew it was him. He commented now and then on videos, especially the original songs, but he used it mostly so he could sit and drink in the sight of Dawson when he was missing him. Just seeing his face and hearing his voice soothed that lonely part of his heart that yearned for more.

Perhaps that made him just as bad as Dawson's stalkerish followers, but he was beyond caring at this point.

He watched the latest clip, not even surprised to see it had over five thousand views already, despite only being posted an hour ago. There were hundreds of comments as well and he scrolled through some of them. What did surprise him was the sheer number of people gushing over *him*. He didn't get it at all. Dawson was the catch of the two of them, with his angelic face, perfect skin, and sweet smile. He didn't understand what the fuss was about himself. Sure, he worked out but he wasn't a muscle hound. His chin was also a little too pointed compared to how square his jaw was, and his Roman nose slightly too big for his face. It was a mystery to him.

He scrolled through more comments, searching for one particular username and stopped when he found it. Without fail, angeltree_06 would comment on every video he featured in and today was no different.

You two are so perfect together! When are you finally gonna be a couple?

As usual, there were numerous replies from other followers.

Ewww, they're brothers!

Um, why would you say that?

Why does someone have to turn everything gay?

That's gross. No. Just no.

Chip ignored the replies and simply liked angeltree_06's comment. He may have been able to hide how he felt from everyone so far, but at least there was one person out there who also seemed to think he and Dawson belonged together.

He closed the app and pocketed his phone, then crossed to the small noticeboard that was on the wall near the front door of the post office. Humming the song from earlier, Chip scanned the posters, and sure enough there was one for the Brockman Bobtails, the local cricket club, advertising for members. He tore off one of the slips of paper at the bottom with the phone number to call and shoved it into his pocket, noting that practice was on Tuesday nights. According to the poster, they only played Twenty20 games in the area which made sense. He knew that even city teams found it difficult to find members, since people were just too busy to give up an entire day on their weekend for a game. It was easier to be able to dedicate half a day though, and with the more exciting version of the game, they got more spectators and greater buy-in from the community.

He really hoped Dawson would join up as well. They used to play together all the time, but after high school had finished Dawson had stopped, citing that he was too busy with uni, his part-time job at Bunnings, and making content and music. Chip got it—he knew how busy Dawson was but the extra exercise and the social aspect would do him good. He tended to lose himself in depressive slumps now and then, and the endorphins of a fun game and being part of a team would hopefully help.

Once Dawson was finished, they headed to the local bakery to grab some lunch before hitting the IGA for their grocery shop. They stepped up to the counter to order when they heard someone squeal behind the older lady serving them.

"Oh my God, oh my God, *oh my God!*" a girl of about nineteen or twenty screeched as she looked at Dawson in awe. She had thick, fake lashes and dark eye makeup which made her eyes look comically wide. "You're Dawson Miller!" she exclaimed, before bouncing up and down.

"Lucy, sweetie," the woman who was trying to serve them said to the girl in exasperation. "Can you *please* try and be professional? We have customers."

"Do you know who he is, Ellen?" Lucy demanded.

Ellen threw Dawson an apologetic look. "Sorry, honey, I don't, except he's a customer. Here for lunch. During the *lunch rush.* So how about you pull yourself together and go and serve some people in the queue."

Lucy looked abashed at the reprimand and Chip felt a little sympathy for her. She was clearly a huge fan of Dawson's, and why shouldn't she be? He was *awesome.* Chip would be excited to meet him too, if he didn't already know him. "Can she spare thirty seconds so I can get a photo of them together for her?" he asked Ellen.

She frowned but finally nodded. "Thirty seconds and that's it. And while you do that, I'm serving the people behind you."

"Deal," Chip said, even as Lucy squealed again and bounced her way around the counter and thrust her phone at Chip.

"Thank you so much," she gushed as she stood next to Dawson for the photo. As excited as she was, she was respectful and didn't plaster herself against him like some fans did. It was Dawson who slung an arm over her shoulder and they beamed at Chip as he took a couple of snaps.

He handed the phone back to her and she slipped it into her pocket. "No worries," he told her.

She glanced over at Ellen and then back at them. "Crap, sorry. Um, what can I get you guys?"

Once she'd run back to the other side of the counter, they ordered a chicken and salad roll for Dawson, a quiche for Chip, and a couple of lattes. They grabbed their number and headed outside to a table, garnering a few sidelong glances from customers as they went. Either more of the locals recognised Dawson than they'd expected, or they were trying to figure out who he was to elicit such a reaction from Lucy.

"I guess there's no point trying to stay under the radar now," Chip lamented.

Dawson bit his lip as he winced. "Sorry."

"It's all good," Chip assured him. "I guess we just roll with it."

A few minutes later Ellen approached with their order. She slid their food and drinks off the tray and gave them a long once-over. "Lucy said your name is Dawson Miller," she said. "Any relation to old Colin Miller?"

Dawson nodded. "Yeah, he was our grandpa."

"He and my dad were mates," she said. "I knew he'd have his grandsons up to visit on school holidays but I don't think I ever saw you with him. I can kind of see the resemblance with you, but not with you, honey," she directed at Chip.

He held out his hand for her to shake. "I'm Tate George. Colin was my step-grandfather."

"Ah, gotcha," Ellen said, nodding. "Your dad married his daughter, Carolyn?"

Chip wasn't surprised she knew all about their family, since Brockman was such a small town and the locals seemed to know everything about everyone. "Yep."

"You boys just clearing out his house?" she asked.

"No, we're actually moving in," Chip told her. "He left it to both of us in his will and in this day and age you gotta be stupid to turn down a free house."

"You got a good head on your shoulders, honey," she told him. "It'll be good to have a Miller still living there. You do know we've had a Miller on that property since it was built, don't you?"

"Vaguely," Dawson told her. "We knew our family had lived here for a bit but we don't know much about it."

"You boys should check out the Historical Society. The Millers have been in this town for as long as it's been here. Ain't nobody been here longer except the Aboriginal people. It's why there's a road, a creek, *and* the rec centre named after your family."

"No way!" Dawson exclaimed, looking shocked. "Miller Road is named after my family?"

Ellen nodded once more. "Sure is. Miller Creek as well. It branches off the Brockman River a few k's out of town and runs through the back of your property."

"Huh. I had no idea but I guess it makes sense."

"As I said, the Historical Society will have more info about them if you want to look into it." Ellen glanced over her shoulder at the line for the counter. "I gotta get back to work but welcome to the area, boys. I'm sure I'll be seeing you around."

They thanked her before she left and then stared at each other in amazement. "That's crazy!" Dawson said.

"Honestly, as if you needed to be *more* of a celebrity," Chip teased. "You're gonna get a big head at this rate."

Dawson threw a piece of lettuce at him. "Shut the fuck up."

Chip laughed and ripped open the paper cover on the bamboo cutlery set. "Just wait until Carolyn hears."

"Oh no," Dawson groaned. "She's gonna want us to write the bloody history of the place now."

"I'll leave that up to you," Chip told him as he shovelled a piece of quiche into his mouth. "It can be part of your memoirs," he said around his mouthful, spitting some of it across the table.

"You're so gross," Dawson complained as he wiped a piece of egg off his arm.

Chip grinned, showing off his quiche-covered teeth and got a faceful of lettuce in retribution. "You love me."

Dawson sighed. "You're just lucky you're cute," he said, then bit into his roll.

"You're just lucky you're cute."

What. The. Actual. Fuck?

That throwaway, teasing comment had been stuck in Chip's head on a loop. Sure, he'd started it by stating that Dawson loved him, but they said they loved each other all the time. They'd done it since they were kids, and it had only escalated when they'd become family. It was the truth. He'd not expected Dawson to come back with a quip about him *physically.* Sure, "cute" didn't necessarily mean anything . . . romantic. He'd not said "sexy" or "hot" or "fuckable". He'd probably meant it in a "cute as in a naughty puppy" kind of way.

Could there be more to it? Dammit, he was too compromised by his stupid feelings to be able to look at the situation critically. The rush of hope that had surged through him was eclipsing any rational thoughts that might have been lurking in the background.

Dawson had acted completely normal around him after the comment, as if it were nothing. They'd finished their lunch, gone and done their shopping, and then headed home. They'd packed away their groceries, made a quick plan for what to make for dinner the next few nights and divvied up the meals they'd each cook. Afterwards, they'd gone their separate ways to do their own thing.

Chip had put on his sneakers and changed into running shorts and had jogged around the property's firebreaks. They were nearing the deadline of when they'd have to be done before the fire season started so it was a good excuse to check them over. He got halfway around and realised he'd not taken anything in, too caught up in reliving that stupid comment over and over again.

"You're just lucky you're cute."

Chip backtracked, concentrating on the breaks, and took a few photos on his phone. He'd seen a small tractor parked behind the shed as well as the ride-on mower in the shed but he had no idea how to drive a tractor. He was pretty sure he'd be able to learn, but this first year they might need to pay someone to get the firebreaks up to scratch for them. There were also a lot of overhanging branches that would need to be cut back, and not all of them were low enough that he'd be able to reach them from the ground. Although he'd taken three weeks off work, he'd not be able to do everything he needed to do in that time. Not only was he a city boy learning how to do everything, but there were a hundred other jobs around the house that he needed to complete as well. He'd never get it all done before the deadline so it looked like he'd need to arrange for a contractor to come in.

He walked the rest of the way back to the house, and when he walked in the back door, he heard the strumming of a guitar and then the murmur of Dawson's voice. It sounded like he was in the loungeroom at the front of the house working on a song, so he walked as quietly as possible into the kitchen and got a glass of water, standing by the sink to drink as he listened to Dawson pluck at the strings of his guitar. Then his sweet, melodic voice got louder and filled the air as he began the song from the start.

It was one of the new songs he was working on, unfinished and unpolished, but it was already a new favourite of Chip's. His style was eclectic—a bit poppy, a little folky, with a hint of country. His lyrics were always filled with hidden depths and this song was no different. On the surface the song was about being yourself and chasing your dreams, but when you dug deeper it was about having the courage to make those decisions despite being told that you'd never succeed. It was about ignoring the naysayers and how hard that could be, but how rewarding it was when you proved to them you could do it.

After the song came to an end and Dawson paused, probably making notes, Chip went down the hall to his room, closing the door behind him. His bed was still unmade and messy from when Dawson had rolled out of it that morning. Chip was pretty anal about making sure his bed was made after he got up but he couldn't even be mad about it. He crossed to the bed, pulled back the covers and climbed under them, inhaling the scent of Dawson.

He hadn't planned on napping, but he'd hardly slept the night before, and he was warm and comfy and surrounded by the smell of what he couldn't have. It didn't take long for sleep to pull him under, the soulful melody from the room on the other side of the wall acting as a lullaby.

CHAPTER 5

Dawson

"Do you mind if I do a Live tonight?" Dawson asked Chip as they stood at the kitchen sink doing the dishes after dinner.

"Nah, 'course not, man," Chip said, taking the dripping dish from him and drying it with the tea towel.

"I was just gonna sing them the new song, is all. I didn't want to disturb you." Chip looked tired and the last thing Dawson wanted was to keep him up. He fished a fork out of the soapy water and scrubbed at the tines with the scourer, rinsed it, and then dropped it into the dishrack.

"It's fine," Chip assured him, putting the plate away. "I heard a bit of it earlier. It's sounding really sweet."

A warm flush spread through him at the praise. "Yeah?"

Chip knocked his hip against Dawson's. "For real, man. It's my favourite yet."

Chip's absolute, unwavering support was the cornerstone of Dawson's belief in himself. There were times when his anxiety got to be too much and he'd spiral, believing that he was a talentless hack who was throwing his life away chasing a nightmare instead of a dream, but Chip was the one who always seemed able to break him free of it. Made him believe once again in himself and his ability. Sure, thousands of fans online would gush over his music and compliment his songs but that wasn't *real* like Chip's enthusiasm was. It wasn't tangible. Chip's support was a warm, comforting presence at his side. Always.

"Thanks," he managed to croak out, unable to even try and voice how grateful he was to him. He finished washing the last pot and pulled the plug from the sink.

"I'm gonna call it a night," Chip told him as he put the pot away in the right cupboard. "I'll have a shower and read for a bit but the house is yours."

"Cool. Yell at me if I get too loud."

"Will do. Night," Chip said and then brushed a kiss against his temple and wandered out of the kitchen.

Dawson stood there, frozen. They were pretty affectionate people, which came from not only being stepbrothers but best friends since they were five. Casual kisses *weren't* part of their usual repertoire though. Something niggled at the back of his mind and he tried to chase after the stray thought. More of a memory. What the hell was it?

It suddenly hit him as he recalled the ghost of a kiss pressed into his hair the night before. He reached up and fingered the spot on his temple lightly, feeling the spot there, knowing it wouldn't be any different to usual but feeling like it *should* be.

Why the hell had Chip kissed him? And why was Dawson wishing it happened more often?

Dawson had been single for over a year now. Things never lasted long with his girlfriends, and he'd only been with the last one, Jules, for a couple of months before he'd broken up with her, citing differences in lifestyles.

She'd wanted to drink and party constantly and he'd been focussed even then on building an online presence. He'd not really been interested in seeing anyone else since, so maybe he was just starved of affection? He and Chip hugged and touched each other casually all the time, but slumping on the couch together while playing games, slapping each other on the back, or even wrestling together was completely different to the touch of a lover. A lingering hug, a soft caress . . . or a kiss.

Was Dawson just feeling antsy because he needed to get laid? He didn't think it was that since his sex drive was quite low thanks to his meds. Even if that *were* it though, why the hell would he be thinking about that after a forehead kiss from his bloody stepbrother of all people? It made absolutely no sense and he was starting to overthink the whole thing. It clearly didn't mean anything to Chip since he'd not turned into a gibbering mess and freaked out over his actions. No, he'd sauntered out of the room and down the hall like nothing out of the ordinary had happened.

Because it *hadn't,* had it? Why the actual fuck was Dawson even associating what had just happened with his lack of a love life? Didn't that mean he was assigning it a hidden sexual meaning when there wasn't anything like that going on? Chip would lose his fucking mind if he could hear what Dawson was thinking. He'd definitely think Dawson was a freak and would probably tell him to go to a shrink to get his head examined.

It was time for a distraction. Dawson went across the hall and into the loungeroom where he'd already set up a tripod earlier. His guitar was leaning against a stool in the centre of the room. A small ring-light was off to one side and he flicked it on, illuminating the space where he'd be sitting since the lighting in the room wasn't the best at night. He attached his phone to the tripod, checked his settings, and then hit *Go Live*.

"Hey everyone," Dawson said to the camera. "What's up? Did you all have a good Fri-yay?"

There were only a couple of hundred people viewing so far but he knew those numbers would skyrocket once his followers were notified that he was Live. A few comments began to trickle in.

Hi Dawson! Hope you had a great day!

How's the new place?

I love you so much!!!

Hello!

"I had a great day, thanks. We went into town for lunch and I got my PO box sorted, which was on top of my to-do list. I'm expecting a delivery in the next week or so from TK Lane with some new kit and I can't wait to show you what they've got in store for summer." He reached forward and picked up the tripod and scanned the camera around the room. "The new place is awesome. I don't think you've seen much of the inside since that first walk-through, but this is what the loungeroom looks like with all our shit in it. Pretty simple but I gotta say, the acoustics are amazing."

Holy shit, r u gonna sing???

Is that your guitar?

Nice! You've been teasing us about a new song for weeks now.

Dawson beamed at the camera, even as he saw the count of viewers online ticking up and up. Over a thousand now. "You would be correct," he told them. "I do indeed have a musical treat for you all tonight and yes, it *is* my latest song. You guys get to hear it before anyone else!" *Well, except for Chip.* "I can't wait to hear what you think. I'll wait a couple of minutes though, to give people a chance to jump online."

Dawson chatted away to everyone online for a while, talking about their plans for the house and a little about the property. Once the numbers had grown enough, Dawson picked up his guitar.

"Alright, guys. This song is called "Just Be." I really hope you like it."

His fingers plucked at the strings and he began to sing, glancing at the camera often to keep the viewers engaged. Comments flooded the feed, faster than he could even read them.

I love ur voice.

This song slaps.

Nice.

I love you!!!

Who's that?

When does it go live so we can stream it?

As his voice soared through the first chorus, he hoped he wasn't being too loud and keeping Chip awake. Sure, he said he was gonna read for a bit but he'd looked so tired over dinner—he could do with a proper night's sleep. He decided he wouldn't let this Live go for too long so he could give Chip the peace and quiet he needed.

This is really catchy!

Marry me!!!

Did Chip get a girlfriend?

Love it!

So good.

I need this, like, yesterday.

You so deserve a record deal, babe.

Dawson wished it was as easy as "deserving" a deal. He had the talent. He had the drive. He had the ambition. Maybe twenty years ago that would have been enough, but it wasn't now. He needed a brand, a following. He needed to be able to guarantee a label would get sales if they signed him. He was close, he knew it. He just had to build it all up, just a little more. He needed his followers to not only like his stuff but to share it. To help him go viral. To have them follow the links to his sponsors. To prove that when it came to Dawson Miller, they were happy to part with their money.

I love this song.

U r sooo hot.

Srsly who's the chick?

Damn, Dawson, you deliver!

I love you so much!!!

Noooooo, Chip can't be taken!

IKR? Devo.

This is seriously good, man.

Best one yet.

She's so pretty!

Through the steady scroll of comments, Dawson kept seeing mentions of a woman. What the hell were they talking about? The song definitely wasn't about a relationship. He couldn't see how it could be construed that way, either. So who were they talking about? Last year, someone had created a fake account, claiming to be Chip. Maybe it had happened again and they'd posted videos of a supposed "girlfriend"? He didn't really see the point, but some fans were obsessed with Chip's *lack* of obsession over social media. Dawson knew that Chip did in fact have a Vewz account, but he didn't advertise that it was him. He rarely commented anyway. Dawson wouldn't be surprised to discover that Chip had created the account simply to help bolster Dawson's following at the very beginning.

Dismissing the mystery woman for now, Dawson concentrated on giving it his all for the final chorus of the song. As the final bars echoed around the room, the steady stream of gifts and diamonds that his viewers sent turned into an explosion across the screen. If he was lucky, his account would get a nice boost from his performance tonight. They'd organised house insurance before they'd moved in and that had been a painful hit to his bank balance.

After answering a few more questions about the song, and chatting a little more, Dawson wound up the Live. "Thanks so much for joining me tonight. Love you all. Peace out." He blew one more kiss at the screen and then hit the *end* button.

Silence settled over the room and Dawson removed his phone from the tripod. He brought up the Live Center on the app and hit replay on the video. Dawson always watched back his Lives after he was done, picking out a few users to mention the following time if they'd been extra generous with gifts, or had been engaging or funny. This time, he focussed more on figuring out who the hell his viewers had been talking about when they mentioned Chip's girlfriend. His eyes flickered over the rapidly scrolling comments, so busy chasing the text, that he missed it the first time. He'd paused and scrolled backwards in the video to double-check a comment when he noticed it.

A woman, standing behind him in the doorway.

Even though it had happened ten minutes ago, Dawson spun around on the stool to face the doorway. It was empty. He glanced back down at his phone and sure enough, there she was. She looked young, maybe late teens, with light brown hair pulled back into a bun on the top of her head. She was wearing a dress, maybe made of linen, but she was thrown into shadows by the ring-light so it was a little hard to tell. His viewers were right—she *was* pretty.

She was also a stranger. Who the fuck was she and how had she gotten into the house?

Dawson slid off the stool as silently as possible, listening hard. The house was still and quiet, and he couldn't hear anything over the sound of his heart thumping loudly in his ears. He reached past the tripod to the fireplace and picked up the old wrought-iron poker. It was heavy and likely overkill for one teenage stalker, but he immediately felt better with it in his grip. Glad he was wearing socks, Dawson crossed the loungeroom as quietly as possible and peered around the door into the hall.

It was empty.

He turned left and crossed the few feet to the front door. Keeping his eyes on the hall, he reached behind him and tried the handle. It was locked. He shuffled over to the kitchen doorway and peered inside. It was dark and he reached up to flick on the light, poker held at the ready in case the girl was hiding behind their small kitchen table.

The room was also empty.

Dawson ventured down the hall, clearing his own bedroom and the bathroom, and even checking inside the linen cupboard. He then crept into the darkened sunroom, his heart still hammering in his chest. He hit the lightswitch, but seeing the empty room did nothing to calm him down. He checked the back door and found that it was still locked. So where the hell was she?

Dawson's breath caught in his throat. Could she have snuck into Chip's room? Had she hurt him? He hadn't bothered to check in there, since he was sure that he would have heard Chip cause a ruckus if a stranger had barged in on him, but what if he'd been quiet because he *couldn't* make a noise? The girl hadn't looked intimidating but she could have a weapon. They were in the country, for fuck's sake. Every farmer and his dog had a gun around here.

Panic took over and Dawson rushed down the hall and barged into Chip's room, slamming the door open against the wall and turning the light on—which was stupid. If the girl *was* in the room with a gun he could have startled her into pulling the trigger, but he wasn't acting at all rationally. He *needed* to see that Chip was okay.

As soon as the light came on, Chip was rolling out of bed and onto his feet, instantly alert. His long black hair was mussed and he was only wearing his sleep shorts, leaving his arms and chest bare. "What is it?" he demanded, taking in the fire poker in Dawson's hand and what he could only imagine was a terrified expression on his face. "What's happened?"

"There was someone in the house," Dawson blurted, hurrying into the room and then turning to face the door, poker at the ready.

"What?" Chip asked. "Who?"

"I don't know. Some chick."

"How did she get in?"

"I don't know."

"Where is she now? Did she take anything? What did she do?"

"I don't know!" Dawson's voice came out sounding slightly hysterical.

Chip examined him closely and then stepped forward and pulled Dawson into a hug. "Are you okay? She didn't hurt you?" he asked, his voice deep with sleep and concern.

Dawson allowed his face to tip forward and lean against his pec. Chip's chest hair tickled his nose but he didn't move away, just breathed in the scent of the body wash they used, still strong on Chip's skin after his shower. "I'm okay," he said. "I didn't even know she was there until I watched the video back. I checked the house but I can't find her anywhere."

"You checked the house *alone?* Why didn't you come and get me?"

"You looked so tired. I didn't want to ruin your sleep two nights in a row."

Chip gave him a long look but then let it drop. "Okay, first things first—let's both check the house again. Together."

They did, but found it just as empty as Dawson had. Chip grabbed a large torch and they went outside, sticking close to one another as they checked the area around the house and the sheds. They found nothing.

Making their way back inside to the loungeroom, Dawson handed over his phone so Chip could watch the video. He knew when he reached the right part as he recoiled and swore loudly, his eyes flying to the doorway. "Holy shit!"

"I honestly thought the commenters were talking about something else. Like, maybe another fake account? I didn't see her behind me when I was filming."

"How could you not see her? She's there, clear as day!" Chip objected.

Dawson shrugged. "Between singing and trying to keep an eye on the comments, I guess I missed her. I didn't hear a thing."

"Well, I guess it's safe to say that you've got another stalker," Chip said grimly, running a hand through his hair and mussing it even more.

"We don't know that for sure!"

The look Chip levelled him could cut glass. "It doesn't take Sherlock fucking Holmes to solve this case, Daw. You have adoring fans, who get a tad too obsessed with you. You pretty much doxxed yourself by giving away so many details about where we moved to. That, plus the fact she wasn't searching the house for the family jewels but *watching you,* tells me you've got another stalker."

"We don't *have* any family jewels," he grumbled.

"*Not* the point," Chip barked.

"Fine, when you put it like that maybe you have a point," Dawson reluctantly admitted. He took a deep breath and then let it out in a rush. "So, what do we do?"

"We *should* call the cops," Chip said and held up a hand when Dawson immediately went to protest. "*But . . .* I know that you won't let me call them, so tomorrow we head into town and see if the hardware has any security cameras. Most farms have them these days so I reckon we'll be able to get something there. I'll pick up a couple of deadbolts for both doors as well, and we'll be vigilant about keeping this place locked up, even when we're home. If she comes back and we catch her on camera, at least we'll have something to take to the cops."

Dawson nodded. "Okay." He crossed his chest with his arms, suddenly realising that he was shaking. The adrenaline must be starting to fade.

"Are you okay?" Chip asked, his brow creasing with worry.

Dawson nodded again, feeling a little like a bobblehead but incapable of doing much else. "Sure."

"Okay, I *don't* believe you. Come on, let's go to bed. You look like you're about to topple over."

Allowing himself to be guided down the hall, Dawson reached up to turn off the lights as they went. When they reached their bedroom doors, he was surprised to feel himself being tugged backwards when he tried to go into his own room.

"Nuh-uh," Chip said. "She'll have been able to figure out which room is yours. I don't want you sleeping in there until we get the cameras and better locks installed. You can bunk in with me again tonight."

Dawson's breath hitched and all he could think about suddenly was the way that Chip's lips had felt, brushing against his skin. "D-don't be stupid," he muttered. "It'll be fine."

"Dawson," Chip said in a stern voice, his hazel eyes boring into Dawson's. "I'm not taking no for an answer."

He knew immediately there was no point arguing. "Can I at least get my PJs, or am I supposed to sleep naked?"

Why the fuck had he asked that? Because even if the world had turned so bonkers that Chip *wouldn't* allow him to enter the room to get clothes to sleep in, the *logical* thing would be to just sleep in the clothes he was wearing now. Not naked.

He must have been more tired than he thought because for a very brief moment he thought he saw a flash of desire in Chip's eyes. He blinked and it was gone.

Instead, Chip just looked amused. "I'll allow it," he said magnanimously.

"You're *too* kind," Dawson drawled, but he couldn't deny that he felt infinitely safer when he walked into the bedroom with Chip on his heels.

It didn't take long to get changed and brush his teeth, and then Dawson was once again crawling into Chip's bed. Last night, he'd joined him without a second thought. Tonight, Dawson's body was thrumming with a weird kind of tension. He could have tried to dismiss it as lingering adrenaline from finding an intruder in their house, but he knew it wasn't that. It was something new, something he'd never even contemplated.

As Chip rolled towards him and slung a warm, heavy arm over Dawson's chest, he couldn't help but wish he'd tug him closer until they were flush together, so he could feel those lips once more against his forehead.

CHAPTER 6

Chip

"**H**ey, I'm Blake. Nice to meet you guys."

Chip shook Blake's hand and grinned. "Thanks for inviting us down."

Blake grinned back, his teeth white against his dark brown skin. Chip estimated he was in his early forties and he had a strong Kiwi accent. He was tall and broad and was wearing cricket whites, but they were showing their age, with grass stained knees and fraying cuffs. "We are *always* happy to have new members," he told them, and then turned and led them across the oval towards the cricket nets. "You guys have recently moved to town?"

"Yeah, just this week."

Blake laughed, deep and booming. "You boys are keen. I love it!"

"It didn't make sense to wait," Chip said, not bothering to explain that he'd not been planning to join up until they were more settled. The events of the night before had left Dawson rattled and he'd been antsy all morning. Chip had suggested they head down to the nets to have a hit after they'd been to the hardware store to burn off some energy. When Dawson agreed, he also decided to call the number on the flyer to let them know that they were interested in joining the cricket club, before he forgot. In a happy coincidence, Blake had told them that a few of the boys were meeting for a casual practice that afternoon and had invited them down.

"So, do you bat or bowl?" Blake asked.

"I'm a batter," Chip said. "Batting average is about thirty-eight, but that's for one dayers. I've not played enough T20 to really know what it is for those. I'm also pretty handy in the slips."

"Nice," Blake said. "What about you, bro?" he asked Dawson.

"Uh, I haven't played for a while so I'm a bit rusty. I'm a fast bowler. Well, I *used* to be. I might only be medium pace now." He laughed awkwardly as he rubbed the back of his neck.

"I reckon we can get you back up to speed," Blake told him confidently.

They'd reached the nets and came to a stop at the edge so they could watch the handful of guys already practising. Like all local clubs, they were a mix of ages, physiques, and abilities. Two of them looked old enough to be retired and were the complete opposites of one another—one was tall, pot-bellied, and had a mane of long grey hair while the other was short, slight, and completely bald. There was another guy who looked to be the same age as Blake, and then two younger guys close to their own age.

When there was a natural lull in activity, Blake gave a sharp whistle to get their attention. "You blokes wanna come over and meet the new guys?"

Everyone ambled over and Blake made the introductions. "This is Noah, Ryan, Raj, Ken, and Bruce. Everyone, this is Tate and Dawson."

Chip was a little distracted by Dawson, who seemed to be retreating into himself shyly, and knew he wouldn't be able to place names with faces if asked immediately. He shook hands, telling everyone, "Please, call me

Chip." He'd always do what he could to take the attention away from Dawson.

When the older, bald man—Chip *thought* his name was Ken—asked where they'd moved into and he'd mentioned their street name, he nodded in understanding. "Ah, the old Miller place."

He shared a look with Dawson. It really was going to take some getting used to, just how much everyone knew about everyone in a country town. "That'd be the one," he confirmed.

"Didn't you used to help out up there at harvest, Ken?" the taller, older gent asked. "Back when they grew oranges?"

"Yeah, I did," Ken confirmed. "I helped Colin out for a few years. He was a good man."

"He really was," Chip agreed.

After a few more minutes of casual chit chat, they got back to practice. Blake and Raj headed out to the oval to do some fielding drills. Ken and Bruce—the two older guys—headed down to the far net with Ken batting and Bruce spin bowling to him. Chip ended up batting against Ryan, who was a tall, lanky guy with bright red hair, while Dawson bowled to Noah, a short, solid blond with a wide smile and dimples, and a golden cross hanging around his neck.

Chip blocked a few balls and let a few others go through as he familiarised himself with Ryan's bowling, before finding his rhythm and getting in some solid hits.

The day was bright and cloudless and the sun high above had a bite to it. After twenty minutes he was sweating heavily, and held up a hand to get Ryan to pause before he pulled off his helmet and wiped the sweat from his face. He tugged his gloves off with his teeth and then pulled his shirt over his head and tossed it to the side. He immediately felt cooler and noticed that Dawson and Noah had done the same. The day had turned out to be hotter than anyone had expected. He quickly pulled his gloves and helmet back on and got back to it. It felt so good to be active once again and he was a little chuffed when they finished up and Ryan complimented him on his form.

Dawson and Noah finished as well and they all moved out to the oval to join Blake and Raj, casually throwing the ball to one another for a while before doing some stretches to finish.

"Our official practice nights are on Tuesdays, here at six," Blake told them as he folded himself in half in an impressive display of agility for such a big man. "We've already started pre-season training and the first game is in a few weeks. Most of us will head here each Saturday for a casual hit like today as well, until games start, so feel free to come down again."

"We will. Thanks," Chip said.

"Fees need to be paid by the first game but they also get you membership to the rec centre, which means you can drink at the bar there. Prices are really cheap and all proceeds go back into the facilities. The bar is open Friday night through Sunday night and it's a great way to meet some of the locals. If you wanna come down before you've paid, just give me a call as we can bring guests so you can tag along with me if you like."

Chip caught the way Dawson blanched and he knew there was no way in hell they'd be hitting the club bar any time soon. Batting practice was one thing but full-on socialising was a little too much for his anxiety, at least until he got to know them all better. "We'll let you know if we want to head down." That was all he'd agree to.

"No worries, bro. You've got my number," Blake said easily. "We've also got a group chat going so I'll get you both added to that to keep you in the loop."

One by one the guys all left, with Noah being the last to leave. "I'm not sure if it's your thing or not, but I'm part of the local church. We have a service on Sunday mornings at nine. If you want me to save you a pew, just let me know."

"Oh, that's really nice of you, mate," Chip said. "But we're not really religious." He tried not to cringe, hoping their atheism wouldn't be held against them.

Noah just grinned at them and slapped Chip on the back. "All good. Just wanted to let you know about other stuff to do in town besides drinking."

Chip smiled back. "I appreciate that. We're kind of homebodies to be honest."

"I totally get that," Noah said. "A few of my friends and I also have jam sessions once a month or so. Nothing serious, but if either of you play at all, let me know."

Dawson's face brightened at this. "That sounds cool."

"Just hit me up, man," Noah said. "Anyway, it was great to meet you guys. I'll see you around."

Dawson gave him a little wave and then they were alone.

"Do you mind if I do a couple of laps before we head off?" Chip asked.

"Yeah, 'course," Dawson said, and flopped down onto the grass. "Do you mind if I don't?" he added with a crooked smile.

Chip chuckled. "You know it drives me insane that of the two of us, I'm the one who works out the most but you're the one with the runway body?"

Dawson had swung his cap around and now peered up at Chip from beneath his long blond lashes. "Runway body?" he scoffed.

Chip gestured vaguely in his direction. "You know what I mean. You've got the chiselled muscles and tiny waist and everything, and I'm just . . . I dunno, thick." He normally didn't get self-conscious, but with them both shirtless and with such a contrast between them, it was hard not to. Dawson was all sculpted perfection and Chip was . . . not. Yes, he was strong and muscular, but he wasn't buff. He tried to suck in his stomach, to make the little roll that always sat above his waistband less noticeable.

Dawson's eyes narrowed. "Okay, firstly, there's nothing wrong with your body. You are fucking *solid* man. You could bench press me with ease if you wanted to. Secondly, when we hit our thirties and my metabolism carks it, you're going to be fucking laughing because working out is just part of your routine, whereas I hate every damn second of it and will do anything to get out of it. I'll end up with a big enough pot belly that I could do one of those pregnancy photo shoots, barefoot on the beach with the long, flowing white dress whipping around me in the breeze with a flower crown on my head."

Chip raised a brow. "That's oddly specific."

His cheeks flushed. "Shut up. You know what I mean."

"Actually, I don't," Chip teased, mercilessly. "My Pinterest page is a lot more boring than yours apparently."

"You don't *have* a Pinterest page," Dawson shot back.

"But if I *did,* it wouldn't have maternity photo shoots on it."

"Weren't you supposed to be running around the oval or something?"

Chip grinned, blew Dawson a kiss, and then took off at light jog. He was feeling better about himself. Dawson always seemed to know what to say, even if Chip didn't quite believe it. He had eyes, after all. It wasn't just his screen presence and voice of an angel that had garnered Dawson hundreds of thousands of fans on social media. He was drop-dead gorgeous and *could* be a model if he wanted to. He'd die, having to be surrounded by people all the time of course, but he'd look good while taking his final breath.

Dawson's social anxiety confused a lot of people. They couldn't understand how someone who had such a big online presence, who was confident enough to make video after video of themselves, could be so socially awkward in real life. Today was the perfect example of how he acted around strangers. He'd said barely a handful of words to their new teammates, and had tried to be as invisible as possible. It was such a contrast to how he was as soon as there was a screen between him and the people he was interacting with. In front of a camera he was relaxed, at ease, and absolutely charming. With no barrier between himself and real, live people in front of him, he resembled a vampire trying to avoid the sun.

Chip got it. They were two entirely different worlds. Dawson could control the narrative on his socials. He wasn't one of those "Insta-elites" who made their lives out to be absolutely perfect and blissful, but unless he was Live he had the opportunity to re-record himself if he stumbled over his words, or if his voice squeaked at the wrong time during a song. He showed his fans how hard it was, how challenging it was to try and carve out a name for himself. He shared with them the good days and the bad. He was honest with them about his sponsorships and how they made it possible for him to make music. And they loved him for it.

Chip had no delusions that people loved Dawson just as much in the real world, but it simply wasn't as in your face so he had trouble seeing it for himself. Unless it was someone like Lucy from the bakery—who was a fan of online Dawson—social niceties made it difficult for Dawson to recognise how other people honestly felt about him. That led to higher anxiety levels, which led to him withdrawing, which led to fewer interactions and a belief that no one really liked him. Chip was trying to help him see his real worth but it wasn't something that could change overnight. It would take time, but time was something Chip had in abundance for Dawson.

He'd made one lap of the oval and passed by close to where Dawson was now sprawled on the grass, his phone in front of him as he recorded a video. Dawson grinned and then turned the phone and before he moved out of range, heard him say, "I think I promised you some Chip eye candy earlier, so here it is."

He wasn't sure if it was his imagination, but had Dawson been saying stuff like that more often recently? It wasn't new—Dawson had always been delighted at how much his fans seemed to love Chip. Again, Chip had no idea *why* they did, but Dawson was always talking him up and telling them how amazing he was. Sure, it did sometimes revolve around his looks, but mostly it was about how funny he was, or how much effort he put into staying fit, or about the coffee table and other small items of furniture he'd made when he'd turned his hand to woodwork. In the last couple of days, he seemed to be making more and more comments about Chip's physical appearance.

Why? Was it just because his fans ate that shit up? Or was it because he was noticing Chip and *liked* what he saw?

Chip snorted at his deluded train of thought. Of course that wasn't the case. Dawson had made it very clear that he thought of Chip as a brother. Not just a stepbrother, but actual *family*. He wasn't going to suddenly develop the same feelings that Chip had just because they'd moved in together. That was utterly ridiculous.

Chip put the thought firmly from his mind and picked up his pace, pushing his body until all thoughts of Dawson were forgotten and all he could think about was the burn in his legs and the hot sun on his skin as he ran.

CHAPTER 7

Dawson

"Ow, it hurts."

"Here," Dawson said, tossing the aloe spray to Chip. "This'll help."

Chip trudged over to the couch and gingerly sat down, being sure not to let the backrest touch his skin. "It's still winter," he whined as he reached up and misted his shoulders with the spray. "How the fuck did we get sunburned?"

"I guess the UV was higher than usual," Dawson commiserated. His own back was slightly burned as well but he'd stopped to apply sunscreen when he'd gotten hot and removed his shirt. Chip hadn't, and he now resembled a lobster.

"Ow, ow, ow," Chip whimpered as he used his fingers to try and spread the aloe.

"Stop that," Dawson chided, and slapped his hand away. "Give me the spray," he demanded and held out his hand. Once he had it, he spritzed the aloe all over Chip's back, getting all the spots he'd missed during his own application. The light smell of the aloe filled the loungeroom, bringing the scent of summer to the early days of September.

"Do you think it'll blister?" Chip asked.

"Hopefully not if we keep applying this every hour. You might want to have another cool shower in a bit as well. Try and get some more heat out."

"That's going to be pleasant," Chip said with a sigh.

Dawson winced. The sun had set and the warmth of the day had fled with it, leaving the night crisp and rather chilly. A cold shower would be truly miserable, but the short-term discomfort would help in the long-term. "Give me a second," he said, and got up to head through to the bathroom. He found a couple of clean flannels and wet them under the tap, then wrung them out loosely. He carried them back through to the loungeroom, trying not to let them drip on the floor as he went—not very successfully. "Here," he said, and then placed the flannels over Chip's shoulders.

Chip inhaled sharply as the rough material touched his skin, but then let the breath out in relief as the cool cloth began to leach out some of the heat of the burn. Dawson patted at it a little and then turned the cloths over to the cooler side. He did that several times, and rinsed out the flannels with more cool water as well, amazed at how warm they got. After fifteen minutes of that, some of the tension in Chip's shoulders eased. "That's feeling a lot better," he said.

"Good. Let me pop on some more aloe spray and then I'll make a start on dinner."

They had a relaxed, casual night. After dinner they headed back into the loungeroom and Chip perched on the edge of the couch and broke out the PS5. He was still shirtless, the skin of his back and shoulders red and angry looking. Dawson made a nest on the floor out of cushions and blankets and got comfortable, leaning up against a chair, catty-corner from the couch. He had his laptop out to do some editing but he kept getting distracted by Chip.

It wasn't the way he got overly excited whilst gaming and would shout at the screen. It wasn't the way he hummed—badly—to himself during the loading screens. It wasn't even the way he tossed popcorn into the air and caught the pieces with unerring accuracy. No, for some reason, Dawson was caught up in something that Chip had said earlier that day, when he'd been comparing their body types. And he'd been . . . upset? Definitely self-conscious. Almost morose.

But why?

Unable to help it, Dawson surreptitiously scanned over Chip's body, but no matter how long he looked, he couldn't see what Chip saw. There was no denying that he was fit. He had wide shoulders and a strong chest, and maybe his torso didn't nip in at the waist like Dawson's did and he didn't have a six pack, but they were actually rare outside of Hollywood or Instagram. His skin was a golden bronze and a dark happy trail led down from his belly button, disappearing under the low-slung track pants he wore.

Yeah, Dawson just couldn't see what he was self-conscious about. Chip had never had a girlfriend or boyfriend though so maybe that was part of it? He'd never been with someone who he trusted, who desired him, who made him feel good. Having random internet users saying you were hot meant fuck all to someone like Chip. Their words meant nothing to him.

"You okay?"

Dawson jerked out of his musings to find that Chip was giving him a quizzical expression. "Huh?" he asked, eloquent as usual.

Chip's mouth quirked up on one side. "You were staring."

"No I wasn't."

"Yeah, you were."

"I really wasn't."

"So, what were you doing while your eyes were pointed directly at me, if not staring?"

Fuck. Dawson could feel his cheeks heating and could tell his face was bright red. He'd always blushed easily, much to his mortification, and he hated his pale skin for that. "I zoned out. Sorry."

"Is something wrong?" Chip asked, the amusement now replaced with concern.

Dawson forced a smile. "Nah, 'course not. I guess I'm just tired."

"It's been a long—*what the fuck?*"

In the blink of an eye, Chip was off the couch and sprinting out of the room. Dawson scrambled to follow, his socked feet getting tangled in the blankets and holding him up while he tried to get free. He ran into the hallway and heard the rear door slam open, and he rushed down towards the sunroom at the back of the house. As he barrelled into the room, Chip came back inside, breathing hard.

"What the hell happened?" Dawson demanded.

"She was back," Chip said, turning and locking the door, before checking the lock once more.

"The girl from yesterday?" Dawson asked, and he suddenly felt sick.

Chip nodded. "I just caught a glimpse of her, walking past the doorway."

"Where is she now?" Crap, was his voice trembling?

Looking bewildered, Chip shrugged. "I don't know. I didn't see where she went." He ran a hand through his dark hair, making his shorter fringe stand up at odd angles. "We need to check the house again." He turned and then swore and kicked at a moving box they'd not unpacked yet. "Fuck! Why did I not install those new locks today? I should have done it the minute we got home but I was too busy bitching about this fucking sunburn."

"Hey!" Dawson crossed to him and laid a hand on his arm. "This isn't your fault. We both thought it wouldn't hurt to wait until the morning to do all of that."

He took a deep breath and then scrubbed his hands over his face. "She must have a key," he said, shaking his head. "We locked up when we got home. It's the only thing that makes sense."

"So we change the locks tomorrow, first thing," Dawson said. "Come on, we'll check the house and then find some furniture we can push in front of the doors for tonight."

"I'm so sorry," Chip said, sounding dejected.

"Why are *you* sorry? If she's one of my stalkers then that makes it *my* fault."

"I should have done *more.*"

"There's no way we could have known she'd be back. Let's just concentrate now on checking that she's actually gone, and tomorrow we can focus on making sure she stays out."

Chip took a deep, calming breath and then nodded. "Okay, you're right. Let's do this."

They checked the house from top to bottom, checking every room, behind every door, and under both beds. Once they were certain that they were the only two living beings in the house, they moved a large bookcase in front of the rear door and wedged a kitchen chair under the handle of the front door.

Feeling utterly drained after the long day, and deciding not to bother even uploading another video, Dawson decided he was going to bed. He was brushing his teeth in the bathroom when Chip came in and joined him. They stood in silence, just looking at each other in the mirror as they brushed. Chip looked drawn and guilty, his hazel eyes dull under his dark brows. Dawson swayed to the side, gently bumping their hips together. "'ou 'k?" he asked around his toothbrush.

Chip removed his brush and then spat into the sink. He looked up as he rinsed the brush under the tap. "Sure," he replied, before scooping water into his mouth to rinse.

Dawson did *not* believe him.

He took his turn spitting and rinsing. When he was done, he turned to face Chip, not noticing until he'd done so how close they now were in the tiny space. "You wanna try that again, with a bit more honesty this time?"

Chip huffed but didn't deny he'd been lying out of his arse. "I don't like the feeling I've let you down."

Dawson frowned. "You haven't."

"I have!"

"At the risk of turning this into yet *another* circular argument, you really haven't."

"I'm not keeping you safe!" Chip burst out and then bit his lip and turned away, like he'd not meant to let that slip.

Dawson could have said a hundred different things. He could have said *"It's not your job to keep me safe,"* or, *"I can look after myself,"* or even, *"We're in this together."* Instead, he just pulled Chip into a hug and held him tight. "It'll be okay."

"I don't know what I'll do if she hurts you." It was said so quietly that Dawson was sure he wasn't meant to hear it.

Again, not knowing what to say, Dawson just squeezed him once more. "Come on, let's go to bed. We can deal with all this tomorrow."

Chip agreed but his face was still creased with worry, and when he tugged Dawson towards his bedroom once again, Dawson didn't argue.

The chattering of his teeth woke him up. Dawson blinked against the murky darkness, waiting for his eyes to adjust. He was shivering uncontrollably, despite the heat from Chip's body next to him. As the room slowly came into focus, the shadows getting less hazy and more distinct, he could see his breath misting in front of his face.

Why the hell was it so cold again? He'd been checking the forecast and it wasn't supposed to be this bad. Was it the house? He'd not really paid much attention to the building report they'd had done when it had transferred into their names. Maybe it wasn't insulated? That was common in older homes, wasn't it? Given that the place was over a hundred and fifty years old, he wouldn't be surprised if it didn't have any insulation at all.

Dawson tried snuggling down further into the blankets but it was no use. He couldn't get warm. He was tempted to plaster himself against Chip's back but that would just be too awkward. It was one thing for him to snuggle up to Chip when they were both awake and consenting but it would just be creepy to do it when Chip was asleep. Then there was the matter of Chip's sunburn—he didn't want to hurt him.

Chip was a bit of a neat freak and had folded the extra blankets from the other night and already put them away. Dawson climbed out of bed and went out to the linen cupboard in the hallway to grab them. He didn't want to wake Chip so he didn't bother turning on the hall light, just placed his hand against the wall to guide his way. He reached the cupboard and pulled the door open and a shout ripped from his throat.

The disembodied head of a young woman toppled towards him. Her eye sockets were hollow, empty voids, her mouth was locked open in a silent, agonising scream, and her neck ended abruptly in a jagged, bloody mess. Dawson stumbled backwards and the head fell from the shelf and into his arms. He fell against the wall, juggling the heavy, slippery weight in his hands before he tumbled to the ground. The head hit the floor with a dull *thud* and rolled away, coming to a stop with the ghoulish features facing him, leaving a blood trail behind it.

Breathing hard, Dawson scrambled backwards, trying to inch away from the macabre sight when suddenly the eyes fluttered closed and then began blinking rapidly. The lashes made a wet *fwup fwup* sound against the empty sockets, and then the jaw creaked and the girl's mouth began to open and close, open and close.

"What the fuck, what the fuck, what the fuck?" Dawson babbled, pushing away from the head but finding his way blocked by the wall at his back. "No, no, no, no, no."

Then the eyes stopped blinking and the mouth snapped closed. Dawson held his breath, waiting. One long moment passed, and then another. He didn't dare move. The seconds ticked by.

And then the head rolled to one side by itself and the girl's mouth began to open and close once more, the movement of her jaw propelling the head across the floor towards Dawson.

He screamed again, turning onto his hands and knees and trying to scamper away up the hall. A sharp pain lanced through his foot and he glanced over his shoulder to see that the teeth had clamped down on his ankle.

There was a crashing noise from the bedroom and then the hall light flicked on. Chip skidded out into the hall and hurried towards him. "Daw? What is it? What's wrong?"

Dawson launched himself into Chip's arms, and in his haste to get away from the head, he sent them both crashing against the wall. "Stay away from it!" he cried, even as he tried to shove Chip away from the danger.

"Stay away from what?" Chip asked, looking bewildered.

"The head! Her head. It's coming for us!"

Strong hands clamped down on Dawson's shoulders and forced him to be still. "Daw, I need you to take a breath. Can you do that for me?"

Why was Chip so calm? Couldn't he see the horror that was coming for them. "We have to go!" he insisted, not daring to look behind him to see the horror of the severed head in the bright light. "It can move by itself."

"What can move by itself?" Chip asked.

"The head! The head can move!"

"Dawson, you're not making any sense," Chip told him.

"Can't you see it? We need to go!"

Those strong hands pushed at Dawson and he found himself being turned around. He squeezed his eyes shut and flinched away from the horror that he knew was waiting for him.

He felt arms slide around his waist and he was cradled from behind. "Dawson? Baby? There's *nothing there.*"

He shook his head, not believing Chip. His ankle throbbed from the bite and he knew what he'd seen. It may have been dark but there had been enough light to see by. A severed head had fallen from the linen cupboard. He'd not imagined that. "No, no, it was there. It was *right* there."

"Baby, come on, open your eyes," Chip said gently, his breath warm against the back of Dawson's neck. "See for yourself. We're alone. There's nothing there."

"I can't," he whispered, unable to bring himself to follow the instructions.

"Yes, you can. I'm here. I'm right here with you. Open your eyes."

His breath hitching in his throat, Dawson forced his eyes to open. He blinked against the bright light of the bulb and then glanced down at the floor in front of him.

It was empty.

His whole body trembling, Dawson turned around in Chip's arms. "What the *fuck* is going on?" he whispered.

CHAPTER 8

Chip

Chip picked up the two mugs of tea and carried them over to the table. He slid one in front of Dawson, who was sitting with his knees pulled up to his chest, arms wrapped around them and his bare feet just hanging on to the edge of the chair. His head was down and his gaze was locked on the table.

"Here, drink up," Chip urged as he took his own seat.

Dawson did as instructed, reaching out and wrapping his hands around the mug before taking a tentative sip. He put the mug back down on the table and then looked up. There was no other way to describe his expression, other than haunted. "I'm not crazy," he said, his voice strong despite the tremble in his hands. "It happened. It really happened."

"I believe you," Chip said, and his eyes fell to Dawson's ankle and the ugly bite mark that marred the pale skin there. He'd been on edge since he'd seen the girl earlier that night, but hearing Dawson scream and finding him in the state he'd been in had Chip rattled. He'd been about to put the whole thing down to a nightmare until he'd seen the bite. It was the perfect impression of human teeth and it had been strong enough to break the skin.

"What the fuck is happening?" Dawson asked. "What did I see? Was it a ghost?"

"I don't know," Chip admitted. "I wouldn't have thought that ghosts could physically hurt you." He paused, carefully thinking about how to phrase the next part. "It definitely was *just* a head? Like, it wasn't the girl I saw and she ran off before I got there?"

Dawson shook his head vehemently. "No. I saw the stump of her neck. There was . . . well, there's evidence." He held up his hands, showing the smears of blood on his wrists. "Oh, God, what am I doing? I need to wash that off."

He jumped up and hurried over to the sink, squirting an obscene amount of hand soap onto his skin and then scrubbing over each forearm. Chip watched as he rinsed and then got more soap, then after rinsing a second time, got even more soap. He stood up and came up behind Dawson, reaching out to still his hand as he reached yet again for the pump bottle. "I think you got it all," he said gently. He tugged Dawson away from the sink and grabbed a hand towel, then gently patted the skin—pink from the scrubbing—dry.

"What do we do?" Dawson asked in a small voice once his hands were dry.

"I don't know," Chip said again. "Maybe it was a one off? An anomaly. Nothing else weird has happened."

"What about the girl we saw? Do you think she's real or a ghost as well?"

He paused, not having considered that. "She *looked* real enough."

"So did the fucking *head* that fell out of the *linen cupboard!*" Dawson snapped, sounding on the verge of hysterics.

"I'm just saying, maybe we need more evidence? What did you want us to do? Head to the church in the morning and ask Noah if the local priest performs exorcisms? You know that's just gonna convince everyone in town that we're crazy."

"I'm *not crazy*! It happened, Tate. It fucking happened!"

Dawson rarely used his real name, so Chip knew he was serious. "I'm not saying it didn't, but other people might not believe us." He guided Dawson back over to the table and into a chair. "I just think we need to sit on this for a bit. See if anything else hinky happens. Record the data. Then if we do need . . . outside help, we'll have more info to give them. Maybe it'll help us figure out what sort of expert we need?"

He took a deep, shaky breath and let it out slowly before nodding. "Okay. Yeah, yeah that makes sense."

Chip reached out and covered one of Dawson's hands with his own and squeezed it. "But Daw?"

"Yeah?"

"Until we get this sorted, we live in one another's pockets, okay? I don't want you alone in this house for a second."

"Won't that get a little awkward?" Dawson asked in what was probably supposed to be a teasing tone, but Chip could hear the relief beneath it that he was taking this so seriously.

"It's you and me—we've been two peas in a pod since kindy. If I gotta wait on the other side of the bathroom door while you shower and shit, well, I'll just make you sing me your latest song while you do so I don't hear you fart."

That got the laugh he was hoping for. "I don't know if that's the sort of percussion I'm looking for on the song."

"People will remix anything these days. Don't discount it yet."

"You're a fucking dag," Dawson said, punching him lightly on the arm.

"Well this dag is potentially living in a haunted house so we take no chances. Got it?"

Dawson nodded, expression serious now. "Got it. We stick together."

"Do you think you'll be able to sleep again now?"

"Maybe? If it's not too cold."

Chip frowned. "There was a lot going on when I woke up, so I wasn't sure if I was imagining it but the room was fucking freezing, wasn't it?"

"Yeah. That's why I got up, to get more blankets."

He reached up and ran a hand through his hair. "Right. So, I guess that's a good reminder—until we work out what the hell is going on here, we can't dismiss *anything* as our imagination."

Dawson nodded. "Agreed."

They stood and placed their mugs in the sink and cautiously made their way down the hall to the bedroom. Dawson was hesitant as he stood in the doorway, his eyes darting from the bedroom to the end of the hall, over and over.

"We'll leave the light on out here, okay? All night," Chip assured him.

Dawson chewed on his lower lip for a long moment. Finally he said, in a quiet voice, "Can we keep the door closed?"

"Of course," Chip agreed easily. He waited by the closed door while Dawson climbed into bed, but before he turned off the light he grabbed the chair from the corner and wedged it under the handle. He then flipped the switch and crossed to the bed, climbing in on the side closest to the door. He nudged Dawson over.

"What're you doing?" Dawson asked in the darkness.

"Shove over. I want this side," he said.

He heard Dawson huff, probably from frustration at being babied, but he *did* move over without complaint. Chip knew him better than anyone and he knew that Dawson was genuinely scared by the night's events. If sleeping between him and the door put his mind at ease even the tiniest bit, he'd happily do it.

They were quiet for a few minutes, both lost in their own thoughts. Eventually, Chip asked, "Are you warm enough?"

He felt more than saw Dawson shrug. "I guess."

Taking that as a "not really", Chip shuffled over and slipped a hand over Dawson's waist, pulling him back against him. He went without complaint, and Chip could feel his body trembling. He didn't know if it was from the cold or the night's events, but either way, it just made him hug him tighter.

Chip stayed awake for a long time after Dawson finally fell into a fitful sleep, determined to protect him from anything and everything.

Except maybe from himself.

It didn't take long the following morning to change the locks over, and only slightly longer to install the new security cameras. They'd gotten four and had planned to set them up surrounding the outside of the house, but they mutually decided that it would be best to have two of them inside. Chip wasn't sure if ghostly activity would show up on a camera but if their intruder came back, she definitely would.

Well, if she was human that is.

He didn't know what had become of his life in the past week that he was now having to question if the person they'd both seen was real or a freaking ghost. He'd never really believed in ghosts before. It wasn't that he thought they weren't real, but Chip had always been an evidence kind of person. He himself wasn't an academic, but that didn't mean he didn't believe in the science of others. If there was hard evidence—preferably peer reviewed, thank you very much—that proved a fact one way or another, he'd accept that before he accepted some conspiracy theory pulled out of the arse of someone who thought vaccines caused Autism.

He glanced down at Dawson's bare feet and scowled at the bite mark there. He really wasn't happy that their evidence had come in the form of Dawson getting hurt. They'd washed and disinfected the wound last night but it didn't seem to have helped much. It was red and inflamed and looked half a second away from being infected. If it got worse, he was going to have to drag Dawson to the doctor, which would go about as well as giving a cat a bath. Dawson *hated* doctors. And how were they supposed to explain who had bitten him? They couldn't play it off as a young niece or nephew getting carried away whilst playing—there was no mistaking the fact that it was made by an adult. A kinky one night stand that got out of hand? Fuck no. Dawson would be mortified, and Chip would really rather *not* imagine him with anyone else. He hated it when Dawson started seeing someone, and would feel queasy for the entire duration of the relationship.

"Um, Chip?" Dawson asked, uncertain.

"Hmm?" he mumbled and looked up.

"You okay?" Dawson was sitting on the couch with his laptop, responding to an email from a potential sponsor. "You were wearing your scary face."

"I don't have a scary face," he argued, trying to school his expression into something neutral. Was his "scary face" due to the bite, or thinking about Dawson with a lover? Or was it a little from column A and a little from column B? No, he'd looked scary, not heartbroken. Definitely the freaking ghost.

"Uh, yeah, you do. It makes you look like you're contemplating hurting someone."

Could you hurt a disembodied ghost head? It had been real enough to break Dawson's skin so perhaps it was real enough to be injured in return? If so, Chip couldn't deny that he'd take a running kick at it and boot it between the goalposts without a second thought.

"Okay, so now you're smiling like a serial killer who's enjoying seeing the photographic evidence of his crimes in court."

He stared at Dawson. "Okay firstly, *again*, that's oddly specific. Secondly, I do *not* look like that!"

"You can't see your own face so how would you know?" Dawson said reasonably.

"I just do!"

"Well, you'd be wrong." Dawson stuck his tongue out at him.

"What are you? Eight?" Chip asked, unable to keep the grin off his face.

"It got rid of your scary expression so I don't mind if it makes me childish."

Chip shook his head and pushed to his feet. "You really are a dag. I'm getting a coffee. You want one?"

"Sure." Dawson pushed up from the couch and followed him through to the kitchen.

As promised, they'd stuck together the whole morning and it had been easy. They orbited around one another naturally and so it hadn't been a hardship to stay close. Once Chip started work again it might be a whole different story but that was still over two weeks away. Would they be able to find a solution to this ghost problem by then? He had no bloody clue where to even start. How did you make a ghost stop haunting you? Was she *actually* haunting them or was it a one off event?

Data and evidence. They needed more of it before they could come up with a game plan. That might take some time, and they also had the issue of the potential stalker to deal with, which added to their stress. Chip figured it could all wait until tomorrow. They were both wrung out from the previous night's events, and now that they'd changed the locks and installed the cameras they could take the rest of the day for themselves.

He opened the cupboard to pull out their mugs and frowned when he found a jumbled mess of Tupperware instead. Chip frowned. He closed the cupboard and turned to Dawson. "Where did we put the mugs again?"

"Right behind you," Dawson confirmed.

Chip stepped to the side, pulling the cupboard open as he did so to reveal the contents.

"What the hell?" Dawson came over to stand next to him as they stared into the depths of the cupboard. "We put all the plastic containers in the corner cupboard."

"It seems like *someone* moved them."

"But why?"

"No idea but they'd better have kept all the lids with their containers because I'm gonna be pissed if they didn't. It took me ages to sort through all of that crap before we moved to make sure I wasn't bringing with us seven random lids that didn't have matching containers."

Dawson shook his head. "You have the weirdest priorities."

Chip shrugged. "Since I can't read a ghost's mind to know why she's fucking with the Tupperware, I figured it doesn't hurt to be practical." He started opening the rest of the cupboards and discovered that all the contents had been moved around. On the third try, he found the mugs and grabbed two. Luckily the pantry hadn't been messed with so he pulled out the coffee and sugar and started making their drinks.

"Since we don't know if she'll move everything again, I say we don't bother putting it all back," Dawson suggested.

Chip nodded in agreement. "So, what did you want to do with the rest of the day?" he asked as they took their drinks back through to the loungeroom, attempting to distract them both from the weirdness that was now their lives. They needed a little bit of normalcy.

"Can you help me with a video?" Dawson asked. "I really need to get something out today but I don't have the energy to do a Live or a song or anything."

"Yeah, 'course, man," he agreed easily. "What've you got in mind?"

"There's a trend at the moment where you play Twenty Questions with a friend, but instead of them answering, you answer for them instead, and they say if you got it right or not."

"A besties challenge?" Chip asked. "I'm down. We'll kill at that."

An odd expression flickered over Dawson's face but then it was gone, replaced with his usual angelic smile. "Awesome. Let's do this."

CHAPTER 9

Dawson

Dawson busied himself with the GoPro, even though it was set up and ready to go. He just needed a minute. *A besties challenge?* Fuck, what had he been thinking? The trend was actually something that couples were doing, proving how well they knew their significant other. Stuff like that had never stopped Dawson before from turning it into a "besties challenge." In fact, his reimagining of a couple of similar trends had been some of his highest viewed videos. It was common for different influencers to adapt trends and alter them to suit their own brand. His viewers knew that Chip was not only his stepbrother but his best friend and they lapped up the brotherly content he posted.

So why was Dawson so nervous now? Why did even the thought of doing a couples' trend with Chip hit differently today? Nothing had changed between them. Except for the ghost thing, but that hadn't changed anything between *them*, had it?

Baby, come on, open your eyes.

Last night had been terrifying for Dawson and he'd been scared out of his mind. He'd been hopped-up on adrenaline from his fight or flight instincts and from encountering a ghostly severed head. But he'd not been so out of it that he hadn't caught on to the fact Chip had called him baby. More than once.

That was definitely new. And for some inexplicable reason, he didn't hate it. Which made absolutely no sense whatsoever. Whenever Dawson had been seeing a girl, he'd *hated* pet names. All of them had called him babe or baby and he'd cringed internally with each use. He'd never said anything, not wanting to upset them, but it always made him feel uncomfortable.

So why was it different when Chip used it?

It was all so confusing. That wasn't the only thing that had changed recently either. It felt like their entire relationship had pivoted somehow and now wasn't as simple as it once was. What had started out as friendship and then brotherhood now seemed charged with something else. Something *more.* Dawson couldn't define exactly what it was but he didn't hate it. In fact, it excited him, energised him. And that scared the shit out of him.

He pushed that thought away for later. Much later. Right now he had content to create, fans to entertain, and sponsors to keep happy. He stopped playing with the GoPro and stepped back over to the couch, sitting down and patting the seat next to him. "Come on," he said to Chip. "Let's get started."

Like he always did, Chip happily complied—no questions asked, always enthusiastic, happy to help. Like supporting Dawson was the highest priority in his life. The warm thrill that went through him at that thought was something else Dawson would unpack later. At the rate he was going he might need to find a storage locker for all those pesky thoughts, since they were growing at an exponential rate.

"Hi everyone," Dawson said to the camera. "Today Chip and I are playing Twenty Questions, with a twist. If you haven't seen this game yet, the rules are simple. We answer the twenty questions from the OG video, *but* we answer for each other. Then the other has to confirm if the answer is correct. Sound easy enough? Cool, let's get started." He glanced down at his phone where he'd pulled up a screenshot of the questions from the original video. "Question one: are you a cat or a dog person?" He smiled over at Chip. "Did you want to answer first?"

Chip nodded. "Sure. Dawson is definitely a cat person. His mum has two cats, and whenever we're back home you're guaranteed to find him curled up someplace warm with them. Dogs are too energetic and chaotic, but he finds cats much more chill."

"Well, Beans and Lou are anyway," Dawson agreed. "Spot on." He grinned. "Chip is a dog guy but he's allergic to them so he can't have one. That doesn't stop him from rolling around and playing with every dog he comes across though. He just gets the worst hives afterwards and then I have to listen to him complain about how itchy he is."

"Eh, patting the dogs is worth it," Chip said with a shrug. "I'm definitely a dog man."

"Alright, question two: what's your favourite season?"

"You prefer summer since you get cold easily," Chip answered immediately.

"And you prefer spring because everything is green, the days are warm but the nights are still chilly," Dawson said. "Though again, you get allergies, so you're miserable the whole time but at least you're liking the weather."

They didn't even have to confirm their responses, knowing they were both right. They fist-bumped.

"Question three: are you ticklish and where?" He turned in time to catch Chip's evil grin. "Don't you fucking dare!" But it was too late. Chip had lunged sideways to pin him to the couch and then used his free hand to reach down and grab at Dawson's extremely ticklish knees. "S-s-s-top it, you f-f-ucker," Dawson cried between giggles.

"You gonna call barleese?" Chip asked as he continued to hold Dawson down with ease.

Normally, Dawson wouldn't surrender quite so quickly during a tickle war, but for some mortifying reason his dick was starting to perk up at how easily he was being restrained. Trying not to panic, Dawson nodded vigorously and shouted, "Barleese! Barleese!"

Chip immediately stopped and let him up, then fell back onto his side of the couch with a smug look on his face. He turned to the camera and said, "Yeah, Daw has super ticklish knees."

"Bastard," Dawson muttered and tried to rearrange his clothing without flashing the entire internet his semi. He cleared his throat. "That fucker over there is *not* ticklish at all and it's really annoying."

"It's my superpower," Chip said.

"I thought your superpower was being a dick?"

"That's more of an everyday skill," Chip shot back, then gave him an impish grin. "So, what's question number four?"

The later the night got, the more anxious Dawson grew. Most of the weird shit had happened once the sun had gone down and he wondered what was in store for them that night.

Chip had just gone in the shower and Dawson was sitting outside in the hallway, waiting, with the bathroom door cracked open an inch. The position put him almost directly opposite the linen cupboard and he couldn't drag his eyes away from the door. He kept expecting that the door would fly open at any moment and the severed head from the night before would come flying out.

His ankle throbbed and he reached down and clasped his hand over the bite there. It had been painful all day, throbbing and hot. He'd slathered it in Savlon after scrubbing it once again, but he was beginning to think there was no way he was going to avoid an infection. Who the hell knew what kind of bacteria a severed head had in its mouth?

The throbbing sped up, keeping time with the thundering of his heart. Dawson's vision seemed to narrow, tunnelling down to the handle of the door across from him. Was he imagining it or did it just shake a little? Was that creaking the sound of the hinges? He stared at the handle until his eyes watered, not even daring to blink, unable to look away.

His breath caught. What was that noise? His ears strained and he was sure that he could hear a *drip drip drip* coming from across the hallway. The memory of the slick blood that dripped from the severed skin of the ghost's throat hit him full force, and before Dawson even knew what he was doing, he was scrambling to his feet and shoving his way into the bathroom.

He slammed the door shut and turned his back to it, sliding down it and bracing his feet against the tiles on the outside of the bathtub-shower combo. It was a head; it wouldn't have the strength to force its way into the room, would it? His breath caught and he squeezed his eyes shut, concentrating on nothing else but his weight against the cool wood of the door, keeping it closed.

He heard movement in front of him. Fuck, how had it gotten in? How had it managed to get past him? Dawson curled in on himself, crying out as he raised his arms to protect his face from the blunt teeth that he was intimately familiar with. Something warm and wet touched his wrist and he jerked away with a cry. "Leave me alone! Please, leave me alone!"

"Dawson? Dawson!" Hands wrapped around his arms and shook him gently. "Baby, come on, look at me. Dawson, please."

Wait, that was Chip's voice. He cracked his eyes open and peered up to find Chip crouching above him. Behind him, the shower curtain had been flung aside and the shower was still on, filling the small room with steam.

"Are you with me, baby?" Chip asked, cupping Dawson's face gently.

Dawson stared at him blankly, and his eyes took in the details before him but his mind failed to process it. Chip's hazel eyes were wide with concern, and his lashes were damp and clumped together. He was soaking wet, and his long black hair was plastered to his neck and shoulders, still dripping with water. Dawson's eyes followed a droplet as it ran down over Chip's chest, slipping over his chest hair before sliding lower, towards his . . .

Oh. Dawson's eyes snapped up as he realised that Chip was naked. His brain kicked into gear and he began to put together the sequence of events that must have occurred.

He'd crashed into the bathroom in a panic. Chip had immediately sprung into action, jumping out of the tub to check on Dawson. He'd not even bothered to turn off the taps, so of course he wouldn't have stopped to grab a towel.

"Come on, Daw. I need you to focus. What happened?" Chip asked.

"I don't know," he said. "I thought it was back but maybe I imagined it."

"What did we say about not assuming we'd imagined anything?" Chip stood, pulling Dawson up after him. For the briefest of moments, while Chip was on his feet and Dawson was still on the ground, his face had been level with Chip's groin.

Dawson was familiar with dicks. He had one, after all. He also watched porn and so he'd seen his fair share before. He'd not paid much attention to them but you couldn't watch a man and a woman fucking on PornHub without seeing the dude's cock. It was just a fact of life. So why was Chip's cock—flaccid, not even standing at attention—now suddenly burned into his brain? After the barest of glimpses?

"I'll go check the hall," Chip was saying and Dawson snapped back to reality in time to grab his hand before he opened the door. "What is it?" Chip asked.

"Um . . ." His voice croaked and he coughed to clear his throat. What had he been going to say? *"Don't go, it's too dangerous? Don't leave me? I don't want you in danger?"* He didn't think any of that would go down well, so instead, he grabbed a towel and thrust it towards Chip. "Here, at least put this on."

Chip took the towel. "You worried a ghost will be offended by my nudity?" he asked, managing to look amused despite the situation.

"Uh, no, not that," Dawson said. "It's just, I know how hard it can bite and I figured you'd want *some* sort of protection."

Chip blanched. "Good point," he said and quickly wrapped the towel around his waist.

While he did that, Dawson reached out to turn the shower off. Their tanks might be full now at the end of winter, but they had a limited supply and needed to conserve all the water they could.

"Ready?" Chip asked, his hand on the doorknob.

Dawson took a deep breath, feeling much braver now that he'd be facing the disembodied head with Chip at his side. "Yes. No, wait!" He reached out and grabbed the full bottle of shampoo, the weight comforting in his hand. "Okay, now I'm ready."

Chip nodded and pulled open the door.

CHAPTER 10

Chip

Chip yawned and scrubbed at his face, feeling the scratch of his stubble against his palms. He'd not gotten a chance to shave last night and he was getting scruffy.

There had been nothing out in the hall when they'd gone to investigate, and Dawson had gotten quiet after that. Chip knew him well enough to know he was second guessing himself and feeling foolish, which in turn made him retreat inwards. Even if there *hadn't* been anything there and it had just been the events of the past couple of days playing havoc with his imagination, that didn't mean the anxiety itself wasn't real. He'd bundled Dawson up in bed, had climbed in next to him, and then they'd watched silly videos on the internet until they'd fallen asleep.

He was growing way too used to waking up with Dawson warming the sheets next to him. It was making him too complacent and he knew that he'd started to let his guard down. He was letting slip too many clues about his real feelings, and if he wasn't careful he was going to fuck everything up between them. Jesus, how many times had he let slip a "baby?" For fuck's sake, he really needed to get a grip.

Beside him, Dawson was beginning to stir. Chip tried not to be creepy but he couldn't seem to stop his eyes from lingering as he emerged from sleep. Long blond lashes fluttered over pale cheeks, which were speckled with freckles and still slightly pink after their afternoon in the sun on Saturday. He yawned widely, reaching his arms above his head in a stretch and only just missing smacking Chip's face with his hand. It made Chip flinch back, and the movement caused Dawson to open his eyes and look across the bed at him with eyes still heavy with sleep. "Hey," he croaked.

"Morning," Chip said, and rolled out of bed. He did *not* trust himself to not lean in and kiss Dawson fully awake. "Sleep okay?" he asked as he pulled his phone from the charger.

"Yeah," Dawson said, sitting up and looking blearily around the room. "Better than I thought I would. Wha' time is it?"

"Quarter past six."

Dawson made a face but started to climb out of bed, and Chip wanted to make a quick escape to use the bathroom. He didn't want to risk leaving Dawson alone though, and so he stood awkwardly by the door and waited for him before he went.

They took turns in the bathroom and then went into the kitchen to have breakfast, only to find that every cupboard in the room was open and the contents strewn across the floor. Tupperware was jumbled together with cans of food, pots and pans, and a handful of brown onions. A bag of flour had burst open, leaving a fine white coating over everything.

Chip glared at the mess and then sneezed twice, then glared some more. "Fuck this," he declared. "I'm not caffeinated enough to deal with ghostly shit right now. Let's go into town and get breakfast."

"Yeah, good plan," Dawson said slowly as he looked, wide-eyed at the mess.

Chip grabbed the car keys, then made Dawson wait while he quickly checked the camera feeds to ensure there was no one outside. The day had dawned misty, and a heavy white blanket lingered over everything. Only when he was confident that the coast was clear did he let Dawson leave the house, then they locked it securely behind themselves.

"I kinda feel like you missed your calling as a secret agent," Dawson teased as they crossed the yard to the car.

"Just for that, you can drive," Chip said and tossed the keys to him.

As expected, Dawson juggled them and then threw them right back. "No thanks."

"You're gonna have to get used to the drive into town eventually."

"The sun's only just risen. Do you really want *me* behind the wheel when there's sure to be suicidal roos every fifty metres?"

Chip frowned. "Yeah, good point."

"I do have them from time to time," Dawson said as he opened the passenger door. "Do you mind if I do a video on the drive in?" he asked as they belted themselves in. "I've been neglecting my subs lately and I need to do something just for them before they abandon ship."

"Go for it." Dawson's subscribers were one of his main revenue generators, and Chip understood how important it was to keep them engaged, entertained, and most importantly, happy to keep subscribing.

It wasn't a long drive and Chip filmed the picturesque countryside they passed on the way, commenting about how beautiful it was in the mist and just making small talk with the camera. Chip was familiar with this type of video. Dawson's fans ate up the "day in the life of" clips, and loved feeling like they were riding along with him as he went about his everyday tasks. It would definitely be a treat for the subs. Chip was proud of Dawson for being his usual charming self and not showing any hint of the anxiety and distress he'd experienced the night before. He truly was an utter professional.

The streets of Brockman were quiet but that wasn't unexpected at just after seven on a Monday morning. There were a few cars already parked in front of the bakery and Chip pulled into a spot beside a Land Cruiser. He held the door open for an older woman who was carrying a tray with four takeaway cups in it and she smiled at him gratefully. He smiled back, and then he and Dawson were inside, breathing in the heavenly aroma of fresh coffee.

Ellen was behind the counter again and she greeted them by name. Chip was impressed by her memory as she must see hundreds of different people each week and she'd spoken to them for less than five minutes. They ordered a bacon and egg roll each, and two flat whites, then managed to snag the empty couches in the corner of the seating area.

Chip put their table number on the small coffee table in front of the couches and sat, sinking down more than he'd expected into the soft cushions. He waited to speak until Dawson had finished grabbing some footage of the bakery. "How're you doing this morning?" he asked.

Dawson sighed and slumped back against the backrest. "Eh."

"That good, huh?"

He shrugged. "What do you want me to say? It looks like we inherited a haunted house, with a pissed-off ghost who seems to have lost her body. On top of that, I may or may not have a stalker. There's a lot going on, dude."

Chip nudged Dawson's knee with his own. "Which is *why* I'm checking in on you. Are you still taking your meds?"

Dawson rolled his eyes. "Yes, Dad. I'm a good boy who takes my anti-mental pills every morning."

Chip tried to ignore the way his cock gave a little twitch at Dawson calling himself a "good boy." It was almost frustrating that it wasn't at all interested in anyone else and only decided to perk up around the most inappropriate person possible. "I wish you wouldn't call them that. Having bad anxiety doesn't make you crazy."

"I'm pretty sure seeing ghosts does though."

"You're *not* crazy," Chip told him again. "We'll figure this out."

Dawson pushed himself up until he was sitting up straight, which was a bit of a challenge with how soft the cushions were. "I'll be better when we have some sort of game plan," he admitted. "Right now, I feel like we're fucking floundering. I mean, where do we even start?"

"I was thinking about that last night," Chip said. "Ellen mentioned the Historical Society. She seemed to think they'd have some info about our family and the house, so maybe they can tell us if anything bad happened there. Maybe if we can identify the ghost, we can figure out what's keeping her there? Unfinished business or something?"

"You mean other than the fact that she was brutally murdered?" Dawson drawled. He was always more sarcastic before coffee.

"We don't know for sure that's what happened," Chip argued.

"Oh sure, sure. Maybe she slipped and fell on a hatchet repeatedly and that's why her head got chopped off?"

Chip sighed. "Okay, valid."

"I just don't know how that'll help though, ya know? So what if we figure out who she was? How is that gonna help her 'move on' or whatever?"

There was an edge to Dawson's voice now. He was getting worked up, starting to spiral. Chip needed to calm him down. He reached over and grabbed his hand, giving it a squeeze. "Hey, we'll figure it out, yeah? I know we have way more questions than answers right now but you gotta give us time to *find* them."

"And what if we don't?"

"We'll work it out," Chip said with as much confidence as he could muster.

"Here you go, boys."

Chip's head snapped around to see Ellen standing next to them. She bent down and placed their rolls and coffees down on the table. When she stood, her eyes lingered on where Chip was still holding Dawson's hand. "How are you two settling in? Are you finding small-town life agreeing with you?"

"Oh, um, sure," Chip replied, quickly dropping Dawson's hand. "Yeah, it's cool here."

"I'm glad," she said, and tucked a strand of grey hair behind her ear. "I reckon you two might enjoy the hillbilly life." Then she winked at them and sauntered off.

Dawson watched her go, an adorable frown on his lips. "Wait, what did she mean by that?"

"I have no idea," Chip lied, glad for his sunburn so Dawson wouldn't notice how bright red he'd turned. How was this his life? He'd been fighting off this attraction since he was a kid, and within days of moving to a new town one of the locals had already seen right through him. The fact that Ellen hadn't clutched at her pearls, scandalised, was something to unpack another day.

Dawson groaned then and rubbed at his eyes. "Urgh, I am really not looking forward to cleaning up that mess at home." He'd already dismissed Ellen's random comment and had circled back to their current issue.

"Yeah," Chip agreed and took a long swig of his coffee. "I'm just hoping it's not gonna be a regular occurrence."

Dawson swallowed loudly enough that Chip heard him on the other side of the table. "What if it doesn't stop? What if it just gets worse?"

Chip considered this. What *were* their options? Sell the house and move back to Perth? That would just lump someone else with their ghost problem. The house wasn't heritage listed so maybe they could demolish it and build something new?

No, even the thought of levelling the house made Chip feel sick. It was old and small and had a hundred issues, but he loved it. He'd loved it growing up when he got to spend time with his new family there, and he loved the memories of Grandpa Miller. He'd never treated Chip any differently to Dawson, even though he wasn't his grandson by blood. He'd just embraced having two rambunctious grandsons to have adventures with when they came to stay.

Simply replacing the house might not even work anyway. The ghost might be linked to the location, not the physical structures. Besides, they didn't exactly have the means to fund a new build even if it *would* solve their issues.

Ultimately, both options left a sour taste in his mouth. Chip knew—like he knew that the sky was blue and coffee was necessary to life—that Dawson would feel the same. They'd been best friends for almost twenty years. He *knew* Dawson. He knew that in this, no matter how scary and bizarre the situation got, they'd be on the same page.

"We'll figure it out," he said, meeting Dawson's gaze. "I promise."

They finished their breakfast and then stopped at the counter to get another coffee each for the road. There was a lull in the rush of customers on their way to work and so Chip took the opportunity to ask Ellen about the Historical Society.

"You'll find it at the Heritage Centre over on Hampton Street," she explained. "The museum is there along with the Men's Shed, CWA, the art gallery and a few other bits and pieces. It's all volunteer run, so they only open on Tuesdays and then Friday through to Sunday."

"Awesome. Thanks for the info."

"You're welcome, poppet." She handed them their drinks. "See you boys again soon."

"I was hoping we'd be able to see them today," Dawson said, sounding dejected, as they made their way to the car.

"We can do it tomorrow before cricket practice," Chip told him. "It'll give us some time today to get a start on a few jobs around the house."

Dawson groaned and slammed the car door behind him as he slid into the passenger seat. "Do we have to?"

"Yes," Chip said. "We took yesterday off, so we really have to make a start on it today before our list gets away from us. Since we've got to clean the kitchen up anyway, we may as well keep going."

Dawson grumbled under his breath but finally said, "Okay, I suppose we should."

"Said like I was giving you a choice," Chip said with a smirk. "Come on, the hardware will be open now so let's pick up a few things and make a start."

After they'd dealt with the mess in the kitchen, they started on a deep clean of the house, doing everything they'd not had a chance to do before the removalists had arrived their first day. Windows and walls were washed, the verandah was swept, the old doormats replaced with new ones, and Chip even cleaned the flue in the chimney. There had been no ghostly activity, so after a break for lunch they decided they'd split up to get more done. Chip sent Dawson outside to mow the grass around the house, figuring that as they'd not seen the ghost out there as yet it was the safer option. Chip then got started on fixing hinges on cupboards and replacing a few cupboard doors entirely. He then changed the washers on all of the taps before dumping Draino down every sink in a preemptive strike against blocked drains.

When he was done, he headed outside to find Dawson beating out the cushions from the rattan outdoor setting that sat under the verandah along the side of the house. The entire area had been tidied, with dead pot plants removed, random tools returned to the shed, and the glass of the small coffee table cleaned. The clouds from earlier had cleared and the late winter sun was doing its best to warm the earth, but it was cool under the wide tin roof.

"It looks good out here," he said, already picturing this space as a good area to wind down after work. "You want a beer?"

Dawson shook his head. "Nah, but I might grab a coffee."

"I'll get it," Chip told him. "Decaf or regular?"

He glanced at his watch. "Decaf. Cheers."

"No worries." Chip headed inside and made them both a drink, and when he returned he found Dawson typing away on his phone. "Busy?" he asked.

"Just replying to a few subs." The subscriber package on Dawson's Vewz gave them priority replies to DMs and he was always diligent in delivering on that promise. It was about ten bucks a month to be a subscriber and Dawson wanted to make sure that his subs got their money's worth. He never engaged in overly long conversations but he'd answer questions or wish them happy birthday. "One of them wants to know how you're settling in and if you like it here."

Chip frowned as he took a seat next to Dawson on the small sofa. "Why do they want to know about *me*?"

He probably should have expected the shit-eating grin he got in return. "You know you have fans, man. This chick seems a little more obsessed with you than the others, but not in a bad way."

Chip arched a brow at that. "That sounds like an oxymoron."

Dawson shook his head. "She's not crazy obsessed, I promise. She never just asks about me when she messages, but always you as well. She's nice." He held out his phone for Chip to see for himself.

His heart almost stopped when he saw the username: angeltree_06. It was the person who always made comments about the two of them being an item. He quickly scrolled through the messages to see if she'd ever sent anything via DM that echoed her comments, but it was all rather benign. As Dawson had said, she always asked about Chip but it was never anything raunchy or scandalous.

"Yeah, she does seem nice," Chip said. "Does she comment much?" Crap, did his voice get squeaky there?

Dawson took his phone back and shrugged, immediately starting to type again. "I guess? I usually only scroll through the first fifty or so comments, so I don't always see the same people commenting. I've seen a few of hers but there's too many to really keep track of."

He nodded. It made sense and it was somewhat of a relief. Dawson might not think so kindly of angeltree_06 if he'd read her opinions about their relationship.

"I mentioned I was going to do a Live for my subs at some point. She's asked if you'll drop by during it." Dawson glanced up at him. "That okay with you?"

He managed a nod. "Yeah. Sure."

"Cool. I'm thinking of doing it tonight, if that works for you."

"I got nothing planned. Sounds good."

They did the Live right after dinner, seated on the couch together with Dawson's phone on a tripod in front of them. Outside, an easterly wind had picked up and was buffeting the house, rattling the window sills and howling under the cracks of the old doors. Chip made a mental note to look at the doors later, since the area was known for the easterlies in summer, and that would get old very quickly.

"Hi everyone!" Dawson greeted his subs. "It's so good to see so many of you here tonight. Thanks for joining us."

Hi guys!

OMG you're so cute!

hey dawson hey chip

Nice shirt - TK Lane?

Yay we get both of you!

As well as the comments, a flurry of emojis filled the screen, as well as gifts.

"Guys, as much as I appreciate the gifts, there's no need tonight," Dawson told them. "You already subscribe so there's no need to do anything extra, okay? This is for you."

More gifts flooded the screen as they blatantly ignored Dawson, and for a brief moment, both of their heads were adorned with sparkly cowboy hats. Chip couldn't help but chuckle. As much as he supported Dawson's role as an influencer, he still found the entire concept a bit crazy. The fact that people willingly threw money at someone simply for doing a live broadcast was outlandish. That they had to purchase coins and gifts from Vewz to do so, giving them a healthy cut before the influencer received the payout, seemed even odder. He was pretty sure these same people would baulk at giving out cash to random internet strangers, yet they were happy enough to do so when they were "purchasing gifts" for them.

No matter how weird it seemed to him, he couldn't fault their loyalty and devotion to Dawson. It was how he earned enough to be able to make the music that he loved. It wasn't always sunshine and roses, but the benefits outweighed the cons.

"Hey everyone," Chip said, and waved at the camera, amused as more heart emojis filled the screen and more gifts streamed in. "How's everyone doing tonight?"

Great now that we get to see you both!

Good thanks

Hi Chip!!!

Good hbu?

How are you liking the new place?

"I'm doing good, thanks," Chip responded.

"We're settling in well," Dawson added. "We spent today doing lots of little jobs around the house."

How are you finding living together?

That last question came from angeltree_06.

Before Chip could reply, Dawson was cheerfully answering. "It's so awesome getting to live with Chip again! I couldn't ask for a better house-mate."

No lover's spats yet?

Chip almost choked at the question but Dawson just barked out a laugh. "Seriously, we get along *so* well, it's almost uncanny. Sometimes he has to kick my lazy arse into doing chores, but otherwise, we never argue or fight."

Do you miss the city? another user asked.

Chip heard a strange squeaking noise over the sounds of Dawson responding and he glanced around the room, trying to figure out the source. There was nothing out of the ordinary and he tried to shake off his uneasy feeling, dismissing it as simply being the wind against the windows. He almost succeeded until angeltree_06 commented again.

What the fuck is that?

Chip frowned. "What's what?" he asked, interrupting Dawson telling a sub about the old orchard on the property.

Behind you, angeltree_06 replied. *The picture is moving.*

Chip twisted around on the couch and looked up at the framed print on the wall behind them. It was indeed moving, swinging from side to side. He met Dawson's wide-eyed gaze and could see the unvoiced question there—*what do we do?*

"Oh, that's from the wind," Chip said, trying to sound completely relaxed. "Not sure if you can hear, but the easterlies are blowing a gale outside." He heard another metallic squeak and glanced up to see that the vintage, textured-amber-glass light fitting over the light bulb was slowly rotating, unwinding itself. The bulb began to flicker and he looked back to the camera, giving an awkward laugh. "Old houses are so funny. Even with the doors closed, the wind blows straight through the house."

That's so funny!

Crazy boo!

I love you soooooo much!!!

Surely the wind couldn't make it swing that badly? And what's with the lights?

Chip ignored the other comments, concentrating solely on angeltree_06's. "It's just a freaky coincidence of the angle of the room and how the wind's blowing in," he said quickly. Next to him, Dawson appeared to be frozen, still staring behind his shoulder at the frame that was swinging from side to side even more wildly now. "We'd better go and try and block the gap up as best we can before the paint gets scratched," he said. "Sorry to cut the Live short but I'm sure Daw will do another one for you guys soon enough! Okay, have a great night. Bye!"

Before any of the viewers could even protest, Chip was reaching forward and hitting *stop* to end the Live. Almost as soon as he did, the framed print swung off the screw entirely and flew forward. He raised an arm instinctively, shielding the back of Dawson's head and the heavy frame crashed against his forearm, the glass shattering on impact. "Fuck," he hissed, pain lancing up his arm.

From above, the metallic squeal got louder and he knew that the light fitting was going to come crashing down sooner rather than later. "We need to move!" he barked at Dawson and grabbed his arm to haul him up off the couch.

No sooner were they standing than the textured-amber light fitting was flying towards them. Again, Chip reached out an arm to prevent Dawson from being hit. The heavy glass disc collided with his shoulder, making him wince just as the light bulb exploded into a thousand pieces. The room was plunged into darkness even as tiny shards of glass peppered their faces. They both cried out as they stumbled from the room, only to find that the lights in the hall were flickering madly as well.

"Chip!" Dawson cried, his voice hoarse with fear and his cheeks wet with streaks of blood.

"Outside!" Chip yelled, shoving Dawson towards the front door. There was a tense moment as he struggled with the new lock, but it soon gave way and they staggered outside into the cold night air. Behind them came the sounds of more bulbs popping and the entire house went dark.

Breathing heavily, they stumbled away from the house, ending up on their arses on the freshly mowed grass. They sat there, panting and shaking, just staring at the house. The house that was supposed to be their home, their safe haven, but was feeling more and more like a nightmare.

"What the fuck is going on?" Dawson asked brokenly. "Why is it doing this to us?"

Chip reached out and grabbed his hand, squeezing it to try and take the sting out of his response. "You mean to you, Daw. Why is it doing this to *you?*"

Dawson shook his head in confusion. "Wh . . . what do you mean?"

"Haven't you noticed, baby? Everything that's happened, has been directed at you." He let out an explosive breath, and ran his free hand through his dishevelled hair, pushing it away from his face. "I don't know why, but this ghost seems to hate you, Dawson."

CHAPTER 11

Dawson

"J ust give me two ticks to grab the lights."

Dawson blinked against the sudden brightness. The room they were in was small and dusty and filled with cardboard boxes. Some of them were plain packing boxes, but others had clearly been sourced from the local shops of yesteryear and included a Campbell's Soup box and a Swan Lager box.

"Grandpa Miller donated *all* of this?" Chip asked, staring at the room with a mixed expression of excitement and dread.

Janet, the president of the Brockman Historical Society nodded, causing her long, silver-blonde hair to bob up and down. "He sure did, just after Lizzy passed."

"And it's just been sitting here ever since?" Dawson asked in horror. "Grandma died twenty years ago!"

She gave a sympathetic shrug but her words were pragmatic. "We're run entirely by volunteers, love, and most of us are old enough to be considered antiques ourselves. Old Colin set aside some of the more interesting family heirlooms, and those are on display in the old Road Boards building of the museum, but the rest of it is waiting for someone to have the time to go through it all and sort the trash from the treasure."

"Aren't there experts from the state museum who would help with stuff like this?" he pressed, shocked at how donations of items that held important local historical significance were being treated.

"Oh, my sweet summer child," Janet said, patting him on the shoulder to take the edge off her condescending tone. "The museum can hardly manage their own collection, let alone those of every small town in the state. Every few years they might put on some training that we can attend, but it ultimately comes down to manpower. The young folk in town are busy with work and family, and if they do volunteer someplace it's generally for the emergency services or a sporting team. History really is left to the old farts, and by the time we take an interest, let's just say that the mind is willing but the body is weak. Sorting through donations like this can be heavy work, as well as being very time consuming. We do our best, but sometimes collections like this one from the Miller Family just have to sit and wait."

It was a depressing thought but Dawson couldn't exactly argue. It wasn't like either he or Chip were clamouring to volunteer for the Historical Society.

"And it's okay if we look through all of this?" Chip confirmed.

Janet gave him an easy smile and gestured with one hand at the stacked boxes. "Of course. Just be gentle as some stuff might be delicate. If you find some bits and pieces you want to look at in depth, I'm happy for you to take them home with you, but we'll just need to document what you're taking."

"Really?" Dawson asked in surprise.

"Technically, the collection belongs to your family," Janet told him. "Nowadays we have forms to fill out to hand over ownership, et cetera, but back then there was nothing like that. It's rare that families would dispute a donation, but it's been known to happen in the past. I try to be as accommodating as possible when descendents want to delve into their family history because it means we're less likely to lose the collection. Just because we've not had a chance to sort through it, doesn't mean that we don't value it."

"Oh, we'd never do that," Dawson assured her. "Once we're done with it, we're happy to leave it with you guys."

"Cheers," she said. "Anyway, you're welcome to use this room while you're here, and I'll drop off some of the sign-out forms for you if you want to take anything away with you. The boxes have been numbered, so if you could take a whole box instead of just individual items from within, that'll make it a little easier to keep track. And if you do happen across anything that's really interesting, make a note so we can take a look. It's much easier to catalogue a couple of items to add to the public display than sort through everything here."

Chip smiled. "Of course."

"I'll leave you to it," Janet said. "Don't forget about Trove, either. It's an online catalogue of newspapers, and other reports and journals. The Millers were an integral part of town life here so there's likely to be a lot about them in the papers of the day. You can access that from anywhere so it'll give you something else to look into."

"You've been so helpful," Dawson told her. "Thank you so much."

"Happy to help," Janet replied. "I find doing a deep dive into my family history fascinating so I'm glad when I can help others do the same." She headed for the door. "I'll be up in the main office. Give me a shout if you need anything."

She was gone a moment later and they were left alone with the room full of boxes. "This might take longer than we thought," Chip said in dismay. He ran a hand through his inky-black hair, the white bandage on his wrist a stark contrast.

It made Dawson's stomach churn at the thought of Chip being injured by their resident ghost, especially as he'd been protecting Dawson at the time. "Yeah. Who'd have thought the family would have so much crap?" He stepped forward and hefted a dusty box onto the small table in the corner of the room, took one of the small box cutters that were sitting in a little jar, and sliced through the yellowing packing tape. He flipped the box open and found a jumble of odd objects, then rifled through them before sighing. "Oh man, I can see why this would be a thankless task. This shit is *so random.*" He picked out a few items and held them up for Chip to see. There was a metal hand beater, a plastic container with a collection of souvenir spoons, a porcelain jewellery box, a cigar tin, and several cookbooks.

Chip grabbed his own box and opened it. "Looks like I've got some photo albums, a few scrapbooks, some school reports, and other documents." He frowned thoughtfully. "This might be a good box to take with us. We're more likely to find relevant info amongst stuff like this than things that were probably shoved in a junk drawer in the kitchen."

Dawson had to agree. He glanced at his watch. "We've got an hour before cricket practice. I reckon we could eliminate a good few boxes before then."

By the time they had to leave, they'd opened more than half the boxes and had piled the majority of those into a "discard pile" on one side of the room. The other, much smaller pile, with boxes that contained promising-looking albums, notebooks, and sheafs of paper, was stacked by the door. They filled out a form for two of the boxes and then dropped it off to Janet on their way to the car, each carrying a box in their arms.

It was a short drive from the historical precinct to the oval, where Chip pulled the car in next to a beat-up farm ute. They could see a small group of guys already gathered by the cricket nets and made their way over.

Blake caught sight of them and waved, his smile bright against his dark skin. "Glad you boys could make it," he greeted, and his eyes went a little wide as he took in the sight of them. Dawson knew they must look a right mess—both of their faces were covered in tiny little cuts from the glass light bulb, Chip had a bandage over the cut on his wrist, Dawson had put a bandage over the bite on his ankle so no one would question how it had happened, and on top of all of that, Chip's sunburn was now at the peeling stage and he looked a little like a snake shedding its skin. "What the hell happened to you two?" Blake asked.

Chip gave an easy smile and answered, saving Dawson from having to stumble through a believable lie. "It's been a crazy week," he said with a chuckle. He held up his hand. "I had a bit of an accident, playing around with changing a saw blade. Dawson tripped over a branch outside and stacked it, and tore up his ankle pretty badly. *Then*, because we're apparently not accident prone enough, we hit a bloody roo the other night driving home from town. My dad had loaned us an old ute for the move and we were in that. The windscreen hadn't ever been replaced so the glass was super old, I guess. It shattered into a million pieces when the poor thing hit it and we copped a faceful." He looked so sincere that Blake and the others bought the story immediately, all groaning and offering condolences about their shitty luck.

"Did you make sure to check the pouch for a joey?" Noah asked, his face creased into concern for the kangaroo.

Dawson couldn't help but feel guilty for making him worry about the non-existent roadkill.

"Nah, mate," Chip said, waving off his concern. "It was a male."

"Before we leave tonight, I'll make sure you guys have got the number for the local wildlife carers," Noah said. "It's always good to have them in your phones, especially if it happens again with a female."

"Thanks for that," Dawson said, giving him a grateful smile.

"Alright, we're burning daylight, boys," Blake said, clapping his hands together. "Let's get this show on the road."

They began with some laps and then fielding drills, before they broke for a drinks break and took some time to go over what the batting order was likely to be.

"Noah, you'll be our opening batsman, and Isaac, you're number two," Blake said. "Then we've got Chip, Raj, me, and Jake, who's also keeping for us. Then Dawson, Ken, Ryan, Johnno, and Bruce. Darcy and Puss will sub for us when needed, since they both work FIFO. We all good with that?"

Everyone nodded.

"Awesome. I'll sort out fielding positions next week, but for now, let's hit the nets."

Dawson hadn't realised how tight his chest was with anxiety until Chip slung an arm over his shoulder and guided him to one of the nets. After the stress of finding out their new home was actually haunted, plus having been spending so much time with strangers, it was no wonder his anxiety was spiking. Chip always seemed to know, sometimes even before Dawson knew himself. For most people, when bowling to someone twenty metres away it probably wouldn't matter if they knew them or not, but when Dawson was bowling to Chip it eased that tightness inside him. Made it easier to breathe.

As for having Chip's arm around him? That felt better than it should have. Dawson found himself feeling bereft when it slipped away and Chip jogged down to the other end of the nets. He watched as Chip tightened the straps on his gloves and elbow guard, and found his eyes lingering as he adjusted his cup.

What the fuck?

He ripped his gaze away, his cheeks burning, and swung his arms around, warming up his shoulders. Why the hell had he been watching Chip do that? And why did he want to do it again, but without the cup in the way?

His memory chose that exact moment to assault him with the image he'd glimpsed the other day of Chip's . . . central wicket, after he'd rushed from the shower to check on Dawson. His dick gave a little twitch as he pictured exactly what that little piece of plastic was protecting, and he had a sudden urge to get up close and personal with it once more.

What the actual fuck? Where were these thoughts coming from? The stress of the past week really *was* getting to him. It wasn't the fact he'd never been attracted to a man before in his life that was both freaking him out and confusing the hell out of him in equal measures. He was well aware that sexuality was flexible and people had self-discoveries at different times in their lives. No, it was the itty bitty fact that they were *brothers*. Sure, they might not be related by blood, but that didn't make them any less family. Harry wasn't his father by birth but that fact wasn't what was stopping Dawson from donning a tartan skirt and calling him *daddy*. No, it was the fact that Harry was more a father to him than the guy who donated DNA material and then fucked off. Dawson didn't find familial connections attractive!

So why the hell was his body reacting this way to Chip?

"Um, Daw? You good there?"

Dawson's head snapped up and he saw Chip standing in front of the wickets, one leg crossed behind the other, leaning on his cricket bat, and a concerned expression making his full lips turn down. "Huh?" he asked eloquently.

Dark brows knit together. "Dude, are you alright? You've kinda zoned out on me."

"Uh, sorry, no, I'm good. It's all good," he said, flipping the ball in his hand a few times, trying to get his mind off how *wrong* it felt to have Chip call him dude and wishing he were calling him baby instead.

Okay, this was venturing into the way-too-fucking-weird category now and Dawson needed to get it together. He took a deep breath and forced himself to get in the zone. He backed up a few metres, not going for a full run up since he had to work back up to his full speed, and slid his fingers into position around the seam in preparation for an inswinger. Chip had taken his batting stance, tapping his bat a few times and was awaiting the delivery.

It didn't take long before Dawson got back into the swing of things and he found himself growing more and more confident the longer they practised. Chip was a much better player than Dawson so he didn't often get the upper hand, but he was happy that he'd managed to take the bails off a couple of times by the time Blake called an end to the session.

Before they left, they spent five minutes with Ken, who was the club treasurer, to pay their fees and order their uniforms. With a promise to Blake that they'd try and get down to the nets on Saturday for another hit, they threw their gear into the boot and climbed into the car to head home.

That thought did not fill him with joy like it should.

Dawson grew more and more tense as they drove the back streets of Brockman towards home. By the time they were pulling into their drive, his chest was tight once more and his breaths were coming short and sharp. As the house came into view, looking dark and foreboding against the darkened sky, the urge to turn and run—run as far away as possible—was almost overwhelming.

Chip pulled the car to a stop and turned off the engine, then he reached over and his hand settled on Dawson's knee, warm and steady. "You okay?"

Dawson shook his head, unable to drag his eyes away from the house. "I'm scared."

Chip's hand squeezed briefly. "I know. So am I."

"What's it gonna do next?"

"I don't know, but whatever it is, we'll face it together."

"You got hurt because of me!" Dawson cried, turning his gaze to Chip. "For some fucked-up reason this ghost has got it in for me, and because of that *you* got hurt trying to protect me." He gasped, trying to get a lungful of air but finding his chest too tight to inhale. "Fuck, Chip. I can't . . . I can't see you hurt."

"Hey, hey, hey," Chip soothed, and he let go of Dawson's knee to reach up and cup the back of his neck. His thumb rubbed in slow circles at the nape of his neck. "I'm okay. It was just a scratch."

"*This* time," Dawson argued. "What about next time?" Oh God, just the thought of what could happen to Chip was enough to make his heart pound erratically and sweat break out on his brow. His nose began to tingle from lack of oxygen even as his lungs burned.

"Okay, baby, I need you to take a breath for me," Chip said. "Come on, breathe in. That's it, now hold it. One, two, three. Good, that's good. Now out. That's great, baby. In again—one, two, three. And out."

Dawson closed his eyes and listened to Chip's instructions, and slowly his chest eased and he felt like he could breathe freely. Chip continued talking, low and soothingly, and he never stopped touching him.

"You okay?" Chip finally asked.

Dawson nodded, keeping his eyes closed so he wouldn't have to see Chip's expression. It would likely be a mixture of worry, concern, and maybe even pity.

"Come on, inside," Chip said. "I'll make us some dinner and we can make a start on looking through these boxes. The sooner we figure out who this ghost is and why the hell she's pissed at you, the sooner we can get this mess fixed."

CHAPTER 12

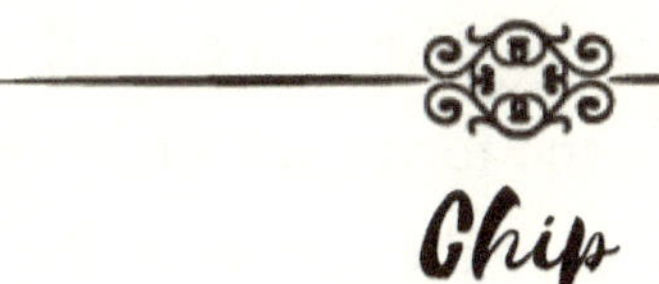

Chip

Chip drained the pasta and poured it into a baking dish, then mixed through some creamy tomato sauce and some diced chicken pieces. He put the pasta bake in the oven and turned on the timer, then wiped his hands on a tea towel. "Okay, that'll take about twenty minutes," he told Dawson. "Let's go shower so we can eat." Dawson flinched a little and his eyes went wide as he stared at Chip, who mentally ran over what he'd said. "Not together!" he said hurriedly, holding out his hands in a stop gesture. "I didn't mean it like that! I meant, we'll take *separate* showers, but I'll stay close, you know, in case of ghostly activity."

Was it his imagination, or did Dawson look disappointed?

Totally his imagination. For fuck's sake, of course Dawson didn't want to shower with Chip, because he didn't have a stupid fucking crush on his *stepbrother*. Chip wanted to smack himself over the back of the head but that would definitely lead to Dawson questioning his sanity.

Luckily, Dawson didn't push the issue, simply got up and led the way down the hall. They separated, to grab clothes from their respective bedrooms, but they made sure the doors were wide open so they could each see the other. Unmolested by the supernatural, they met up again in the bathroom.

"How are we gonna do this?" Dawson asked.

"You go first," Chip said, gesturing at the shower. "I'll wait outside until you're in and then I'll come in and wait until you're done."

"Thanks," Dawson said with a grateful smile.

Chip stood just outside the door, and when he heard the shower curtain close, he popped into the room and took a seat on the closed toilet lid. The sounds of water splashing onto the bottom of the bathtub mixed with a melodic harmony that Dawson was humming under his breath, and Chip tried his best to not picture what was happening behind the curtain. "What's that song?" he asked, to distract himself. "I don't think I've heard the tune before."

"Just something I'm working on," Dawson replied.

"It's nice." He winced a little at how banal that sounded but Dawson didn't seem to mind.

"Thanks. I'm hoping I'll have something more concrete by the end of the week."

They chatted about inconsequential things, and Chip ducked out of the room as Dawson got out and wrapped a towel around his hips before they swapped positions. Chip kept his shower brief, wanting to spend as little time as possible naked in the same room as Dawson. His dick did *not* need any more fuel for the fire, thank you very much.

Once they were both dressed, they pulled the pasta bake from the oven and loaded up their plates, eating at the table in comfortable silence. Only once they were done and the dishes were cleared did they pull a box from the Historical Society onto the table to begin sorting through the contents.

"What are we even looking for?" Dawson asked after a while, a pile of old documents on the "looked at" pile by his left elbow and a faded sepia wedding photograph of his grandparents, Colin and Elizabeth, in his hands.

"I'm not sure," Chip admitted. "I guess anything which might indicate that a tragedy happened here or something?"

"Grandpa's fashion in the seventies sure was a tragedy," Dawson muttered, tossing the photo onto the growing pile next to him.

Chip glanced over, taking note of the bell-bottomed suit Colin was wearing and shuddered. "You're not wrong."

They worked their way through the first box and found nothing of interest, either to their current predicament, or that Janet would want for the museum. It was all mostly from the last fifty years and was relatively boring, although Dawson did seem to get a kick out of seeing his mum's school reports from high school.

The second box was mostly photo albums interspersed with old scrapbooks. Chip opened one that had an intricately hand painted cover that read "Miller Family History in Brockman." On the first page inside was a handwritten inscription: *A wedding gift to my beloved husband, Colin - Four generations of Millers in Brockman, by Elizabeth Miller.* "Holy shit," he whispered, carefully flipping through the heavy pages. "This is hardcore."

Dawson came around the table and leaned over Chip's shoulder so he could see. His curls had dried now and a lock of hair tickled against Chip's cheek. "How long must this have taken her?" he asked in awe.

Each page was beautifully decorated by hand, from delicate borders of vines and flowers, to small pictures depicting a family member or event. There were photos from throughout the generations, a detailed family tree, and then a double page dedicated to each family member with anecdotes, newspaper clippings, quotes, and information.

They flipped through page after page, reading each blurb, enraptured by history brought to life by Elizabeth's flare for writing. It could have been dry and impersonal but she made them feel real enough they could walk off the page and into the room. She hadn't written a chronological account of their lives but shared the important bits, the parts that had made their mark upon the world.

"I don't really remember Grandma well," Dawson commented. "I was so little when she died. But I heard from Mum how she struggled with her mental health all her life. It seems that when anyone speaks of her, that's what they remember. They never speak of her humour or her creativity." He sounded sad, and Chip felt a pang for the woman he'd never met.

Chip turned another page once they'd finished reading about Dawson's great-great-grandfather and how he'd helped the police find three men who had robbed a train and had hidden out on his farm—when they both froze.

Staring up at them from the scrapbook was *Dawson*.

"What the hell?" Dawson whispered, staring at his doppelganger.

"Jacob Edward Miller, born ninth of June, 1884," Chip read, but his eyes were drawn back to the photo, unable to look away for long.

Jacob was the spitting image of Dawson. Or, Chip reasoned, Dawson was the spitting image of Jacob. The photo was black and white but his hair was very light, and his curls were as wild as Dawson's and fell to shoulder length. The shape of the jaw, brow, and nose were the same. His eyes looked pale and were likely the same shade of blue. If he took a photo of Dawson right now and applied a black and white filter to it, they could have passed as the same person. Except for the expression.

Despite his anxiety, Dawson smiled often and was a ray of fucking sunshine. Jacob scowled at the camera, his mouth twisted and his eyes narrowed. Sure, it was a single photo, one moment captured in time, and they couldn't judge his entire personality from that alone. There was just something about it though, that made Chip believe any other photos of Jacob would be the same. He just didn't look like a nice person.

"That's really uncanny," Chip said as diplomatically as possible.

"I think you meant to say it's fucking freaky," Dawson said, his voice shaky.

Chip turned and really looked at Dawson, and it was only then that he noticed he was trembling. "Hey, are you okay?"

He shook his head. "No. I don't know why, but I just have a really bad feeling about this."

"What do you mean?" Chip asked, more to distract himself from the urge to pull Dawson onto his lap and hold him tight. He was pretty sure Dawson's bad feeling was the same as his own.

"He wasn't a good man," Dawson whispered, his eyes still glued to the page. "Jacob Miller did some terrible things." He stated it like he knew without a doubt in the world that it was true.

"What do you think it mea—" Before Chip could finish his sentence, the lights flickered and the kitchen door slammed closed, before opening again and banging against the wall. The empty plates from dinner that they'd placed on the sink to be washed once they were done were flung against the far wall, shattering into pieces. The temperature plummeted and their breaths misted on the frigid air.

Chip and Dawson's eyes met just as the scrapbook rose into the air and was flung at the wall, and a ghostly scream of rage echoed throughout the room.

They'd fled the kitchen and were holed up in Chip's room after deciding they'd clean up the mess in the morning. The ghost appeared to have gone for now, but they were both unsettled. They lay in bed, facing one another, and Chip couldn't help but relish the way their knees touched and their breaths mingled.

"I guess, at least now we have something solid to start looking into," Dawson said.

"For sure. Jacob is definitely the key to all of this," Chip agreed. He paused and then asked, "How are you feeling?"

The laugh that Dawson barked out sounded on the verge of hysteria. "I'm fucking freaking out, Chip. Isn't that obvious?"

He couldn't help it. Chip shuffled forward and wrapped his arms around Dawson, holding him close. "It kinda is, which is why I'm so worried about you."

"I think she thinks I'm him," he whispered. "I think that's why she's hell bent on me."

"Yeah, that's what I figured too."

"What do we do?" Dawson asked in a small voice.

Chip blew out a breath and it puffed up a lock of Dawson's hair, filling his nose with the scent of his shampoo. "Maybe we can try and reason with her? Explain that you're not him, and if she stops haunting us maybe we can figure out a way to help her?"

"You really think that would work?" Dawson asked, sceptical.

Chip shrugged. "Dunno until we try. I'll also check out Trove tomorrow and see if there's any news articles about Jacob."

"Okay."

Dawson sighed and snuggled in against Chip's chest, and Chip wondered if he could hear the erratic thumping of his heart. He silently begged his dick to behave, not wanting the traitorous bastard to betray him now and make the moment awkward. It was so *nice* to have Dawson in his arms and Chip just wanted to enjoy the moment. He wanted to pretend that none of the other bullshit was happening and to imagine, just for a second, that they were cuddling because Dawson simply wanted to be close to him.

"I'm sorry," Dawson murmured.

Chip frowned, not sure he heard him correctly. "For what?"

"This is all going to shit because of me. It was supposed to be a new start for both of us. A new home, new town, new adventure."

His arms tightened and Chip pressed a kiss to the top of Dawson's head. "You have nothing to be sorry for, Daw. I'd rather be here with you, in a haunted house, than anywhere else."

"Really?"

"Yes, really." He closed his eyes, and gathered his courage. "You are the most important person in my life. I would live in literal Hell if it meant I got to spend time with you." It was as close to a declaration of love as he could get without scaring Dawson away.

"Same," Dawson said.

It wasn't exactly a return declaration but Chip would take it. "How 'bout we try and get some sleep? It's been a long day."

"Okay. Night, Chip."

"Night, Daw."

He expected Dawson to unfurl from his arms and roll away, but he didn't. He stayed right there, with his head pillowed on Chip's chest, and that's how they fell asleep.

CHAPTER 13

Dawson

Dawson yawned widely, and then took a sip of his coffee before leaning back in the old wicker chair on the verandah and resting one foot on the opposite knee. The morning was cool and crisp, and the lawn and trees were sparkling with dew. Chip sat in the other chair, his laptop balanced on one knee as he searched the online database for newspaper articles about Jacob Miller. Dawson was checking his Vewz account for messages, being sure to reply to his subscribers to keep them happy.

One of the messages he had was from angeltree_06.

> angeltree_06: I just wanted to make sure that you and Chip were okay after the other night. I know Chip tried to pass it off as the wind but I know what a haunting looks like. If you need to talk, my DMs are always open.

He stared at the message for a long time, absently rubbing at his ankle where the healing bite was itching. Finally, he held the phone out to Chip. "Check this out."

Chip took it and read the message, his eyes widening a little. "Huh," was all he managed.

"Do you think she's for real?" he asked, taking his phone back.

"She seems pretty confident about what she saw," Chip said. "Maybe she's had experience with ghosts?"

"Do you think I should reply?" Dawson asked.

Chip pursed his lips and Dawson found his eyes lingering on them. They were so full and soft looking. He wondered what it would be like to kiss them.

Hold up. *What?*

"I don't think it would hurt," Chip said. "I reckon we need all the help we can get, so it's worth asking her what she knows."

It took a moment for his words to sink in, since Dawson was still reeling from the direction his mind had gone in. Seriously, what the hell was wrong with him? Why was he having these sorts of thoughts about Chip lately? First he'd wanted to see his dick again, and now he was thinking about kissing him?

"Daw?" Chip asked.

And there his mind went, wandering off again. He gave himself a mental shake. "Sorry, just thinking. Um, sure, I'll reply back."

Chip didn't turn back to his laptop like he expected, but kept his eyes on him.

"What?" Dawson asked, feeling exposed and vulnerable under that scrutinising gaze.

"I just want to make sure that you're doing okay. I'm worried about you," Chip admitted.

From anyone else, even his mum, Dawson probably would have bristled at that. His back would have been up from others thinking he couldn't cope and for making a fuss. It was different with Chip. He didn't know why, but it didn't piss him off. Instead, he wanted to assure Chip and to allay his worries. "I'm okay, I promise. I'm not gonna lie, my anxiety is through the roof, but I'm doing okay despite that."

"Will you let me know if I can do anything to help?"

His heart clenched a little at that. Chip was the best person he knew. He always wanted to help, to take the load off, but he never pushed. He was happy to wait until he was asked, instead of just barging in and taking over. "I will," he promised. The silence that followed was charged and he shifted uncomfortably. That bloody urge to kiss Chip was still there and he just didn't understand it. He needed to get away, just for a minute, to clear his head. Replying to angeltree_06 could wait until later. "Do you mind if I grab my guitar? I wanted to work on that song a bit more but I won't if it'll disturb you."

"I don't mind, dude," Chip told him. "I find it relaxing." He went to stand up.

"It's okay," Dawson told him, holding his hand out to stop him. "I'll be in and out of the house in less than a minute. No need to get up."

Chip didn't look convinced. "You sure?"

"I'm not dumb enough to be like one of those silly college kids in a horror movie that decides to check out the basement alone," Dawson said, trying for levity.

"We don't *have* a basement," Chip shot back.

He grinned. "Exactly. I'm grabbing my guitar from the loungeroom and then I'll be back. No problems."

Chip didn't look convinced but he did sink back down into his chair. Dawson went around the front of the house and let himself in through the front door. He paused just inside, listening intently, but he didn't hear anything. The house was dim as they'd closed all the blinds and curtains to keep the heat in, so he couldn't see much. But from what he could see, there didn't seem to be anything ghostly. Feeling confident, he walked around the corner into the loungeroom, flipped on the light, and jumped backwards, letting out a little scream and then— *"Fuck!"*

There was a crashing sound from outside, probably the rattan chair being knocked over, and then the front door slammed open. Dawson felt a hand grasp the back of his shirt and he was yanked backwards as Chip threw himself in front of him. "Stay the fuck away from him, you ghosty bitch!" He then looked around the room slowly, trying to see what had startled Dawson.

Unable to help it, Dawson began to laugh. He laughed so hard that he doubled over, pressing his hands over his stomach as his whole body shook with it.

"What happened?" Chip demanded, his brow marred with a mixture of worry and annoyance.

Dawson tried to speak but he couldn't get the words out between his laughs.

"Dawson!" Chip barked when his patience reached the end of its rope. "What the fuck happened?"

He straightened up and took in a deep breath, his stomach aching from laughing so hard. "Sorry," he wheezed. "Didn't mean to scare you."

"What. The. Fuck. Happened?" Chip growled.

Dawson's dick chose that moment to twitch in his jeans and it sobered him instantly. Add to today's list of fuckery—Chip's growly voice was kind of sexy. "Huntsman," he said, pointing to the wall next to the light switch.

Chip turned and caught sight of the large spider, and he reeled backwards in shock. "Jesus fucking Christ, that's a big one!"

"Another couple of centimetres and I would have mistaken him for the switch," Dawson added.

"Want me to put him outside?" Chip offered.

He shook his head. "Nah, I don't mind sharing space with him. He just took me by surprise is all." He then smirked at Chip. "It was very sweet of you to barrel in here like you did and yell at the—what was the phrase you used? Oh, that's right. The *ghosty bitch*."

Chip's cheeks went bright red. "Shut up," he muttered.

"I almost swooned," Dawson teased.

"Daw," Chip whined, covering his face with his hands.

He grinned then, enjoying seeing Chip so embarrassed. "Shall I call you Kevin from now on? I don't mind singing to you." He held his hands wide and belted out, *"And I . . . will always . . . love you!"* Given how early it was, he was impressed with himself that he managed the high note without sounding like a muppet.

"Stop it!" Chip begged, but he was laughing.

Dawson kept singing but it cut off abruptly as Chip tackled him and took him to the ground, his hands going straight for his knees. "Chip!" Dawson squealed as he was tickled, his whole body jerking and twitching as he tried to escape.

"I believe that's Mr Costner to you," Chip said, his evil fingers digging into the most ticklish spots with ease. He leaned down and whispered into Dawson's ear, "Do you surrender, *Whitney*?"

The hot gust of air against his ear sent goosebumps rippling over Dawson's skin and he shivered, before his leg jerked and he tried again to yank himself away from his attacker. "Chip! St-t-t-op i-i-i-t," he squealed.

"Nope!" Chip cried gleefully.

Dawson tried once more to free himself and almost managed it, wriggling onto his knees and crawling for half a metre. Then Chip grabbed him around the waist, flipped him onto his back and quickly straddled his hips, holding him down. His fingers now dug into Dawson's ribs, and he squeaked and giggled even as he squirmed and wriggled to get free. His hips bucked up, and they both froze as he felt something hard and warm pressing against him.

Holy fucking shit, Chip had an erection.

In the blink of an eye, Chip was up and off him and was backing towards the door. "I'm gonna get back to searching this database," he said, hooking a thumb over his shoulder, unable to meet Dawson's eyes. Then he was gone.

Dawson lay on the floor, breathing hard and trying to understand what the hell had just happened.

Even though he was never far away, as they'd agreed once the haunting had begun, Dawson knew Chip was avoiding him. He'd remained in the same vicinity and he replied when Dawson spoke to him, but he didn't hold eye contact and he didn't initiate conversation.

It was clear he was mortified.

Dawson hated seeing Chip so uncomfortable but he had no idea how to fix it. Was it best to just ignore it and pretend it had never happened? Reassure him they were both men and so he knew that boners had a mind of their own and he knew it didn't mean anything?

But what if it did?

He'd been strumming on his guitar and his fingers slipped as that errant thought crossed his mind. He froze, and tried to understand why his heart was now thumping in his ribcage. No matter how inappropriate it was, given that they were *family,* Dawson couldn't help but be . . . pleased? Was that the word? Happy? Excited? Urgh, he didn't know how to describe it exactly but he *liked* the idea that Chip was possibly attracted to him.

That his erection was not simply an accident but specifically because of his proximity to Dawson.

As far as Dawson knew, Chip had never even kissed anyone. They told each other everything, and Dawson was certain that if Chip had had *any* kind of experience he'd have told him. So there was a real possibility it had simply been the instance of a close, warm body and the friction of their tickle war that had caused Chip's hard-on, though Dawson couldn't help but wish it was because of him.

But why? What the hell was he going to do about it if it *did* turn out Chip was attracted to him? He knew what that meant. Chip was demisexual. For him to be attracted to Dawson it would mean he'd have to have strong feelings for him. Stronger than mere friendship or the bond that came from being stepbrothers. *Romantic* feelings.

It was always an ego boost when you discovered that someone thought you were good looking. Dawson was honest enough with himself to admit that hearing his fans and other random commenters online tell him they thought he was hot made him feel good about himself, and gave him a boost of serotonin. So if it was true, and Chip really was attracted to Dawson, was it just his ego preening that made him like the idea? Or was it something more?

Was Dawson attracted to Chip?

They were both in the sunroom and Chip was at his desk, still trawling through old newspaper articles on his laptop. Dawson swivelled in his chair, his guitar resting on his lap, and let his gaze roam over Chip, considering him. He'd always known Chip was good looking. He had eyes, after all. Chip's black hair was always so shiny, and his hazel eyes were captivating as they seemed to change colour in the light. His smile was so broad and joyous that whoever it was aimed at couldn't help but smile back. Even his Roman nose didn't detract from his attractiveness, but added to it. He was so solid and warm, and Dawson loved being hugged by him. Especially when Chip held him as they slept . . .

Okay, so Dawson *might* have a bit of a crush on his stepbrother. Huh. That hadn't been on his self-discovery bingo card this year. Go figure. The question now was, what was he going to do about it?

His phone vibrated and he glanced at the screen to see he had a reply from angeltree_06. He opened up the message thread and skimmed through the past few messages.

> angeltree_06: I just wanted to make sure that you and Chip were okay after the other night. I know Chip tried to pass it off as the wind but I know what a haunting looks like. If you need to talk, my DMs are always open.

> Dawson: Normally, I try not to share too many personal or private details with my subscribers but I'm at the point where I can admit we need help. Is that something you can do? Help us?

> angeltree_06: Glad to hear from you. Gotta admit I was getting a little worried. First of all, are you both okay? You've not been injured?

> Dawson: We have no major injuries.

> angeltree_06: But you *have* been injured by the ghost?

> Dawson: Yes. Nothing life threatening, but we've got some scrapes and scratches.

angeltree_06: Okay, good to hear you're both relatively okay but it's bad news that you're being physically harmed by this spirit.

Dawson: How so?

angeltree_06: It's too complicated to explain in a message. Any chance we can FaceTime at some point? I'm sure you have questions about me and my experience and I can explain everything.

He stared at the message. It made sense to actually speak to angeltree_06, but he didn't want her to pick up on the new tension between him and Chip. She seemed perceptive enough that she'd spot it immediately. He reached down to scratch at his ankle and decided the ghost was dangerous enough that they didn't exactly have much of a choice.

"Chip," he called across the room. "This chick wants to speak to us over video chat today so she can explain how she can help. Is that okay with you?"

Chip paused in his scrolling of the archive but he didn't look over at Dawson. It made Dawson's chest ache but he couldn't dwell on that right now. "Um, sure. I guess."

He sighed but typed out a message.

Dawson: Sure. Send me your number and the best time for you.

angeltree_06: I'm at work but I finish at 4. Would 6 work for you?

Dawson: Sounds good. Oh, and what should we call you?

angeltree_06: My name is actually Angel but my friends call me Angie.

Dawson: We'll speak to you at 5 then. Thanks, Angie.

CHAPTER 19

Chip

Angel—Angie, she said she preferred—was younger than Chip had pictured. He didn't know *why* exactly, but he'd gotten the vibe from her comments and messages that she was in her thirties or forties. He certainly hadn't expected her to be younger than them, probably twenty-one or twenty-two. She seemed to be one of those old souls, mature beyond her years. Not that a casual observer would think that if they simply judged her on her looks.

Angie was striking. She was slender, angular, and androgynous. Chip was grateful that Dawson had been polite enough to introduce the both of them using their pronouns so she'd felt comfortable to share hers. She had platinum-silver hair that was shaved on one side and longer on the other, and even at the end of a long work day it was still perfectly styled. She had multiple piercings including her septum, tongue, and left eyebrow, and her make up was minimalistic, except for her eyes which were lined with dark eyeliner. She wore a grey-knit jumper, and several tattoos peeked out from the neckline.

"Has anything else happened today?" she asked them, after they'd all introduced themselves.

Chip tried not to wince outwardly as he mentally relived the mortification from this morning. He still couldn't believe he'd gotten hard while tickling Dawson. Okay, so that was a lie. It wasn't hard to believe *at all.* He was just stupid enough not to have considered the fact that being so close to Dawson would have his body reacting that way. He'd gotten complacent and now things were awkward as fuck between them.

But Angie hadn't been asking about *that.* "She's been quiet today," he said.

"She?" Angie asked. *"You've seen her?"*

They nodded, and Chip wished they'd used his laptop for the call, since they had to sit too close together to both be seen on Dawson's phone. "A few times," he confirmed. "At first we thought it might have been a stalker or creepy fan breaking in, but we're pretty sure now that we were actually seeing the ghost."

"I think you've seen her," Dawson told Angie. "Did you see the Live, where I sang 'Just Be' for the first time?"

Angie nodded. *"Yeah."*

"Everyone in the comments kept talking about seeing a woman in the background. That's the first time she appeared."

Angie's jaw dropped, and they saw the glint of a barbell on her tongue. *"Holy shit, that's your ghost?"*

They both nodded. "That's her," Chip confirmed.

Angie ran a hand through her hair. *"That's not good guys. She looked* real. *Having a ghost powerful enough to manifest so solidly is really dangerous."*

Chip huffed. "No shit. Considering what she's done already, we've figured that out on our own."

Dawson elbowed him, and when he glanced his way, Chip saw that he was glaring at him for being rude. "Sorry," Dawson apologised for him. "It's been a bit stressful here."

Angie just smiled. *"All good, I get it."*

"Can you tell us *how* you get it?" Dawson asked. "You said earlier that you'd explain about how you know about ghosts?"

"Yeah, of course," she agreed easily. *"It's nothing super crazy or anything. Like, I don't have a secret YouTube channel investigating the paranormal and I'm not a ghost hunter. I just grew up in a haunted house."*

Forgetting the awkwardness between them, Chip turned to exchange a look with Dawson before returning his attention back to the phone. "Um, what?"

Angie snorted. *"I grew up with ghosts,"* she reiterated. *"I actually still live with ghosts since I've not moved out of home yet. Like, who can afford to do that these days?"*

"Yeah, there's a reason we live in Bum Fuck Nowhere," Chip agreed.

"Are your ghosts dangerous?" Dawson asked her.

Angie shrugged. *"Some of them have been. I think my house was built on some sort of rift or something because it's not like we just have one or two ghosts who have a connection to the house. Yeah, there are some who've been here for years but we always have new ones appearing, then leaving after a while. It's those ones who usually cause the trouble."*

Dawson was staring at Angie with a mix of fascination and horror but he didn't say anything. Chip understood how he felt. After what they'd been through in the last week, he couldn't begin to imagine what it must be like to have been dealing with that for twenty-odd years. "What do you do when they're violent?" he asked.

"It depends. Sometimes we've not done anything as they've moved on before we've been able to come up with a game plan. For one really bad one, we tried

an exorcism, but the dude who performed it was a dud," she said. *"It didn't do anything but piss the ghost off even more and things got even worse. In the end, I found a guy online who walked me through how to do a house cleansing."*

"A what?" Chip asked.

"A house cleansing. It's the broad term for several rituals and ceremonies that help ghosts and spirits move on."

"What sort of rituals?" Dawson asked, sounding sceptical. "Like spells and séances?"

Angie picked up the hesitance in his voice. *"Look, I get that this sort of stuff sounds like hocus pocus, but given that you're being attacked by a ghost, I'd think you'd have more of an open mind."*

Dawson flushed at being called out—no matter how nicely—for being rude. Chip's protective instincts immediately flared and he jumped in to defend him, despite having been the recipient of *Dawson's* glare a minute ago for also being rude. "Cut us some slack, would ya?" he said, trying not to snap since he was well aware how much they needed Angie's help, but not willing to let it slide. "This is all new to us and it's been a bit of a steep learning curve."

Angie's expression was sympathetic and her tone reasonable as she replied. *"I get it, okay? I know it's hard but you gotta trust me on this."*

"We don't even know you," Chip told her.

"True," she allowed. *"So I guess I should have said to have faith in me. I can help you, but it'll mean going out of your comfort zone and participating in some stuff that you might think is a load of shit. All I can do is promise I'm not taking the piss. This isn't a scam. I don't want anything from you other than to help."*

Chip and Dawson exchanged a long look. They'd been friends for long enough that they didn't have to speak to know they were on the same page.

It was a risk to trust Angie, but ultimately, they knew they had no choice if they wanted this ghost dealt with. They didn't know anyone else to turn to and neither of them had the expertise to do it themselves. Chip raised a brow in question and Dawson gave a subtle nod. Agreed, he turned back to the phone. "Alright," Chip told her. "We're on board. What happens now?"

Angie looked determined but then she grinned. *"How do you feel about a house guest?"*

Dinner had been a quiet affair. They'd cooked a stirfry together but Chip had withdrawn once again. They'd arranged with Angie for her to come and stay over the weekend, possibly longer if needed, so she could help them cleanse the house, and she'd arrive on Friday night. Whilst discussing the details with her, things had almost felt normal between them, but once the call had ended and it was simply the two of them, Chip's mortification from that morning had returned and he put distance back between them.

The downcast expression on Dawson's face as they ate didn't escape Chip's notice. He'd hurt him. A lot. It was unusual for them to be at odds but Chip was terrified that the damage was already done. Dawson was not only his stepbrother, but he was also *straight.* There was no way he'd not have an issue with Chip's reaction to him that morning. He was just too nice to come out and say anything.

When they'd finished eating, Dawson wordlessly took their plates over to the sink and began filling it with hot water.

"Leave them," Chip said. "I can do the dishes later."

Dawson shook his head. "Why give her more shit to break." His tone was clipped. Annoyed. Chip couldn't blame him. "The rate we're going, we'll need to buy more fucking crockery."

"I'll dry then," Chip offered, standing. Of the two of them, he was the neater one, so seeing Dawson aggressively washing dishes was a red flag. He wasn't just upset with Chip but *angry.*

"I got it," Dawson all but barked.

It was as clear as day that he didn't want to be around Chip. He should have been relieved, since he was the one who was keeping his distance, but instead, Chip just felt sad. This was all so fucked up and it was all his fault. If his stupid body hadn't betrayed him at the worst possible time, this wouldn't be happening. They'd probably have spent the whole of dinner talking and making plans. Connecting.

Fucking hell.

"Okay, sorry," he said and retreated back to the table.

Dawson's back and shoulders were stiff and the plates chinked loudly against one another in the sink but he didn't respond.

Not wanting to just stare at Dawson like a creeper, Chip spied Elizabeth's scrapbook sitting on the buffet. He'd retrieved it from the floor when they had once again cleaned up after the angry ghost but hadn't looked at it again, spending the day searching the online archives instead. He didn't have his laptop or phone with him to continue his digital search so he figured he may as well see if there was anything else of use in the scrapbook.

He flipped through the pages until he reached the entry about Jacob but didn't linger there. Not only did he not want to risk the ghost throwing another tantrum, but he didn't want to look at the man's photo. Dawson was such an uncanny copy of him, except for the expression. Chip loved looking at Dawson's face but he never wanted to see such a look of arrogant contempt marr his features. Even if Dawson turned around now, as upset as he was, Chip knew that he'd never see Jacob's expression mirrored there. He just didn't have it in him.

The paper of the scrapbook was both thick and fragile. It had been good quality but age had impacted it and Chip tried to keep his touch delicate. Until he caught a glimpse of the ghost looking up at him from the following page. He recoiled so fast from the scrapbook that his chair overbalanced and he went crashing to the ground with a cry.

Before he'd even managed to regain his senses, wet, soapy hands were on him, hauling him to his feet and pulling him across the room. "Are you okay? What's wrong? What happened?" Dawson asked, his eyes wildly searching the room even as he held Chip to him.

Chip allowed himself to lean against Dawson for a moment, enjoying his subtle strength and the warmth of his body. It wasn't often that *he* was the one needing soothing and he enjoyed being within the protective circle of Dawson's arms, especially since all of Dawson's annoyance with him had dissolved in an instant. He tipped his chin towards the scrapbook, still sitting innocently on the table. "It's her," he said.

"She's here?" Dawson asked, frowning. "Where?" His eyes scanned the room again even as his arms tightened around Chip.

"Not physically here," Chip corrected. "She's in the scrapbook." He could feel his cheeks heat in embarrassment. "It startled me."

"Of course it would," Dawson agreed, as if it were obvious that anyone would have reacted that way. It made Chip relax just slightly.

"I guess we should take a look," he said, even though it was the last thing he really wanted to do.

"Yeah, we should," Dawson agreed easily.

Chip hated the instant that Dawson's arm dropped from around his shoulders as they moved back over to the table. He righted the chair and they sat down next to one another, the scrapbook open in front of them.

"Huh, it really is her," Dawson said, and he reached out to trace his fingers over the black and white photo on the page. His voice had gone hollow, his bravado from the moment before gone. "I didn't think I'd recognise her, since we only caught glimpses of her, but I'd recognise that mouth anywhere."

Chip tried not to flinch at that thought. He'd not seen the disembodied head that had rolled from the linen cupboard and latched onto Dawson's ankle, but he supposed there was no forgetting certain features after such an ordeal. "Charlotte Miller," he read from the page. His eyes skimmed over the text and his heart ached for the girl. "She was Jacob's younger sister. Whatever fucked-up shit was done to her that's caused her to haunt this place was done to her by her *brother.*"

"I can't . . ." Dawson pushed back his chair abruptly and stood. "I can't do this right now." His voice was pitchy. "I need to . . . I can't . . . " He trailed off but his breathing was heavy and laboured, and then he darted from the room.

Chip followed as Dawson hurried down the hall and into his own bedroom, and watched as he pulled open a drawer and rummaged through it. "What can I do?" he asked, not bothering with empty platitudes. Dawson wasn't in a state to accept them. He'd not quite tipped over into a full-blown anxiety attack as yet, and when he was on the cusp he always preferred action. Chip had witnessed it dozens of times before and Dawson had explained once that it gave him some semblance of control, made him feel like he was doing *something* to deter his body's fight or flight instinct. It rarely worked, but that was beside the point.

"I'm going to have a shower," Dawson told him. "Will you sit with me?"

Chip had to tell his dick that Dawson was only taking precautions against the ghost and it didn't mean anything, but the appendage didn't quite get the memo. Just the thought of Dawson in the shower got him chubbing up. *Not the fucking time!* "Of course," he said.

Dawson paused, his back still to Chip, and he took several deep breaths. Then he plucked a pair of track pants and a long-sleeved shirt from the drawer and turned and walked past Chip towards the bathroom.

CHAPTER 15

Dawson

Once he'd stepped into the tub and pulled the shower curtain closed, Dawson called out to Chip to tell him to come in. He heard the bathroom door open and then the toilet lid creaked so he assumed Chip had taken a seat on it. They didn't say a word to one another.

Dawson was so bloody confused, which wasn't helping his fucking anxiety at all. As he stood out of reach of the spray, waiting for the water to heat up, he found himself clenching his teeth together and tried to make his jaw relax. It was easier said than done. He concentrated on taking deep breaths, even though what he really wanted to do was to scream and cry and run as far away as possible.

He wanted to run into Chip's arms and stay there forever.

And just what the actual fuck was that all about? He reached up and scrubbed at his eyes, trying to figure out what the hell was going on in his head. He was *mad* at Chip for acting like such a fucking arse all day and *ignoring* him. So why the hell did he want nothing more than to curl up with him under the blanket and hide from the world? Before he could stop himself, he blurted, "What the fuck, Chip?"

There was a beat of silence and then Chip said, "I know. It's so fucked up. I can't believe Jacob is her brother."

"I'm not talking about the ghost!" Dawson snapped, even as he tested the spray and found it finally warm enough to step under. "I'm talking about *you*. You've ignored me all day. Why?"

The silence this time was much longer. When Chip spoke, his voice was strangled. "Are you really gonna make me say it?"

Dawson glared at the shower curtain where he knew Chip was sitting just on the other side. "How long have we known each other? Today wasn't the first time you've had a fucking boner in front of me so I don't see what the big deal is." Which was a total lie. Sure, teenage hormones had wreaked havoc when they were younger and they'd found themselves getting erections at the craziest of times, but that was just puberty. Chip had never gotten an erection because of *him*.

"You know why today was different," Chip muttered, and Dawson barely heard him over the sound of the water.

He squirted body wash onto a loofah and began scrubbing himself down. "I thought I meant more to you than this," he said, even though he knew it was a low blow. The gasp that echoed around the room told him he'd hit the mark. "I know you were embarrassed but it's *me*. You know I'm not going to judge you for something as trivial as that so why the hell have you been avoiding me all day. Do you think so little of me?"

"It's not like that," Chip said and he could hear the hurt in his voice.

"Then tell me what it's like."

"It's not that simple."

"Why the fuck not?" Dawson snapped.

"Because it's you!" Chip cried, and Dawson immediately felt bad for starting this conversation while he was in the shower so he couldn't even look at Chip while they spoke. "Fuck, Daw, I can't lose you!"

"Nothing you can do would ever make me ditch you, Tate," he said, using his proper name to hammer home how serious he was. "Nothing. You hear me?"

It took a long time for Chip to speak and when he did, his voice was trembling. "You can't promise that."

Dawson sighed and closed his eyes as he rubbed shampoo into his hair. He wasn't dumb. He'd noticed over the past few days that his own feelings for Chip had begun to change, and he could read the signs. It was becoming very apparent that A, those feelings were mutual and B, it was much more than just a simple crush.

He opened his mouth to speak but got a mouthful of warm water from the shower spray. He went to spit it out but suddenly gagged at the thick, coppery liquid in his mouth. Dawson's eyes shot open and all he could see was a red haze. He reached up and wiped his eyes but it didn't clear it, then jerked his head to look up at the shower head and whimpered as he saw that he was no longer being showered in water but blood. As he instinctively stepped backwards, away from the spray of blood, his ankle hit the side of the bath and he began to fall. He cried out, even as he grabbed at the shower curtain, but it was already ripping free of the railing and he was falling.

Arms caught him and Dawson felt himself being pulled free of the tub, but he was half wrapped up in the plastic curtain with his arms trapped at his side. Panic set in and he kicked and squirmed, trying to get free.

"Hey, Daw! Calm down, I've got you," Chip said, but Dawson didn't hear him. He needed to get away—away from the blood, away from the cloying thickness of it and the way it sat heavy on his tongue. He struggled even harder and found himself falling again, but this time only the half metre to the tiled ground.

It was then, as he was clawing his way out of the shower curtain, that Chip noticed the blood. "Fuck, what happened? Are you hurt?"

Dawson shook his head, even as he scooted away from the shower as far as he could, with his back pressed up against the closed bathroom door.

Chip crouched down in front of him, his hands held up as if he wanted to comfort Dawson but didn't want to startle him. Then he glanced over his shoulder at the still-running shower and he blanched. "What the fuck?" he uttered as he took in the blood pouring from the shower head. As if on instinct, he stood and reached for the taps, turning them off.

The flow of blood stopped, except for the occasional drip.

Dawson stared up at Chip and he could feel the blood cooling on his skin, clumping his eyelashes together and beginning to thicken even more. His stomach roiled and he fought down the urge to vomit. He tried to form words, to beg Chip to help get him clean, but he couldn't. All that came out of his mouth was a strangled moan.

Then Chip was moving. He pulled Dawson to his feet and pulled the shower curtain away, tossing it behind him into the previously white tub which was now stained a pink hue with red streaks up the sides. Dawson didn't have a chance to feel exposed before Chip was wrapping a towel around his shoulders. He threw another towel over his own shoulder and then tried to guide Dawson away from the door so he could open it.

Dawson couldn't move.

Without missing a beat, Chip scooped Dawson up into his arms, and managed to get the door open and them both moving. Dawson closed his eyes and hid his face against Chip's shoulder, not wanting to risk seeing the ghost of Charlotte Miller. He heard the back door open and then they were outside in the chilly night air. Chip didn't slow, just carried Dawson across the back yard towards the shed where they'd set up their gym equipment.

Dawson began shivering. It was so bloody cold and the towel wasn't anywhere near big enough to cover him. Even once they reached the shelter of the shed, the tin structure and concrete floors did nothing to insulate against the cold September night. He huddled against Chip's warm, broad chest, but he couldn't stop his teeth from chattering.

"Sorry," Chip murmured. "We'll get you warm soon."

Dawson was lowered to the ground and he flinched as his bare feet touched the freezing floor. Chip looked around and quickly grabbed a sweat towel and placed it on the ground for him to stand on, then turned to the small sink in the corner and began filling it with water. They'd left a stack of flannels and fresh sweat towels in a small cupboard next to the sink for after their workouts, and Chip took a flannel and dunked it in the water.

"I'll try to work quickly to get the blood off you," he told Dawson in a gentle voice. "But it's probably gonna get a bit nippy."

Dawson's arms were wrapped around himself to try and retain heat, and his teeth rattled. "'Sokay," he managed to say. "Nips have f-f-frozen o-o-ff already."

Chip chuckled, even as he squeezed the excess water out of the flannel. "Can you wrap the towel around your waist so I can start?"

It was only then Dawson realised that the towel had been wrapped around his shoulders like a cape and he was clutching it closed at the front—his arse had probably been exposed the entire way out of the house—and he snorted as he dropped it down and secured it at his hip.

"What's so funny?" Chip asked.

He shrugged. "Think I m-m-mooned the ghost."

The bark of laughter that left Chip's mouth was not at all polite. "Fucking bitch doesn't deserve to see your arse."

"But you do."

Chip froze at Dawson's words, looking like a roo caught in headlights. Despite Chip's obvious shock, Dawson didn't regret the words. With everything going on at the moment, the epiphany about his growing attraction towards his stepbrother, plus Chip's interest in him, was the only bright spark in his life. It made him feel giddy in a way that none of his girlfriends had ever done. There was a constant, low hum of excitement in his belly each time he took out those thoughts and examined them. So maybe it was time he did something about it?

"Let's get this blood off you before you freeze," Chip said, suddenly businesslike.

Okay, so maybe *right now* wasn't the best time, but it would be soon. "'Kay."

The first stage of cleanup was brutal. Chip bent Dawson over the sink and they cleaned his hair as best they could. The water was warm but it cooled quickly as it ran in rivulets down over his chest, and even after being towel dried, his hair was damp enough to cause heat to seep from his body.

After changing the water, Chip took Dawson's chin in one hand and began to gently wipe over his cheeks and jaw. His expression was intense but his eyes were soft as he wiped away the blood. "Close your eyes," he murmured, and his breath was a warm puff against Dawson's chilled skin.

He let his eyes close and Chip ran the flannel over them, removing the clumping blood from his lashes. He kept them closed, even when Chip moved on to his brow and then his ears. He tried not to think about anything else but the soft touch of Chip's hands and how good it felt to be looked after like this.

The flannel had already cooled by the time Chip began to drag it across Dawson's shoulders and chest and it sent goosebumps rippling across his skin. He was so fucking cold. Luckily, Chip didn't dawdle, and he rinsed the flannel again before bringing the now-warm cloth back to clean down Dawson's flanks.

Once his torso was clean and dry, Chip rinsed the flannel once again and held it out to Dawson. "Um, I'll let you do the rest," he said, now unable to meet Dawson's eyes.

As much as Dawson was beginning to want *more* with Chip, he didn't want having Chip's hands on him for the first time to be like this, so he accepted the flannel with a soft, "Thanks."

"Will you be okay here for five minutes?" Chip asked. "I want to run into the house and grab you some warm clothes."

Dawson nodded. He knew Chip would be safe enough, since he didn't resemble the man who had once done terrible things to Charlotte Miller. He watched as Chip left the shed and then hurried to clean off the rest of the way. It wasn't perfect and he would have loved to have had a proper shower, but there was no way he was risking that tonight. It would have to do.

Chip was back almost as soon as he was done, and he was carrying a bundle of clothes as well as Dawson's phone. "Here," he said, as he dumped the pile onto the ground and then tossed a few items over to Dawson.

It was fresh trackies and an oversized hoodie that belonged to Chip. Dawson pulled them on then nodded at the pile. "What's the rest for?"

Chip held up a couple of fleece blankets. "I don't want you to have to go back into the house until I've cleaned the bathroom properly but it's too fucking cold out here. I figured these would keep you warm until I'm back."

His heart squeezed at that, knowing how much Chip looked after him. His annoyance from earlier entirely forgotten now, he crossed over to Chip and threw his arms around him. "Thank you," he whispered.

The few inches of difference between their heights meant that Chip's face was against Dawson's neck and he shivered as warm breath gusted over his chilled skin when Chip spoke. "Anything for you."

He had to wonder how true that statement was. How far would Chip go for Dawson? Attraction was one thing, but would he be willing to act on it? Would he be willing to cross that line? He could only hope.

Once they broke apart, Chip didn't simply hand the blankets over to Dawson, but took the time to wrap them around him, making sure he was warm. He then gave Dawson a soft smile and left to go and clean up the bathroom.

Dawson sat himself down on their shoulder-press machine to keep his bare feet off the concrete. He leaned against the backrest and closed his eyes, allowing himself to drift in that state in between resting and dozing. He was so freaking *tired*. They'd been in their new house for almost a week now and he was emotionally drained, not to mention the physical stress he'd endured. His ankle was itching from the healing bite, the small cuts on his face had scabbed over, and he was exhausted. If Angie couldn't help them, he didn't know what they'd do.

His eyes snapped open as he realised he should alert Angie to the latest occurrence. He grabbed his phone from where Chip had laid it and opened the private messages function on his app.

> Dawson: So, we have a name for our ghost - Charlotte Miller. Didn't have much of a chance to learn anything about her yet except for the fact that she can turn our water into blood. My shower was not as cleansing as I'd hoped.

Given the late hour, he'd not expected a reply until the following morning but the message status turned to *Read* and then he could see her typing.

Angie: Things appear to be escalating . . . that's not good.

Dawson: Not at all.

Angie: I think you need to try and make contact tomorrow. If things are escalating this quickly, you can't really wait until I get there.

Dawson: Make contact? What does that involve? I don't own a ouija board.

Angie: Nothing as extreme as that. You simply have to try and talk to her.

Dawson: What do you mean?

Angie: Well, when air moves up your trachea and through the larynx, it causes your vocal cords to vibrate which creates sound. If you move your lips and tongue in certain ways, you form words. This is called communicating.

Dawson: Wow, sarcastic much?

Angie: Daft much? Talking means exactly what it sounds like!

Dawson: What the hell am I supposed to say?

Angie: How about something along the lines of "I'm not Jacob Miller, please stop being mean to me?"

Dawson: You reckon that'll really work?

Angie: No idea, but it's better than doing nothing until I get there.

He took a deep breath, keeping himself from asking her if she could just come sooner. They didn't know her and she didn't owe them anything. She was already doing them a favour so he really didn't want to push the envelope too far. It was only two more days—Angie would be arriving Friday night. Surely they could manage for two more days. Right?

Dawson: Okay, I'll give it a go.

Angie: Keep me posted.

Dawson: I will. Thanks.

CHAPTER 16

Chip

The bathroom looked like a murder scene, and Chip spent the entire time cleaning wondering whose blood it was. If forensics ran a DNA test on it, what result would come back? It was definitely blood, but maybe it was animal blood? But did the ghost kill some poor critter or did she just manifest the blood? How would she do that? Did it just appear out of thin air? Or was it the blood of Charlotte Miller? Or Jacob? If so, did she reanimate the blood from dust?

The fact that his house was not only haunted but also apparently defying the laws of science was really getting under Chip's skin.

By the time he was finished, his back was aching, his fingers were pruned, and he stank of Domestos, so he took a quick shower himself before he headed out to the shed to collect Dawson. He was worried that now the shock of the bloody incident was wearing off, the tension that had simmered between them all day would return and make things awkward. His worry was baseless. Dawson told him about his text exchange with Angie and her suggestion, and they tossed around ideas for how to start a conversation with a ghost as they made their way into Chip's bedroom and started getting ready for bed. Dawson then climbed under the covers, and as soon as Chip turned off the light and got into bed himself, he wriggled across the mattress and plastered himself against Chip. Then he promptly fell asleep.

Chip lay there for the longest time, silently analysing the move. Was it just a need for comfort after the bathroom incident? Was it simply because Dawson was exhausted and not thinking? Or did it mean something more? *Could* it mean something more? As much as Chip wished for that fairytale ending, he knew reality didn't work like that. The chances of Dawson ever returning Chip's feelings were practically non-existent and getting his hopes up would just lead to disappointment.

In the dark of night, with the heat of Dawson's body pressed against him, though, it was difficult to keep his hopes from peeking out and testing the waters. Especially after Dawson made that comment earlier about Chip being deserving of seeing his arse.

Chip didn't fall asleep until late, but as soon as Dawson stirred just after dawn he was up. Not quite awake, but up. He shuffled, zombie-like to the bathroom to take a piss, and then followed Dawson down the hall and into the kitchen. The kettle took an age to boil and he sighed when he finally took that first sip of coffee.

"So, what's the plan for today?" Dawson asked from across the table. He was paler than usual and looked drawn. His lower lip was red and chapped from where he'd been chewing it during the night—a sure sign that his anxiety was bad.

"I don't really know," Chip admitted. "Angie didn't say we need anything special to do this, did she?"

Dawson shook his head and sipped his own coffee. "Nope. No ouija boards or those funky static-machine things that ghost hunters use. She said to just have a conversation and explain that I'm not Jacob."

Chip frowned. "If it were that easy, you'd think she'd have already figured it out since we've spoken about this a *lot.*"

Dawson shrugged. "Maybe she doesn't eavesdrop and we need to actually address her specifically?" he suggested.

"Oh, so she's a polite ghost now?" Chip asked, unable to hold back his sarcasm. "She won't eavesdrop on a private conversation, only try and drown you in blood." He immediately felt bad when Dawson flinched. "Fuck, sorry." He rubbed a hand over his eyes and then removed his cap, which was perched backwards on his head. He smoothed down his hair before he replaced it. "I'm tired and not thinking clearly."

It was Dawson's turn to look concerned. "You didn't sleep?"

Chip shook his head. "Not much. Was a little too worked up."

"Urgh, we need to get this sorted," Dawson said. "Now."

"Okay," Chip agreed, placing his coffee on the table and standing up. "Come on. Let's go and see if we can sense her anywhere in the house."

They walked from room to room, both on high alert for any sign of the ghost. They'd swept the house from front to back and then back again, and had ended up in the loungeroom with no results. Chip took a deep breath and reached out his hand to Dawson, who took it wordlessly. His grip was tight though, and Chip gave it a reassuring squeeze. "Charlotte?" he said to the room. "Are you here? We'd like to talk to you."

Nothing.

Chip and Dawson exchanged a look. "Charlotte Miller?" Chip tried again. "We'd like to talk to you about your brother, Jacob Miller."

The atmosphere in the room changed instantly. The pressure dropped, causing Chip to wince as his ears popped, and the lights began to flicker.

Although the windows were shut tight, with the curtains drawn to keep out the cold, a chill breeze swirled around their legs. The door to the room banged shut, then opened of its own accord, before slamming closed again. It continued to open and close another handful of times but Chip's attention was drawn to a shimmery mass that had appeared in front of the fireplace. He took a hesitant step forward but stopped as the mass began to swirl and twist in agitation. "Charlotte?" he asked softly.

The lights stopped flickering.

"Charlotte, it's nice to meet you," he told her. "My name is Chip and this is my stepbrother, Dawson Miller. I haven't worked out exactly how you're related yet but I think he might be your great-great, maybe great again, nephew?"

The lights flickered a few more times and the breeze in the room intensified as it began to circle them, buffeting their bodies with the force of it.

"We're not here to hurt you," he assured her. "We just want to help you."

The wind increased again, forming a mini tornado around them. Dawson's curls were flying around his face, the flickering lights almost strobelike against his pale skin, and Chip's cap was flung off his head and across the room. He immediately pulled Dawson to him, wrapping his arms around him to keep him safe from whatever Charlotte was doing, and Dawson tucked his head against his chest, hiding his face. When the wind intensified *again* and threatened to knock them off their feet, Chip decided it was time to put an end to the temper tantrum. *"Enough!"* he thundered at the ghost.

The room was shocked into silence. Everything ceased—the wind, the flickering lights, everything.

"Charlotte, we need to talk to you so we can help you but we can't do that if you're going to attack us every time we try," he told her. "Can you please just give us a chance to explain a few things?"

There was no reply—not that he'd been expecting one—but there were no further wind attacks and the lights stayed steady. He took that as her acquiescence.

"Thank you." It didn't hurt to be polite to the powerful ghost. "Firstly, can I please just reiterate that Dawson is *not* Jacob. I know he looks very much like him, but they aren't the same person. Not only did Jacob die a very long time ago, but Dawson is kind and sweet and gentle. He may look like Jacob, but he's completely different to him."

The lights flickered twice, and it almost felt inquisitive.

"We don't know what Jacob did to you, but whatever it was, I can guarantee you that Dawson would never do anything like it. He's not evil. He's the complete opposite of evil, I promise you this." There was no response from Charlotte but the atmosphere in the room remained calm, open almost, like she was willing to hear them out. "I would very much like it if you would stop hurting Dawson. He's very special to me and I don't like seeing him hurt, especially when you're punishing him for crimes he didn't commit."

No response.

"Please, Charlotte," Chip said. "I need you to assure me that you won't continue to hurt Dawson. I want to help you but I'm not going to if you can't make me that promise." He gestured up at the light above them. "Make the lights flicker once if you can make me that promise."

Nothing happened for a long time. Both Chip and Dawson tilted their heads back to watch the globe with bated breath, awaiting Charlotte's response. Just when he thought she wasn't going to respond, the light flickered once.

The relief was immediate.

Dawson sagged against Chip's chest, and he held him tight, supporting him. Without even thinking about it, he pressed a kiss to Dawson's blond curls. "Thank you," he whispered to Charlotte. After a few more seconds of just holding Dawson, Chip straightened and turned to the fireplace, then almost jumped out of his skin.

Charlotte had manifested in front of the fireplace, looking as solid as either of them.

She looked so much younger than in her photo. Chip wasn't sure if that was because historical photos always looked formal and severe or if it was because of the lost expression on her face. Her light brown hair was loose around her shoulders, as opposed to the tight bun she'd been wearing when they'd seen her on the Live video the first time. It was curly, the same as Dawson's, and looking at her now, the familial resemblance was unmistakable. Where Jacob could be Dawson's twin, Charlotte could easily have been Dawson's sister. The round, cherubic face, the pale blue eyes, the arch of their brows. It was all the same.

"Hi."

Chip glanced over at Dawson, who was now tucked under his arm, and found that he was looking at Charlotte in wonder. He'd not spoken until now, both of them worried at how she would react.

For her part, Charlotte was staring at Dawson, examining him closely. She drifted closer, her plain cream dress moving gently around her legs. She stopped about a metre in front of them and continued to stare intently at Dawson. Finally, she offered him a small smile and the rest of the tension in the room faded. It appeared they'd finally convinced her of the truth.

"How can we help you, Charlotte?" Chip asked her. She didn't seem able to speak and he hoped they'd be able to figure out what she needed so she could rest.

There was a bang from behind them, and both Chip and Dawson whirled around to see that the loungeroom door had banged open and the scrapbook was floating into the room. It stopped just in front of them and

Chip managed to snag it from the air as it suddenly dropped. It was still open to Charlotte's page. He looked down and read quickly over the entry, specifically the final part.

"Charlotte was only seventeen when she was killed in a tragic horse-riding accident. She and her brother, Jacob, had been returning home after checking on a flock of sheep, when Charlotte fell from her horse and she became entangled in the lead rope. Despite Jacob's attempts to halt the horse, he was unable to do so and Charlotte was dragged to an untimely and gruesome death."

When Chip finished reading the passage aloud, Charlotte became agitated, pacing back and forth, and the lights started to flicker once more. Blood began to trickle down from her throat, staining the top of her dress with its vivid colour. He didn't need the details to be able to deduce that she had been decapitated by the rope around her neck.

"He didn't try to save you," Dawson said softly to her, echoing Chip's thoughts. "Jacob instigated the whole thing."

She stopped abruptly and turned to him, nodding. Her head wobbled alarmingly.

"Yet everyone believed that he was the hero," Chip noted.

"Do you know *why* he killed you?" Dawson asked the ghost.

She nodded.

"If we figure it out, and expose the truth of what happened, will that be enough for you to rest?"

There was a longer pause and then she nodded again. The blood slowly began to fade from her dress, and she appeared whole once more.

"Okay, so we just need to solve a murder that happened over a hundred years ago," Chip said, blowing out a long breath. "Piece of cake." He looked over at Charlotte. "Do you have anything that can help us?"

She smiled then. It wasn't a joyous smile but one of determination, and she disappeared from where she was standing. A moment later, they saw the back of her disappearing through the doorway. They followed and caught sight of her at the end of the hallway. By the time they got down to the sunroom, she was gone.

"Really?" Chip snapped, annoyed that she'd disappeared so suddenly. "What the hell are we supposed to do now?"

From outside, there came a loud knocking sound.

They both cocked their heads to listen.

"Where is that coming from?" Dawson asked.

Chip frowned. "The side of the house?"

They headed outside into the dreary, overcast day. The clouds were low and heavy, rain imminent. It was cold and the wind whipped at their hair. Chip wished he'd thought to grab his cap to keep it contained.

They followed the noise of the knocking, which was getting louder, around the side of the house. It was the side that had a pile of junk stacked against it—a jumbled heap of items that had never been discarded on the off chance they'd come in handy one day. The knocking continued, growing deeper and louder, and it appeared to be coming from behind the deepest part of the pile. Chip rolled his eyes. "Typical," he muttered, but immediately began to move items out of the way.

They'd rolled away three forty-gallon drums, a roll of ring-lock fencing, and numerous planks of nail-studded wood when they came across some large sheets of rusted tin. "What do you think our chances are of getting this moved *without* needing a tetanus shot?" Chip asked dryly.

The knocking got even louder, making the tin quiver.

"We'll just have to be careful," Dawson told him, and took a tentative hold of one side of the tin.

They carefully lifted it away from the house, inching backwards so they didn't trip, and manoeuvred it to lean up against the drums. They then turned back to the house and Dawson gasped.

They'd uncovered a set of wooden doors, inset into the ground at an angle, a little like the outside basement doors that Chip had seen on American television shows. It was the last thing he'd ever expected to find at an old farm house in rural Australia. The knocking reached a crescendo as the doors were revealed and then suddenly—it stopped.

"I guess this is what she wanted us to find," Dawson said, peering at the doors.

"I guess so," Chip agreed.

CHAPTER 17

Dawson

Dawson pulled out his phone as they stared at the doors. He held it up and looked over at Chip. "I know it's not the best time to be thinking about stuff like this, but do you mind if I record this? I've hardly posted in the last couple of days and I'm worried that I'm going to start getting stern letters of consternation from my sponsors."

Chip gave him a warm smile. "Of course, dude."

"I'll be sure to edit out any freaky stuff if I capture anything," he assured him quickly. "I get that this probably isn't something you want broadcast to the world."

"It's okay, Daw," Chip assured him. "I trust you. And I get that you gotta keep your sponsors happy. No judgement here, 'kay?"

He nodded and hit record on his phone, pointing it at himself to begin with. "Hey everyone! Hope you're all well. I've been pretty busy doing stuff around the house. Luckily for me, I'm decked out in the comfiest shirt from TK lane—it really makes it easy to move about." He held up his wrist to show off the watch there. "And of course, my Quest is capturing all the important info to track my day." With a plug to his main sponsors done and dusted, he moved on to the fun part. "So, you'll never guess what Chip and I found today while exploring the yard." He hit stop and then flipped the camera and started recording the outside of the house, panning around to show the junk and the doors. "Grandpa Miller kept a *lot* of shit, as you can see," he said. "Behind it all, we found this weird trapdoor thingy. Have you ever seen anything like this before?" he asked, panning across to Chip.

Chip shook his head as he looked at the camera. His hair was windswept and wild looking and he was absolutely stunning under the bright light from the overcast sky. "I haven't," he told Dawson's viewers. "I'm guessing it's some kind of cellar that they used for food storage back in the day."

"How about we find out?" Dawson said, turning the camera back to the doors. "Wanna do the honours, Chip?"

He filmed with a steady hand as Chip hefted open first one door and then the other. Having the camera between himself and reality helped to keep him calm, and Dawson didn't even jump as Chip let go of the second door handle a little early and it thumped down against the ground. He stepped up close, allowing the camera to film the gloomy depths of the room below.

Chip pulled out his own phone and turned on the flashlight function to illuminate the way. There was a set of stone steps made from coffee rock that led down into the cellar, and Dawson followed on Chip's heels as he descended into the darkness.

The room they found themselves in wasn't overly large, maybe four metres squared. It had stone walls and a low ceiling. Dawson could only just stand upright, his curly hair brushing against the roof. Shelves lined all of the walls and as Chip turned in a circle, the light from his phone illuminating the space, Dawson caught sight of a single window high in one corner that was black with grime. He filmed the entire room and then hit stop so he could speak to Chip without recording it. "What do you think she wanted us to find down here?" he asked.

Chip had stepped close to one of the shelves and was inspecting several wooden crates. "I'm not sure. There's nothing here but these, so I'm guessing it'll be something in here."

He lifted one of the crates down, his biceps bulging as he did so. Dawson had been aware of Chip's strength before, but now he found that he couldn't drag his eyes away from the glorious sight before him. The long sleeved shirt he wore pulled taut against his muscles, and as he lowered the crate to the floor, Dawson could see the long line of his spine. He had the strongest urge to push the shirt out of the way and run his tongue up every single bump.

The crate had a lid on top, but it was warped with age and was easy enough to lift off. Inside, the contents appeared to be much the same as one of the boxes they'd gotten from the Historical Society. It was full of books, loose paper, and some old photos.

Chip reached in and picked up a few of the books, and a photo fell from the pages of the top one. Dawson picked it up and examined it. It was black and white and showed two young girls, maybe early teens, standing in front of a church. The girl on the left was definitely Charlotte. They were both wearing smart dresses and had hats pinned to their hair. They had serious expressions on their faces, but Dawson could just tell that was simply because they had been instructed so for the photo. There was a lightness to the girls, a shine to their eyes that spoke of hidden mirth.

He flipped the photo over and saw that an inscription had been written on the back in a spidery cursive.

Charlotte and Abigail at the church fete.

While Dawson had been looking at the photo, Chip had flipped through several of the books. "I think this is what we're after," he told Dawson.

"Oh?"

Chip held one up. "These are diaries. *Charlotte's* diaries."

A chill wind swept around their legs, causing Dawson to break out in goosebumps, but as quickly as it had come, it was gone. A simple confirmation that this was what Charlotte had wanted them to find.

It had started to rain by the time they emerged from the cellar, and they made a mad dash back inside to prevent the old diaries from getting wet. They settled in the kitchen and Chip got the kettle boiling so they'd have a cuppa while they looked through the diaries.

There were five in total and each notebook was full from front to back. They looked through them to find the most recent diary, and discovered that the last date was 23rd December, 1904.

"What year did Charlotte die?" Chip asked as he double checked the dates on the other diaries.

Dawson grabbed the scrapbook and opened it up to her entry. "January 16, 1905," he read.

Chip frowned. "Charlotte?" he called to the room. "Are you still here?"

There was silence for a moment and then the light flickered.

"Did you continue your diary into the new year?" he asked. "Flicker the lights, once for yes and twice for no."

The lights flickered once.

"We're missing her latest diary," Dawson muttered, feeling crestfallen.

The diary was yanked from his hand and fell open as an invisible hand flipped through the book. It was discarded on the table and each of the other diaries was subjected to Charlotte's scrutiny. When the last diary was checked, the atmosphere in the room changed immediately. The room grew dark, cold, and oppressive, and then suddenly the diaries were flung across the room and against the wall with impressive force, causing the bindings to break and loose pages to scatter. All the cupboard doors slammed open and the contents spilled out to smash upon the ground, and the globe above them shattered.

"For fuck's sake," Chip spat, even as he leaned over Dawson to protect him from the temper tantrum. "Calm down, Charlotte!"

She ignored him and continued her path of destruction, pulling the cutlery drawer out and sending knives, forks, and spoons flying. Dawson was simply grateful that none of it headed in their direction, as the last thing they needed to deal with was knives flying at their heads.

A full minute passed until Charlotte's anger abated, and they were assaulted with a wave of frustration and grief before the oppressive force over the room dissolved and she was gone.

"I'm getting *real* sick of cleaning up after her," Chip growled as they got to their feet.

Dawson surveyed the mess with a sinking feeling. "Did she break *every-thing*? Is there a single plate remaining?"

Chip crossed to the cupboards, broken glass crunching under his shoes as he walked, and he peered inside them. "Nope. Everything is ruined."

Dawson sighed. "Until we get this sorted, I'm not buying more crockery. We can eat off paper plates until we can be guaranteed that our plates and cups are safe from Charlotte."

"Agreed," Chip said. "I'll start on this. How 'bout you try and piece together the diary entries? We might not have the entries from the last fortnight of her life but we might find some clues in the lead up to the end of the year."

"Yeah, good idea," Dawson agreed, and he began collecting the sheets of paper that now littered the room.

It took them over an hour to get the kitchen put back to rights. Dawson had separated the loose pages into years but only put 1904 into date order, since they'd start there and only go further back if needed. Before they had a chance to start looking through them, there was a knock at the door. "Expecting someone?" he asked Chip.

"Ah, fuck, yes. I'd arranged for a contractor to come out and give us a quote for the firebreaks. Sorry."

"No worries. I'll spend some time editing today's video while you do that. The diary can wait."

The afternoon flew by as Dawson finished his video and then spent some time replying to DMs and responding to a few emails from sponsors.

Chip poked his head into the sunroom after the contractor left. He was towelling his hair dry, having gotten wet from the rain that was falling steadily from the sky. "Hey, I've gotta make a run into town to grab a few things from the hardware. You wanna come?"

Dawson was feeling confident that Charlotte wouldn't do anything to him and he was honestly ready for a little bit of time to himself. "I might stay here, if that's okay?"

The way that Chip didn't protest told Dawson he needed a bit of alone time as well. "Of course. Can I get you anything?"

"I've got a few parcels to pick up from the post office. Would you mind getting them?"

"Of course. Where's your key?"

"On the hook in the kitchen. Well, it was. God only knows if it survived Charlotte's tanty."

Chip chuckled. "I'll go look. Call me if anything happens."

Chip was only gone for an hour and a bit, but it was enough time for Dawson to get his thoughts in order. They'd been a mess for the past week, especially when it came to their evolution in regards to Chip, but he'd decided he was going to do something about that and was feeling much better with a plan in place.

By the time Chip was back, Dawson had started making one of Chip's favourite dishes for dinner—a Malaysian rendang—and they ate from paper bowls. "I guess it makes dishes easier," Chip drawled as they cleaned up after dinner.

"True that," Dawson agreed.

They took the 1904 diary through to the loungeroom and sat together on the couch. The rain had picked up even more and was hammering against the tin roof, and Dawson shuffled over until their legs were pressed together. Chip threw him a look but didn't comment, just asked, "How far back do you think we'll need to go?"

"I'm not sure," Dawson admitted. "How about we start in the middle of the year, and if it feels like we're missing context we can backtrack?"

He leafed through the pages until he found the start of July, and they began to read. There was an entry for each day, and most were mundane things, recounting what had happened each day on the farm. They'd only read three entries when Chip left to find the scrapbook so they could cross check against the information there. Charlotte often mentioned someone called William and they realised that he was not only the eldest brother, but also Dawson's great-great-grandfather. He was eight years older than Charlotte and appeared to work the farm alongside her father.

From the entries, they determined that Charlotte had finished school the previous year and now helped her mother with the housework, and was also a junior member of the Church Committee, a group of community-minded ladies who planned events and helped support families in town that had undergone tragedy. There was often mention of Abigail Wiltshire, the girl from the photo, and she was not only Charlotte's best friend but was also on the Church Committee with her mother.

It was in July when Charlotte finally made mention of Jacob in more than simply passing.

17th July 1904

It has rained nigh constantly since my entry yesterday and I am quickly growing weary of the weather. Father is quick to remind me that after the harsh summer that befell us, the rain is most welcome, yet it does so get tiresome! I do hope it passes before week's end as Mama has promised me that Abigail can come for a visit and supper on Saturday. My brothers will be busy helping Father with repairs to the fences and so we will be free to visit without them bothering us. William never causes us too much distress but Jacob appears to go out of his way to intrude. He is, on his best days, rather foreboding and Abigail has confided that she finds his company unsettling. If all goes well, we shall avoid him for most of the day and will only have to bear his presence at supper.

It is our hope that we shall be able to put our heads together and come up with some grand ideas for the Committee so we can prove our worth. Some days we both feel as if we are humoured by the older ladies yet we both feel we have some excellent ideas that would benefit our community. In private, Abigail likes to refer to Mrs Cumberland as Mrs Curmudgeon and I must confess that I must try not to giggle each time she frowns at us and tells us in her most condescending manner that our ideas have no merit!

"I wonder if Abigail had Jacob figured out?" Dawson asked after they'd read the entry.

"She was clearly uncomfortable around him," Chip agreed. He yawned and stretched his arms out above his head. "I'm gonna go make a cuppa," he said. "You want one?"

"Tea would be nice. Thanks."

"Keep reading," Chip said as he stood. "You can catch me up on anything important when I'm back."

Dawson grunted, already reading the next entry, getting lost in the memories of what life was like in Brockman at the turn of the previous century.

When Chip returned, he was carrying two tin cups that he'd pulled from his camping supplies, both steaming with hot tea. "Anything?" he asked as he sat down once more.

"Yeah. Not anything more about Jacob, but it appears Charlotte had a temper in life as well as death. She makes mention of it here." He pointed out the entry in question and allowed Chip to catch up.

31st July 1904

A savage storm assaulted us overnight and we woke to much damage around the farm. A fairly large tree fell onto the stables, causing damage to the roof and upsetting the horses. For the first time in my memory, we were unable to attend mass this morning as we were all required to assist Father in the cleanup, even

Mama and I! It was laborious work, and I was utterly filthy by the time we had finished for the day, but I must confess that I thoroughly enjoyed myself. Mama tells me that it isn't fitting for girls to muck about in the dirt but it is freeing to be able to exert myself in such a manner. How thrilling is it to have a goal in mind that is achieved, especially with many hands working together? The feeling of accomplishment today far outweighed that of completing a piece of needlework or fixing supper for Father and my brothers.

I made mention of my enjoyment to William once we had cleaned ourselves of the mud and debris that clung to us. Of the family, he is the one who indulges me the most, and in this it was no different. He has promised me that he will speak to Father about allowing me to help more often. It may only be in the form of surveying the stock or checking for orphan lambs but I shall eagerly accept any opportunity that arises, especially if it allows me to take to horseback. I do so prefer being astride a horse than being confined to the buggy, even if Mama does consider it unladylike. Given how I am quick to temper at the best of times, she is often at her wits' end when it comes to my unladylike manner and so if I am to be allowed to assist William, I must make more of an attempt to please Mama. I shall need all of God's grace to assist me.

"She sounds like a firecracker," Chip said with admiration. "Good on her for wanting to do more than just cook and clean."

It was in August that things got interesting.

16th August 1904

Father is angry with Jacob and I do not understand why. It has made the day most uncomfortable, with neither Father nor Jacob speaking to one another. Mama has been most quiet also which leads me to believe that he has also upset her. Alas, I am not surprised as Jacob's tongue can be lashing when he so wishes, and we have all felt the brunt of it at one time or another. William helped me in the kitchen after supper so Mama could rest, and when Jacob made a scathing remark about William belittling himself by undertaking women's work, William berated him most sternly for his lack of respect for Mama. Jacob appeared most angry, but William is not only older but also towers over him and so he did not cause a fuss. He left us be, but the entire incident has left me feeling unsettled and agitated. It is not a feeling that I am fond of and I do so hope this veil of anger that appears to have settled over our house has lifted come morning.

17th August 1904

Tensions are still high today and Jacob has refused to apologise for his rudeness to both Father and Mama. Father is furious and has made his displeasure known, but Jacob is stubborn and quick to anger. A family trait that we both share, but I do not hesitate to say that our differences lie in our execution. Whereas I will sulk and then apologise, I rarely take my anger out directly on another. Jacob unleashes his own on whomever has the misfortune of being close by, and never admits fault. Today was much the same. Neither capitulated and nothing was resolved. Mama has been quiet and withdrawn all day and I do so worry for her. She has not been well for some years now and this has drawn her strength more than it warranted.

William took pity on me and asked me to help him move the flock to a yard closer to the homestead. It was hard work, but I felt accomplished once we were done and he told me he was proud of me and that I had proved my mettle. He promised me that I can help again in future and that he would placate Mama so she would not raise a fuss.

Two ewes had lambed overnight and William allowed me to hold one of the dear little things as he checked over the mother. It was such an extraordinary feeling to hold her close and feel her tiny body tremble against me. She is perfect in every way. Even the black fleece on her ear does not detract from her perfection, yet accentuates it. I asked William if we could keep her at the house but he simply laughed and told me not to form an attachment to the poor thing. I am not naive. I know the destiny of these animals, yet I wish that I could shower them in affection if but for a short while. It was a lovely distraction from the black cloud that has fallen over the household and I was ever grateful for the reprieve.

18th August 1904

I accompanied Father and Mama into Brockman today to gather the post and to collect some items from the general store. Whilst there, we ran into Abigail and Mrs Wiltshire, and Father graciously escorted us to the tea rooms for luncheon. It was a treat to see Abigail again and I most enjoyed spending time with her whilst our mothers chatted. I do miss our schooling days when we would see each other almost daily, but I am lucky that our friendship has remained ever strong. Some days I feel like she is the only person who truly understands me, and I her.

22nd August 1904

Have you ever felt like you wish you could erase a day from your memories? Today was one such day for me. I feel ill even recounting it here, but I challenged myself to write each and every day and if I cannot bare my soul within these pages, then where shall I? Perhaps the act of committing the horrors to paper will be much like lancing a lesion and I shall feel cleansed afterwards?

I had risen early to get the bread in the oven and William asked if I would like to check on the lambs while he fed the flock. Of course I was eager to accept, and we went together out into the yard. It was still moments before dawn, and quite dark, so I stayed close to William as he was familiar with the path to take. The flock were huddled around the large gum tree by the well but as we approached it became apparent that there was something terribly wrong. They were agitated and wary, crying out in alarm, yet staying close to one another.

William and Father have been concerned as foxes have become more common in recent years, migrating across from Victoria. William shared his fears with me that perhaps our flock had been victims of such an attack, but the reality was much more horrific.

The little lamb that I had only days before held in my arms, the one with the black ear, was some distance away from the flock and she had been torn apart. I could not bear to witness the horror and so turned away as William examined the poor soul. It was only moments later that he let out a string of curses I had never heard fall from his mouth before. He was in a rage and he stormed towards the house, leaving me hurrying in his wake. When he reached the house, he tore inside and to the rear room that he shares with Jacob, and I watched on in shock as he pulled a slumbering Jacob from his bed. Father and Mama heard the commotion and came running, but not before William had struck Jacob ferociously around the head, knocking him to the ground.

The following moments were chaotic as Father restrained William, who was shouting at Jacob, accusing him of being the perpetrator of the horrific act. Mama was crying and demanding to know what was going on, and William explained about the attack on the lamb and how he had seen that it had not been caused by an animal but by a human, as the cuts were deliberate and precise.

I was full of confusion as to why he had immediately suspected Jacob of the heinous crime, but both Father and Mama immediately suspected him also. It did not take long until Jacob confessed, and he became teary with remorse.

Mama hurried me from the room and I did not see what happened next, but I did overhear that Jacob will be meeting with Father O'Reilly after mass each week to atone for his sins.

William will not look at Jacob and I have spent most of the day crying over the little lamb. He came to comfort me this evening and told me that he buried the poor soul down by the dam.

I just cannot fathom what possessed Jacob to do such a thing to an innocent creature. My brother has always been different but I still loved him. Now I do not feel like I know him at all. Did I ever?

"Holy shit," Dawson said softly as they came to the end of that entry. "That's some sociopathic bullshit right there."

"Sounds like the family knew it as well," Chip agreed.

"Poor Charlotte. Imagine discovering that about your brother." Even after all she'd put him through, Dawson's heart still ached for the girl.

"Okay, I'm calling it," Chip said, gently tugging the remaining diary pages from Dawson's grasp. "That's enough for tonight."

"But there's still so much to get through!" Dawson protested.

Chip shook his head. "What we both need is a good night's sleep. We can read the rest tomorrow, and do some more research. We should even try to find the missing diary."

Dawson couldn't help throwing Chip a sceptical look. "Where the hell do you even plan on looking for it? If it wasn't with the others, I wouldn't think we'd have any hope of finding it."

He shrugged. "It won't hurt to check those other boxes from the Historical Society and have a look through them. There was a lot of stuff in there."

Dawson nodded. "Okay, yeah, that sounds smart. We'll need to make sure we're back in time for Angie's arrival though."

"We'll have plenty of time," Chip assured him. He led them down the hallway to the bathroom where they brushed their teeth, standing side by side. Dawson couldn't help but stare at his stepbrother in the mirror, drinking him in.

Chip looked tired. There were dark bags under his eyes, and he had several days' worth of stubble on his wide jaw. The numerous small cuts from the bulbs exploding at the start of the week were mostly hidden by the growth, but the ones that were still visible were mostly scabbed over. His eyes, normally so bright and beautiful, appeared dull, their shine gone.

It hurt Dawson's heart to see him so exhausted and drained.

They finished in the bathroom and headed down the hall, but Chip paused when they reached the bedroom doors. He looked at the door to Dawson's room and swallowed hard. "Oh," he said. "I guess with Charlotte behaving, you'll be back in your room." He sounded disappointed.

Dawson had thought of that earlier in the day when Chip was in town. He shook his head and took Chip's elbow, guiding him into his room. "Nope. I've already made up my bed ready for Angie to stay in there, so I'm still bunking in with you."

"Oh." Chip couldn't quite keep his happiness at that hidden, and it was the last sign Dawson needed to know that what he was about to do would be welcomed. He stepped in close and reached out to cup Chip's chin. Chip was several inches shorter than him and he tilted his head up to gaze at Dawson in confusion. "Daw?" he asked.

Without overthinking it, Dawson leaned down and pressed a soft kiss to Chip's lips. "I think it's about time you took me to bed, Chip. Don't you?"

CHAPTER 18

Chip

What the fuck was happening? *Was* this really happening?

Dawson pulled back a moment, his blue eyes appearing darker than usual due to the shadow falling over his face. He scanned Chip's face—looking for what, Chip didn't know—but he apparently found it, as he leaned back down to kiss him again.

Dawson was *kissing* him. Holy fucking shitballs! This kiss was more than just a press of lips. Dawson's mouth moved, sliding against his, and Chip did his best to keep up. Considering he'd never kissed anyone before, he wasn't exactly sure what he was doing. He hoped he wasn't making a complete mess of it, but from the small whimpers Dawson was making, he couldn't have been fucking it up too much.

The kiss didn't deepen—there was no tongue involved. Eventually, they broke apart and Chip found that he was breathing hard. Dawson looked his usual gorgeous self, and entirely too composed for what they'd just done. As far as Chip knew, this was the first time Dawson had kissed a man, and then there was the small little detail about them being stepbrothers. Surely he'd be freaking out even a *little* over one of those things? Right?

"Why aren't you freaking out?" he found himself asking.

Dawson had the audacity to fucking *shrug*, looking way too nonchalant for the situation at hand. "I've been thinking this over for a little while now and I made my decision. You know what I'm like once I've decided on something."

"Yeah, but this isn't something like the release date for your new song, or an extra tier for your subs!" Chip protested. "I mean, I thought you were straight?"

"We both know that sexuality is fluid, Chip. Up until now, I've only ever been attracted to women. Now I'm attracted to you. Does that make me bi? Pan? Something else? I don't know, yet. I'm not going to get the Dymo out and print out a label to stick to my forehead tonight, so I'm not gonna worry about it just yet."

Chip frowned, wondering how the hell Dawson was being so calm about all of this. "What about the whole, 'we're kind of related' thing?"

He hadn't been expecting Dawson to laugh. Well, snort, really. It wasn't a very dignified sound, whatever it was, but it was full of mirth. "Dude, it's not like we're related by blood. Our parents got married, so what? If it's okay for Greg and Marcia, then it's okay for us."

"Did you seriously just compare us to *The Brady Bunch*?" Chip demanded.

Dawson grinned. "I did. Got a problem with that?"

"Maybe," Chip admitted, but he was lying. He knew that eventually, he'd see the funny side like Dawson did, but right this very moment, he was still a little too stunned to be thinking clearly at all.

It wasn't even the broadening of Dawson's sexuality or the fact they now both appeared on the same family tree that was messing with his head the most. It was the fact that what he'd wanted for *so long* was apparently happening. He'd been in love with Dawson since before his voice had broken. He'd only *ever* been attracted to Dawson. No one else. He was a twenty-four-year-old virgin who had just been kissed for the first time, and Chip's head was spinning a little at the sudden change.

"What does this mean?" he asked, sounding dazed and confused to his own ears.

Dawson's expression softened and he pulled Chip into a warm hug. "Whatever you want it to mean."

"That's not how this works," Chip protested. "You get a say as well."

His arms falling away, Dawson stepped back and took Chip's hand, leading him over to sit on the side of the bed. "I told you, I've made my decision, Chip. Now it's up to you."

"You said that, yeah, but what *exactly* does your decision entail?" he asked.

Dawson snorted. "Entail? What the hell are you? Sixty?"

"Fuck off," Chip huffed, shoving his arm. "You know what I mean."

"Okay, Grandpa, calm down."

"No, just *no*. It's bad enough that we're stepbrothers—don't go bringing granddaddies into this."

Dawson sniggered but relented. "Fine." He bumped their shoulders together. "Look, for whatever reason, my feelings towards you changed recently. I'm attracted to you now, and I kept wondering what it would be like to kiss you. I decided that I wasn't going to let fear of societal backlash hold me back. We're not technically related, it's not illegal for us to be together, so fuck what anyone else thinks. If we both want to do this, then why shouldn't we give it a try? Why shouldn't we be happy?"

"You want to be *together*?" Chip hadn't even considered that. His initial thought was that Dawson was just experimenting with him. What was he saying? Did he want them to *date*?

"Fuck, Chip, don't do me dirty, man. I care about you way too much to just want something casual with you. Of course I want us to be together."

"But we've only just kissed!" Chip protested. "You've never done that with a guy before and I've never done it with *anyone* before! Surely it's too soon to decide something like that."

Dawson's face fell and he looked hurt. "I thought you felt the same way."

Chip let out a long breath and rubbed at his eyes. "I do," he said. "But I also know that this isn't a fairytale and things like this don't generally have a happy ending. I want you, Daw, so freaking much, but I also love you too much to risk losing you. If this goes south . . . fuck, I don't think I could handle you never speaking to me again. I've loved you from afar for half my life. Isn't it better to *keep* loving you from afar if it means I get to keep you in my life?"

"Oh, Chip," Dawson said, and he snaked an arm around his waist in a one-armed hug. "I *promise* you, no matter what happens, you won't lose me. If this doesn't work out, then we'll just go back to what we were."

"It's easy enough to say that now, but how realistic is that?" Chip asked.

"I'm not saying it wouldn't be awkward, but we'd get past it," Dawson promised him. "I don't think it'll come to that, though. You're my best friend in the whole world. We know each other inside out already. I honestly believe we can make this work, Chip. You just gotta have a little faith in us."

Chip took a moment to think about it. This was his dream come true, handed to him on a silver platter. Sure, other things in his life were a little fucked right now—he lived in a haunted house and had been tasked with solving a murder that was over a hundred years old—but did that mean he couldn't be happy? He could have this. He could. He just had to take that leap of faith.

"Okay," he whispered.

"Really?" Dawson's face lit up with joy and he leaned in and smashed their lips together. Chip didn't quite tilt his head enough and their noses squished together painfully, but he didn't care, too happy to worry about the brief flare of pain. It didn't take long for them to find a rhythm and Chip allowed Dawson's lips to guide him. He didn't think he'd win gold at the kissing Olympics, but if it felt good, did it really matter?

Dawson turned and gently pushed Chip down on the bed, and he went willingly. The weight of Dawson on top of him, the warmth of his body, the connection that sparked between them, it was all a little overwhelming but in the best possible way. He wanted more of it, for as long as he could get it. Chip could feel Dawson's arousal against his thigh, but Dawson didn't push for more. Chip was grateful for that. He wanted more, he did, maybe even tonight, but he didn't want to go from his first kiss to his first sexual encounter in less than ten minutes.

Dawson's lips were soft, except for one side of his bottom lip where he chewed on it when his anxiety was spiking. The skin there was chapped and a little rough and it dragged deliciously against Chip's own lips. He tentatively licked it with his tongue and Dawson moaned, pressing down against Chip even more. His own tongue delved into Chip's mouth and he revelled at the odd but welcome feeling. It was hot and wet and made him feel sexy as fuck. Desired. The fact that it was *Dawson* who was making him feel so desired was still blowing his mind.

Daw wants me back.

They both moved their heads at the same time and their teeth clacked together, and they pulled back, grinning and laughing. Chip felt a surge of affection for Dawson. In the few minutes that their relationship had done a complete one-eighty, it hadn't changed. They could still laugh together, and that was a huge relief. Sure, it was just the beginning, but he was hopeful that they'd continue as they had always been, just with the added extra of a physical relationship.

Dawson leaned down and began the kiss again, and this time one of his hands drifted down over Chip's chest and stomach to snake under the hem of his shirt. His fingers were cool against the hot skin of Chip's stomach but they were gentle as they explored. "Is this okay?" he murmured against his lips.

Chip moaned out a breathy "yes," and allowed his own hands to explore. Dawson was still wearing his hoodie, but Chip could feel the knobs of his spine as he ran his palm down the centre of his back. Dawson had always been lean, bordering on skinny, but his workouts—no matter how begrudgingly he did them—had honed his muscles, and they were strong beneath his skin.

One of Dawson's hands dropped down to skim under the waistband of Chip's jeans and his breath hitched in anticipation. Then it was gone, a finger tracing around his belly button, and Chip wanted to groan in frustration but his mouth was currently busy devouring Dawson's. His stepbrother continued to tease, every now and then his clever fingers dipping down to tickle at Chip's happy trail but never going further. He was achingly hard and now totally on board with moving the schedule along to the "first sexual encounter" portion of the evening, but Dawson appeared to be in no hurry.

Chip bucked his hips, pressing his hard cock against Dawson. He'd never been bothered by their height difference before, but now he was finding it frustrating. In the porn he'd watched, guys had frotted against one another, their cocks rubbing together. Even fully dressed, he wanted to be able to press against Dawson, feel his hard dick against his own. But he couldn't. Dawson's cock was currently aligned with Chip's thigh and his own with Dawson's stomach. If he scooted down the bed so their cocks were facing one another, kissing would either result in a crick neck, or wouldn't be possible at all. He wouldn't be entirely sure of the logistics until he tried it, but he wasn't in any rush because he rather enjoyed kissing Dawson, even if he *did* want their dicks to get to know each other.

It was time to be a little more strategic.

Chip pulled back from the kiss and then pushed Dawson gently away. "Up," he instructed. "Let's lose the clothes."

Dawson's eyes gleamed as he hurried up off the bed, and by the time Chip was standing, he'd already lost his hoodie and shirt. Chip grinned, excited by Dawson's enthusiasm, and he quickly stripped off his own clothes. He didn't allow himself to stop and analyse how it felt to be naked with an erection in front of someone else for the first time, because he was with Dawson and he trusted him. He knew he was safe. Instead, he took charge, guiding Dawson back to the bed, leading him until he was sitting against the headboard. Then Chip climbed up and straddled his lap, linking his arms around his neck.

Dawson's pupils dilated even more at the move and Chip felt his confidence soar at being able to affect him in such a way. He shifted his hips forward just a little and they both moaned as their cocks rubbed against one another. "Oh yeah," he said, his eyes falling shut at the sensation. "This is so much better."

"Holy shit," Dawson said, sounding awed. "I had no idea what to expect, but this is amazing."

Chip tried not to think about how Dawson was comparing this to his past sexual encounters with women. It was natural for him to do so—this was new and different. But still . . . nope, he wasn't going to venture down that path at all. Instead, he pulled back to put a little distance between them so he could wrap a hand around both of their cocks.

"Fuck," Dawson cried, his eyes glued to the sight between them.

Chip couldn't look away either. Dawson's cock was longer than his own but not as thick and he was dripping with precum. It glistened on the tip before running down the length of him, and Chip gathered it with a finger and rubbed it over the tip of his own cock, mixing it with his own. The added lubrication felt amazing, so he reached over to the side blindly, digging in the top drawer of his bedside table for the tube of lube he kept there. It was awkward, trying to snap the lid open with one hand, but he wasn't willing to let go of their cocks for even a moment. Dawson was no help, too entranced with the view, and he didn't even seem to notice Chip's plight. Finally, he got the tube open and he squeezed a healthy dollop right onto their tips.

"Jesus, fuck, that's cold, man!" Dawson's entire body had jolted and he glared at Chip, who gave him a sheepish look.

"Oops. I didn't think it would be that cold." He glanced down at their laps and began spreading the lube over their shafts, which despite the cold shock were still rock hard. It made the glide of his hand so much easier and they both groaned as he worked them over.

Dawson reached between them and covered Chip's hand with his own, getting in on the action. "Fuck, I never realised how much bigger your hands are compared to mine."

Chip looked, and noticed that Dawson's hand wasn't quite big enough to wrap around them both, even without Chip's own hand in the way. He didn't feel the need to add to that comment, but seeing as Dawson sounded awed by the fact, he just put it to good use. He began pumping them in earnest now, not entirely sure if what felt good for him when he jerked off would translate to jacking both of them simultaneously. It seemed to be doing the trick as they were both breathing hard and bucking against one another, fucking into the tight circle of Chip's palm.

Dawson came first, his breath hitching before he cried out and spilled over Chip's cock and fist. Chip watched, fascinated, as his cock continued to twitch and pulse, slowing down his movements just a little. Dawson pulled away when he became too sensitive, but he knocked Chip's hand away and used his own to take over jerking him.

It only took a minute longer before Chip came silently, his eyes closing as his orgasm rolled through him. He shook and trembled as Dawson worked him through it, and then he felt soft lips press against his forehead and he opened his eyes to find Dawson looking at him in wonder.

They took a few moments to clean up with some tissues, and Chip turned off the light while Dawson turned on the lamp on the bedside table. Then they climbed into bed and cuddled up against one another.

"That was amazing," Dawson murmured.

For some inexplicable reason, Chip suddenly felt shy. "I'm sure you've had better," he muttered, looking away.

Dawson cupped his jaw and turned his head so he could look at him. "Chip, you don't understand. That was seriously good. Do you know how long it usually takes me to get off?"

Chip frowned. "What do you mean?"

"Because of my meds," Dawson explained. "They mess with me so bad. A lot of the time I can't even come, let alone that fast." He ran a hand through his hair. "Fuck, with Jules, I couldn't even get off with her half the time and had to fake it." He grimaced. "Shit, sorry, the last thing you want to hear right now is about my ex. I just wanted you to know how good it was for me."

A few minutes ago, Chip had been hating the idea of Dawson comparing him to any of the women he'd slept with, but now, knowing that he'd made

Dawson feel so much better than they had? Yeah, he was preening. Did that make him a bit of an arsehole? Probably, but he never pretended to be perfect. He leaned in and kissed Dawson. "It was amazing for me too," he told him. "Thank you."

Dawson reached up and pushed his hand through Chip's hair and it felt so good that he wanted to purr. But it didn't feel as good as the next words Dawson spoke. "You mean everything to me, Chip. Thank you for taking a chance on us."

As if Chip was ever going to do anything else. Dawson was the only one who had ever caught his interest and he was certain that he would be the only one to ever capture his heart. "It was the easiest decision I've ever made," he whispered, before leaning in to kiss Dawson once more.

CHAPTER 19

Dawson

"Wanna stop in at the bakery for lunch?" Chip asked, looking over at him hopefully.

Dawson chuckled. Chip's appetite seemed bottomless at times. Nodding, he said, "Sure. I could definitely go a pie."

Chip grinned and hefted a box into the back of the car. They were at the Historical Society to pick up the remaining two boxes that held documents and photos, hoping they might just find the missing diary inside. Janet hadn't been there but she'd let the other volunteers know that they were welcome to check out the boxes and they'd picked them up with no issues. They were planning on spending the rest of the day searching through the documents, reading the rest of the diary entries they had, and prepping for Angie's arrival.

"We should also stop by IGA and do a grocery shop," Dawson said as they got into the car.

Chip snorted. "Yeah. We should stock up on paper plates since we've hardly any left. I don't trust Charlotte not to lose it again, even if she did agree to behave, so I reckon we should keep using them for now." He popped the car into reverse, slung an arm over the headrest of Dawson's seat, and began to deftly reverse out of the parking spot.

"Yeah," Dawson agreed, absently. His attention had suddenly been diverted to the proximity of Chip's arm and the scent of his deodorant. He wondered if it would be appropriate to reach across the console and lay his hand on Chip's thigh, or even hold his hand once they were driving. Would Chip mind?

He didn't think so. When they'd woken this morning, Chip had hugged Dawson close and kissed his cheek before hurrying off to brush his teeth, and then he'd kissed Dawson properly a little later on. He'd seemed completely on board this morning, with no regrets from the previous night, but they'd not discussed how they would act in public. Dawson had never been a big fan of public displays of affection with his girlfriends, but even if he did get the urge to kiss Chip in public, they had the added complication of being stepbrothers. It wasn't illegal—they weren't related by blood—but there was still a social stigma surrounding it.

They weren't in public right at this moment though, were they? They were in the relative privacy of the car. Surely it would be safe enough here?

Before Dawson could draw out his internal debate even longer, Chip took the matter into his own hands. He put the car into drive and then reached over and twined their fingers together, deftly manoeuvring the car one-handed out of the Heritage Centre car park. Dawson turned to look at him, knowing that he was grinning like an idiot, but unable to stop himself.

Chip didn't say anything, just lifted their joined hands to his lips and pressed a kiss to Dawson's knuckles before turning his attention back to the road.

The bakery was relatively quiet when they arrived and Dawson decided he may as well make some content while he was there. They'd had nothing but great food and exceptional service from them and he wanted to promote them if he could. Since the bypass was built, the town didn't get as much through traffic as before, and if Dawson could tell his followers about how good the bakery was, it might encourage them to detour for lunch when heading up north.

He filmed himself and Chip entering, got footage of the menu above the counter and the seating area, and then filmed the cabinets, showing off the display of pies, sausage rolls, cakes, and pastries.

"Hey guys," Lucy greeted them with a huge smile. "How's things?"

"Yeah, good," Chip replied.

"Are you filming for your page?" she asked Dawson, an excited gleam in her eyes.

"Sure am," he told her. "Don't worry, I won't film any of the staff without asking them first."

"You can film me!" she said, bouncing on her feet. "I'd love to be on your Vewz!"

He smiled and nodded. "Sure. Your boss won't mind?"

She shook her head. "Nah. He's pretty cool about stuff like this. Anton is a big believer in not turning down free publicity."

Since there was no one waiting behind them, Dawson filmed Lucy greeting them, and asked her a few questions about items she'd recommend. Her enthusiasm was perfect for the camera and she was a complete natural. He told her so. "Have you thought about starting your own channel?"

"Oh, nah," she said, waving him off, but she had started to blush. "No one wants to hear about my boring life."

"Hey, what might seem boring to you is different and interesting to others," he told her. "If it's something you want to do, I'd be happy to give you some pointers."

"Really?"

"Really," he told her. "Just let me know."

"I will," she said. "Thanks. So, what can I get for you guys?"

They got their pies and found a seat outside, since the rain from yesterday had stopped and the sun was trying its best to peek out from behind the clouds. They ate in companionable silence, with Dawson getting the odd bit of footage. Once they were done, they headed to IGA, and got enough to feed themselves and Angie over the weekend before heading home.

The boxes they'd picked up from the Historical Society were a bust. They found the original deed for the property in a faded old envelope, which they put aside as something that Janet may want to display, but otherwise, nothing else of importance.

Dawson received a message from Angie, that she was leaving work for the afternoon and was on her way, so they didn't bother starting on the remaining diary entries. Dawson edited together his video while Chip hit the gym. Seeing him return to the house, sweaty and flushed, was a much different beast now and Dawson distracted Chip with several kisses before he allowed him to get into the shower.

Throwing a simple chicken curry together and onto the stove to simmer, Dawson did a final tidy up of the house as he nervously waited for Angie to arrive. Was this all a mistake? They were inviting a stranger into their home on her word alone that she could help them. What if she couldn't help? What if she was making it all up and her interference would actually make the situation worse? What if she *was* genuine but wanted to blackmail them and would withhold her help until they gave in to her demands? What if . . .

"Hey," a soft voice said, breaking into his rapidly spiralling thoughts, even as strong arms wrapped around his waist from behind. Chip nuzzled against Dawson's throat and then said quietly, "Your breathing is a little fast. What's wrong?"

Dawson slid his own hands over Chip's and held on to them tightly. "Just nervous, I suppose."

"It's gonna be okay, baby," he murmured.

Dawson hummed, immediately buoyed. "I like it when you call me baby," he admitted.

"Really?" Chip asked, sounding pleased. He pressed a soft kiss to the shell of Dawson's ear. "I'll have to remember that."

From outside came the sound of tyres crunching on gravel, announcing the arrival of Angie. Chip squeezed Dawson tightly for one more moment before stepping back, and Dawson followed him out into the hall and to the front door.

Angie was pulling a large backpack from the boot when they went outside, and she waved over at them. "Hey!"

"Hi," Chip said, stepping forward, holding his hand out.

Angie gave a wry smile but took his hand and shook it. "Thank you so much for coming," he said. "I'm Chip."

She smiled even wider. "I know." Her metallic-silver hair shone under the setting sun, which also glinted off her numerous facial piercings. She was wearing low slung, wide-legged pants made from a black, heavy denim which had chains hanging from one side. She wore a tight-fitting top that showed off an inch or two of skin on her stomach as well as a black, faux-leather jacket. "Good to meet you."

Dawson took one last deep breath and then moved closer. "Hey," he said, but didn't offer his hand. "Nice to meet you in person. Did you find the place okay?"

She nodded. "Yeah, it was super easy." She looked around at the house and the yard. "It's beautiful here. How big is the property again?"

"About eighteen acres," he explained. "Nowhere near as big as it was originally but still more than enough for us." He gestured over his shoulder. "Come on in and I'll show you where you're staying."

She followed Dawson inside and down the hall to his room, where she dropped her bag. After a quick tour, so she knew where the bathroom was, they all gathered in the kitchen. "It's really nice," she said, her eyes constantly roaming around the walls. "You can definitely feel the presence of spirits though."

Chip looked at her with a raised brow. "Spirits? As in *plural*?" He sounded as shocked as Dawson felt.

Angie nodded and accepted the beer Chip handed her. "There's one that is definitely more present than the others, but I can sense others in the vicinity. They might not have shown themselves, and they may never do so, but they're on this side of the veil."

"Okay, so that's disturbing," Chip said, echoing Dawson's thought. "Are they dangerous?" He cast a worried look in Dawson's direction.

Angie closed her eyes and appeared to be concentrating. "I can't tell. I'm guessing the strong presence I can feel is Charlotte, and I can definitely feel violence in her aura, but the others aren't strong enough for me to be able to tell that."

"You know, this isn't something they warn you about home ownership," Dawson muttered as he checked on the curry.

"Yeah," Chip agreed as he slid into a seat at the table, gesturing for Angie to do the same. "I was under the impression our biggest issues would be termites or dodgy wiring."

"Any idea who the other spirits are?" Dawson asked as he joined them. "Dinner won't be long," he added as an aside.

"In a house this old, multiple ghosts aren't just common but to be expected," Angie told them. "And just like with pest control or crappy electrics, there are people who can help."

"How can you sense them?" Dawson asked, hoping he wasn't being rude. "I know you said you grew up in a haunted house, but have you had some training or something?"

"No, nothing like that," she said, leaning back in her chair and hooking a foot over her knee. "It's just experience, I guess? Maybe I'm naturally more open to the spirit world, I dunno. All I know is that since I was a kid, I could tell when there were ghosts around. Not just the prominent ones that caused a fuss or made their presence known, but *all* ghosts. My mum's the same but my dad can only see them when they make themselves known to him. Maybe it's genetic on my mum's side? Or maybe it's luck of the draw? No clue. But yeah, I can just tell when they're around, and sometimes I can sense what they're feeling—if they're malevolent, stuff like that."

"What does it feel like?" Dawson's curiosity was piqued.

Angie frowned and took a sip of her beer, her lips lingering on the rim of the bottle while she thought. It was weird. Two weeks ago, Dawson would have been captivated by her. She was striking and her androgynous beauty appealed to him, but now he felt no buzzing of attraction or stirring of interest at all. Well, not for *her*, anyway. If he looked to his left at Chip instead, there was a very good chance he'd start drooling.

How things had completely changed in such a short matter of time.

"It's so hard to explain," Angie said, finally. "Like, you know when you're out in the bush and you just *know* that there's someone around? You can *feel* someone watching you? It might just be a roo but it could be a person, and even if you don't see *anyone*, you know, without a shadow of a doubt, that there's *something* there? It's like that, I guess. Base animal instinct or a sixth sense? I'm not sure what you'd call it, but I just know they're there. When they're particularly strong, I can sense their emotions." She glanced over her shoulder to the doorway. "For example, right now Charlotte is confused, a little scared, and a little bit mad."

Dawson's eyes flew to the doorway but he didn't see anything. "She's here right now?" he asked.

"Yup." Angie didn't take her eyes off the seemingly empty spot.

"Why is she upset?" Chip asked. "We spoke to her yesterday. She knows we're trying to help her."

Angie cocked her head to one side, as if listening. "I don't know what you're trying to tell me," she murmured, but it wasn't directed at either Dawson or Chip.

The room suddenly went cold and an invisible wind swirled violently around them, sending loose papers flying and Dawson's hair whipping around his head. The pan on the stove rose into the air by itself, and hovered there for a moment before it was flung across the room. Dawson threw a hand up to protect his face from the hot curry that was now airborne, but he was knocked out of the way as Chip barrelled into him, taking him to the ground. Angie had ducked for cover as well and they huddled under the table, watching as the kitchen was once again systematically destroyed.

The cupboards were wrenched open by an invisible force and the contents sent flying around the room. Metal pans clattered against the wall and plastic bowls thunked down next to them. When the stacks of paper plates and cups hit the wall, there was a dissatisfied cry and the temperature plummeted even further. Dawson gasped as a figure materialised within the centre of the vortex caused by the ghostly wind and debris that was being drawn into it. Charlotte was standing with her hands clenched into fists at her side and a look of absolute fury on her face. She pointed at the fridge and the door opened, and she smiled triumphantly as the milk flew across the room and exploded against the far wall. A jar of jam hit the table with a thunk and rolled down to land next to Dawson's foot, and he scooted backward so he was completely sheltered by the table.

Once everything inside the fridge had been thrown around, Charlotte turned her attention to the drawers next to it and she shouted in glee as she began to fling knives around the room. Chip reached out and pulled the chair in to try and shield them, but they could do little but wait for Charlotte's temper tantrum to end.

"What's got her so pissed off?" Dawson asked.

Chip and Angie looked as bewildered as each other. "No clue," Chip replied.

"I have a feeling she doesn't like me," Angie said. "But I have no idea why."

Charlotte's rage finally petered out once the kitchen was an absolute shambles. She stalked towards the table and they waited, not even daring to breathe, for what would come next.

There was a loud *thump* on the wood above their heads and all three of them flinched. The chair was ripped away and it flew against the far wall, falling into a broken heap upon the floor. Another thump, then another, and then something dropped from above to land on the floor next to them.

It was Charlotte's severed head.

Dawson screamed and tried to scramble backwards but they were bottlenecked beneath the table and no one could move fast enough. Just like that first night, her throat just beneath her chin was a mess of torn and bloody flesh. Her eye sockets were empty and gaping, and her mouth was open in a horrific rictus.

There came the patter of what sounded like rain above them and then liquid was pouring off the sides of the table, pooling onto the floor. The overwhelming smell of hot copper filled Dawson's nostrils and he knew it was blood. Charlotte's mouth opened and closed to propel itself across the floor and Dawson froze in terror as it got nearer and nearer. There was a scraping noise behind him and the warmth at his back was gone, but he couldn't look, couldn't speak, could do nothing but watch and wait as Charlotte's severed head moved towards him.

Suddenly there was a roar from above and the table above him was gone, flipped over by a furious Chip. He'd clearly managed to get out from under their hiding spot and he was in full protective mode. He grasped Dawson's elbow and hauled him to his feet, then did the same with Angie before stepping in front of them both. Blood was still raining down from the ceiling and it ran into Dawson's eyes, obscuring his vision.

"Charlotte, *enough*!" Chip thundered.

This time, chastising her didn't work. Charlotte's face contorted into a snarl and drops of blood pooled into the hollows of her eye sockets, but instead of draining out of the gaping maw of her throat, it seemed to be increasing, solidifying, forming into something.

Eyes. The blood was forming into eyes.

Dry lids blinked over the newly formed, blood-red eyes, making a sound like sandpaper scraping across coarse chipboard. They didn't focus on Chip, or even Dawson, but on Angie. Her mouth opened and closed again, propelling her forward, and as one, they all took a step back. "Don't come any closer!" Chip warned her, holding out a hand, even as he shuffled backward.

"Can't you do something?" Dawson whispered to Angie.

She looked pale beneath the blood dripping from her hair and she shook her head. "All of my equipment is in my room," she told him, sounding apologetic. "I'm so sorry. I thought after your discussion with her, it would be safe. I miscalculated."

"It's okay," he assured her, even as he wondered what they could do.

"Charlotte, I'm warning you," Chip said, sounding stern. "If you don't cut this out, you'll regret it."

Her eyes rolled in their sockets until she was glaring up at Chip from the ground. The tattered shreds of her throat were lost in the puddles of blood on the floor, and her matted hair hung in clumps against her face. "You dare to bring a witch into *my* house and then threaten *me*?" she screeched, her face contorted in rage. It was the first time they'd heard her speak, and her voice had a pitch to it that hurt Dawson's ears.

"A witch? I'm not a witch," Angie told her, addressing Charlotte directly for the first time.

"Lies!" Charlotte screamed. "Witch!"

"Charlotte, this is your last warning," Chip told her. "Stop this. Now."

"I will not let you ruin me, witch," Charlotte snarled at Angie. "I will destroy you before I succumb to your magic! I will tear the flesh from your bones. I will—"

They didn't get to hear the rest of her threats. Chip had backed up another step and then he skipped forward and kicked her head across the room. He'd never played much footy, so Dawson was impressed by his aim as he sent her head directly at the window. Glass shattered, they heard a soft *thump* from outside, and immediately it stopped raining blood, the wind died out, and the temperature returned to normal.

They stood in silence for a long moment before Dawson looked over at the upturned pot in the middle of the floor. "I was really looking forward to that curry," he said dejectedly.

CHAPTER 20

Chip

"**I** am so fucking sick and tired of cleaning up this room." Chip arched his back in a stretch and wiped at his brow. "You know how there's that meme about how being an adult with your own place means forever cleaning your kitchen? Well, this isn't exactly what I had in mind."

Dawson was tying up a bin bag that they'd filled with ruined food from the fridge, and Angie was wiping down the table. "Yeah, it's really starting to piss me off now," Dawson agreed. "I'm so sorry that this was your introduction to us," he said to Angie.

She shrugged and tossed the Chux at the sink. "It's all cool."

Chip threw down his own cloth. "Right, let's get cleaned up, then head into town and check out the food at the pub. I'm starving and we're not bothering to cook again just to give Charlotte something else to wreck."

The Brockman Arms stood on a corner in the middle of town, opposite the IGA and the Bendigo Bank. It always looked busy when they drove past but it appeared especially busy tonight. Chip guessed that was to be expected on a Friday night, seeing as it was the only pub in town and there wasn't much else to do. The car park was full so they parked outside the closed bakery and walked up. There was a wide verandah with iron lace facings around the sides of the building that had street frontage, with picnic bench style seating all the way along. It was a fairly typical pub, found anywhere in country WA—two storeys tall, with the bar and restaurant downstairs and accommodation upstairs. The inside was dark but cosy, with wood panelling and high ceilings, and a fire had been laid in the large fireplace in the main bar.

A family was leaving as they entered, so they were quick to snag the booth they'd vacated at the rear of the room. They slid onto the jarrah benches on either side of the table, Chip and Dawson on one side and Angie on the other. Dawson's leg pressed up close against Chip's thigh but neither made a move to put space between them.

They quickly browsed the menu and Chip headed up to the bar to order—a steak for him and Angie and a parmi for Dawson—and when he returned, he found that Dawson had pulled out the reassembled pages of Charlotte's diary.

"We seem to be missing the last one," Dawson was telling Angie. "She died in January of 1905, but we only have diaries up to the end of 1904. From the way she reacted when we realised we didn't have the last one, it's obvious that it's got important info in there."

"We looked for it today but didn't have any luck," Chip said, as he handed over the drinks he'd brought back and slid back into the booth. "So at the moment, we're just going on the entry from the scrapbook from Elizabeth and the 1904 diary. I haven't had any luck on Trove but I was mostly searching for Jacob. I haven't searched for Charlotte yet."

"Probably worthwhile doing that next," Angie suggested, before taking a sip of her cider.

Chip pulled out his phone. "How about I do that search now and you catch up on the diary entries we've already covered, then we can finish the diary together?"

"What about me?" Dawson asked. "What can I do?"

Chip dropped a hand under the table and gave his leg a squeeze where Angie couldn't see it. He was pretty sure she wouldn't be at all surprised by their new relationship status, but he didn't think Dawson had cottoned on to that yet. Until he did, Chip certainly wasn't going to play their hand and risk upsetting Dawson. "I'm sure you've probably got a tonne of emails and DMs to catch up on if you wanna do that?"

"You sure? I don't wanna lump you guys with all the work."

"Until Angie's caught up to us, there's not a hell of a lot we can do, dude," Chip told him. "No need to feel guilty."

By the time their meals arrived, Chip had gotten the hang of the search function on the archive site and had found several newspaper articles about Charlotte's death. He waited until the waitress had left, then said to the others, "Journalism back in the day was absolutely *brutal*." He shook his head in disbelief. "They really didn't hold back. They're all much the same, but this is from the *Swan Gazette* three days after her death." He pinched his screen, to enlarge the article to make it easier to see, and then began to read.

"A most horrible end—A girl named Charlotte, aged seventeen years, met with a frightful death in Brockman this Monday past on her father's farm. She was on a horse, assisting her brother with the feeding of their sheep, when the animal took fright and bolted. Although her brother tried valiantly to halt the terrified creature, the girl slipped from the horse's back and the lead rope became fastened around her neck. She was dragged around the paddock until she was decapitated in a most gruesome manner, resulting in her immediate death. Great sympathy is felt for the family."

He looked up to find both Angie and Dawson looking horrified.

"That's awful," Dawson whispered.

"So, we're all on the same page, yeah?" Angie asked them. "We all think Jacob tied that rope around Charlotte's neck and staged the murder as an accident?"

"From the way Charlotte's been acting, I'm guessing so," Chip agreed. "From the snippets of insight into his character, I certainly wouldn't put it past him. At the very least, he certainly didn't try to help if it truly *was* an accident."

"Yeah, I don't think it's much of a stretch to assume that murder is beyond someone who tortures animals," Dawson added. "We just need to figure out his motive."

Angie held up the diary. "I've reached the page you've marked to show which entry you got up to. Want me to read us some more while we eat?"

Chip glanced around them. It was crowded and noisy, and over in the far corner, karaoke was being set up. There was no way anyone would overhear them. He nodded. "Sure. I guess we want to mostly read any that mention Jacob or any issues around the house."

"No worries." Angie took another bite of her chicken, skimming through the following entries. Once she'd chewed and swallowed, she began to read.

"8th September, 1904. Father and Mama are travelling to Perth next week for a business meeting with a gentleman recently arrived from Sydney. I had hoped they may allow me to go with them as I have only been to the city once before and it was most exciting, but I have been told it is not appropriate and I am to remain behind under William's charge. I must confess that I was most put out at the news this morning and I caused quite the fuss. Mama was very displeased

at my behaviour and I ran to my room in tears. Father must have taken pity on me as he came soon to see me and told me that if I wished, he would ask Mr and Mrs Wiltshire if Abigail can visit with me whilst they are gone. I would have preferred he ask if I could stay with Abigail's family instead, but with Mama gone I will need to prepare meals for William and Jacob. I do so wish that her parents agree so I do not succumb to boredom whilst they are gone."

She turned the page and her eyes flickered over the next entry. "Okay, looks like for the next couple of days not much happened, just stuff about helping her mum. The entry for the tenth is literally two lines about pickling beets." She turned another page and then grunted. "Okay, here's some more, from the 11th.

"Father approached Mr and Mrs Wiltshire after mass this morning and they agreed that Abigail may stay with me whilst they are in Perth! I am so greatly relieved. Mama has told me that I must be on my best behaviour until then, and I assured her I would be. My good fortune continued after noon as William requested that I accompany him to the north paddocks to check on the flock. It did feel somewhat bittersweet. I have not spent any time with them since the morning we found the lamb Jacob had killed, and I battled my melancholy even as I played with the lambs that have been born since. There are nine in total now and they are darling.

I am still mystified as to the motive behind Jacob's horrible attack on the creature. No one has spoken of it since but I have observed that William is still at odds with Jacob and has yet to forgive him. Jacob is ever his surly self, even *more so after his meetings with Father O'Reilly. I do not think he is as devout as we are, and the meetings leave him more angry than before. I just hope that he is on his best behaviour when Abigail comes to stay as it would be mortifying if anything of the sort occurred whilst she was here."*

"Okay, so who else is getting the feeling that this visit isn't going to end well?" Dawson asked.

"Yeah, it's sounding pretty foreboding," Chip agreed.

"Spoiler alert, but I think you're right," Angie said, reading ahead. Thankfully, she began to read aloud.

"14th September. Father and Mama left this morning for their trip to Perth. All morning I was filled with excited anticipation for Abigail's arrival. Just after luncheon, she arrived by buggy with her father. Mr Wiltshire and William spoke for a long while, mostly gossiping about the neighbours, but also discussing the upcoming summer and the predictions of drought.

Once we bid Mr Wiltshire farewell, Abigail and I retreated to my room. She showed me a new book of poetry that she had received from her grandmother, and we enjoyed reading from them. Some were almost scandalous and we spent some time giggling. It seems that we upset Jacob with our 'girlish nonsense' and he was most cross with us. He stomped into my room without even the courtesy of knocking, so he could growl at me. I must confess that I was rather curt with him and demanded he leave us in peace. William came to see what the disturbance was and after hearing us out he told Jacob to leave us be, which did nothing but make Jacob even more angry.

Abigail helped me prepare dinner, and William and I attempted to make it a civil affair, but Jacob sat across the table from me with the countenance of a thundercloud, making it an awkward experience. Abigail was most gracious, dismissing my apology over my brother's behaviour, but I still felt terrible. She, too, keeps a diary, and I do worry that even as I write this she is recording her own version of the day's events that shows our family in a shameful light."

"Jacob really was an arsehole, wasn't he?" Chip observed, as Angie paused so she could eat more of her parmi before it went cold.

"Definitely," Dawson said. "William seems like a great dude but Jacob is the total opposite."

"Of *course* William was a good guy," Chip said, bumping their shoulders together. "He's your great, great, grandfather. If *you're* descended from him, he had to be cool."

Dawson rolled his eyes and shoved at Chip, dismissing his statement, but even in the dim pub lighting he could tell he was blushing.

"Aww, you guys are adorable," Angie cooed. Chip looked over to find her leaning her chin on one hand and looking at them with hearts in her eyes.

Dawson blushed even harder and Chip winked at her.

"Oh my God, I didn't expect to see you guys here!"

They turned their attention to the newcomer and it took Chip a moment to place her. It was Lucy from the bakery. Instead of the checked shirt and neat black cap of her uniform, she was wearing tight jeans and a fitted jumper and her hair was loose around her shoulders.

"Hey Lucy," Chip said, and from the corner of his eye, he saw Angie tuck the diary away into her bag. "How was your day?"

"Busy," she said, rolling her eyes. "Fridays are always crazy." She glanced over at Angie. "Hi! I'm Lucy, nice to meet you!"

Angie gave Lucy a slow once over, and then gave her a disarming smile. "Hey. I'm Angie. Nice to meet you too."

"Are you meeting friends here?" Chip asked her.

Lucy was looking at Angie and biting her lower lip coyly, and she replied absently. "Um, I was but they bailed on me. I was just heading home."

"Oh, in that case you should join us," Angie said, patting the seat beside her. Belatedly, she looked over at the others. "You guys don't mind?"

Chip snorted, since Lucy had already sunk onto the bench opposite them and was gazing at Angie in adoration. "Nah, it's cool."

They finished their meals and Lucy ordered some wedges to snack on, and they spent the next hour or so chatting. At one point, Angie and Lucy headed for the pool tables so Angie could "teach" Lucy how to play. From what they could see, it was really just an excuse for them to be up in each other's personal space. Huh, maybe Chip could try that sometime so he had an excuse to be that close to Dawson in public?

They saw Blake and Ryan from the cricket team as well, and Chip made their excuses for not joining them tomorrow for casual practice. "Our friend asked us at the last minute if she could come for a visit," he said, gesturing over to where Angie was. "We don't want to bail on her, sorry."

"All good, man," Blake said easily, clapping him on the back. "You'll be there on Tuesday night?"

"Yeah, of course."

"No worries. We'll see you then!"

It was getting late, and when Chip spied Angie and Lucy emerging from the women's loos looking much more dishevelled than when they went in, he waved them over to the table. "We'd better be getting back," he told them.

"Sure thing," Angie said, and she turned and kissed Lucy on the cheek. "Don't lose my number," she told her in a husky voice.

"Oh, there's no way that's happening," Lucy told her with a huge grin. She turned to the boys and waved at them. "Have a good night. See you round."

"Yeah, catch you," Chip said, then he put a hand on Dawson's lower back to guide him as they made their way out of the pub.

As they walked down the street to the car, Angie threw them a sheepish look. "Sorry about that. I kind of derailed the evening there."

Chip laughed. "All good. It's not like the diary is going anywhere."

"Yeah," Dawson added. "We can read more when we get home. You and Lucy seemed to be having a good time."

Angie grinned. "We were. She's really sweet. I hope she calls me." They got into the car and Angie pulled out her phone and switched on the flashlight. "How about I get us back on track by reading some more while we drive?" They both hummed in agreement so she started to read.

"15th September. Today began much better than yesterday. William took Jacob with him to inspect the shearing shed as that time is almost upon us. Whilst they were gone, Abigail and I made a pudding for after luncheon. While we were baking, she confided that last week, her parents had invited over the Murray family, including their middle son. We had gone to school with Thomas, and Abigail had always had a keen eye for him. She is almost certain that both her parents and his are hopeful of a union between the two of them, especially as the Murray's have extended an invitation to the Wiltshire's for luncheon after mass on Christmas day.

Abigail is beside herself with excitement over this development and we spent many hours discussing what their wedding may look like and even names for their children. It was most enjoyable.

Of course, Jacob simply had to ruin it. He and William returned for luncheon and walked in as we were still talking about Thomas. Jacob had much to say on the matter, casting aspersions on both Abigail and Thomas, despite the fact that as far as I'm aware, he's not even met Thomas before. Abigail was in tears and was begging to go home, but William and I calmed her down and convinced her to stay. William took Jacob aside and had harsh words with him, which had Jacob storming off in a snit. By this stage, our luncheon had gone cold and we'd all rather lost our appetites.

Come the afternoon, we assisted William with the flock, mostly to distract Abigail from Jacob's churlishness by way of sweet little lambs. Her family runs cattle, so she rarely gets to see lambs up close and she fell instantly in love with the wee things. After supper, we played a few games of Jubilee, and by the time we retired for the evening Abigail appeared much happier."

"Jacob strikes again," Chip murmured as they turned off the highway and began driving past the old cemetery. He briefly wondered if Charlotte was buried there and made a note to mention it later.

"16th September," Angie continued. *"Today, William escorted Abigail and myself into town so we could attend a ladies' day picnic that was being hosted by*

the Church Committee. It was a lovely day, with the sun bright, though lacking warmth. Our arrival caused rather a fuss—all because of William! He has long been known as Brockman's greatest bachelor and many a lass has been devastated that he remains unwed at twenty-four. As we arrived, it appeared that every eligible woman in town descended upon us, giggling and fluttering their eyelashes, trying to win his favour.

Abigail and I watched in great amusement, and we did observe that William showed very little interest in the chattering swarm, but he DID appear quite taken with Winifred Johnson. Winnie, as we knew her at school, is one year older than Abigail and me, and by all accounts is a sweet, gentle girl, who has quite the talent for sketching and is being trained by her mother in the art of midwifery. By the time the picnic had finished and we were ready to depart for home, William had asked to escort Winnie to the Spring Ball next month. Abigail and myself were perhaps the only ones—besides William and Winnie, of course—who were delighted when she acquiesced."

"Do you think Jacob was jealous of William?" Dawson mused. "He seems to have been the golden child of the family and Jacob was the black sheep."

"I wouldn't put it past him," Angie said.

"Yeah, I reckon he would have been," Chip agreed. "But I doubt he'd ever have taken his frustrations out on William. He strikes me as the sort of coward who only picks on those smaller and weaker than himself."

They'd reached their place, and as they turned into the driveway they both heard Angie gasp from the back seat. "Oh no," she whispered.

They were all silent as Chip parked the car, and then they sat there in the dark, waiting for Angie to continue. When she spoke, her voice had a slight tremor to it.

"17th September. Something has happened overnight and I do not know what.

I woke this morning to find Abigail gone from my room. At first I was not overly concerned, thinking that perhaps it was simply a call of nature, but when I went into the kitchen to put the bread in the oven, I found Abigail curled up in front of the stove. She was in a fugue state, awake but not coherent, with the remains of tears on her face. A cursory check showed that she was not obviously injured but she was unable to tell me what had occurred.

I cried out for William and he came immediately to my aid, but when he suggested he get the buggy to take Abigail to Doctor Harrison's, she roused enough to protest most vehemently. She begged us to simply take her home and after some attempts to persuade her otherwise, we did just that.

By the time we reached her home she had regained some of her faculties, yet she still refused to share what had occurred. When I asked her if Jacob had done something, she went quiet and did not say anything. As much as it pains me to suspect my brother of a vile act, I cannot shake the suspicion from my mind. I did not pry further, attempting to respect her wishes of privacy, and it was a solemn return journey home. William and I did not speak of it, but I could tell that he shared my concerns, as upon our arrival he immediately confronted Jacob and demanded he disclose what he did. Jacob was quick to deny the accusations but his entire countenance had changed. Instead of the solemn, churlish attitude of the previous days, he appeared brash and cocksure. It has done little to dispel my fears that he is the cause of my friend's distress, and yet I cannot prove anything. I can only hope that my dearest Abigail recovers from her ordeal and forgives me for allowing such misery to befall her under my roof."

CHAPTER 21

Dawson

They gathered in the loungeroom, unanimously agreeing that they wanted to get to the end of the diary that night. While Dawson made them all tea, Angie curled up in one of the armchairs and skimmed through the entries, searching for any mention of Abigail. She assured them she couldn't sense Charlotte nearby, and so they held onto hope that they wouldn't have to deal with her anger whilst they recounted her memories.

"Anything?" he asked, as he returned and handed them their camping mugs.

Angie's face scrunched up, in what he assumed was an expressive form of, *eh*. "The entries right after are mostly her worrying about Abigail and trying to figure out what exactly Jacob did. She mentions she's seen Abigail with her family at church but that she avoids Charlotte and her family and how much that upsets her. In October she also says Abigail has not been attending Church Committee meetings and that she didn't attend the

Spring Ball." She then smiled. "Spoiler—William is officially with Winnie after the ball and Charlotte is very excited about that."

Dawson sat down on the couch next to Chip, enjoying the warmth of his hip pressed against his own. "I guess it's not really a spoiler, since if they didn't get together I wouldn't be here."

"True," Angie agreed. She flipped through the diary, towards the very back. "I only got through to late October, sorry. Give me a second."

They waited patiently as she flipped through the pages, watching as her eyes slid down the page, searching for a glimpse of Abigail's name.

"Nothing about Abigail yet, but in early November they found a dead cat on the property that had been partially skinned. No prizes for guessing who they suspected of doing it, but apparently, this time Jacob didn't admit to it."

"Probably didn't want more one-on-one time with Father O'Reilly," Chip muttered.

"She mentions here how she misses Abigail and hopes she's doing okay," Angie mused, but continued to turn the pages. A few pages later, she sat up a little straighter and concentrated on the words on the page. "Okay, okay, I think this is it." She looked up at them and her eyes were filled with sadness. "I don't think either of you will be surprised at this outcome."

Dawson's eyes fell closed and he could already feel his heart breaking for this poor girl from the past. He knew this was going to be hard to listen to.

Angie began to read.

"5th December. Today was the first time in months that I saw my dearest Abigail, but alas, it was not the joyous reunion I had hoped for. I was in the front yard, beating the rugs, when I saw a figure approaching the house from the road. They appeared to be moving as if in a trance, stumbling almost, as if they

did not see the track before them. It did not take me long to recognise Abigail and I ran to her, overjoyed to see her even if I was confused as to why she was on foot. It is some distance between our farms and she must have been walking for quite a while, and given the heat of the day, this would be most unpleasant.

When I reached her, I immediately saw this was not the friend that I had known. Her face was sunken and gaunt, and there were deep bruises beneath her eyes that told of her exhaustion. Her eyes, always so bright with mirth and laughter, were dull and listless, and at first I do not know if she even recognised me. Something however, had propelled her to seek me out, and I knew that whatever it was, it was not joyous news. I took her arm and led her towards the house, but as soon as we placed foot on the verandah, she grew agitated and upset and refused to go inside. Knowing I needed to get her out of the sun and somewhere cool, and also knowing that it would give us some modicum of privacy, I led her to the cellar.

I begged Abigail to tell me what had distressed her, and although I had prayed it wasn't so, her words confirmed it for me. 'Your brother.'

It took some time to coax the story from her, and by the end, I understood how she had come to be in such a state. For, when she had stayed with me (and oh, how I am ridden with guilt that it was because of me that she is in this dire situation) she woke to find Jacob standing above her, covering her mouth with his hand to prevent her from crying out. He dragged my sweet Abigail from her bed and out into the night before forcing himself upon her in a most carnal manner. Once done, he left her to the elements, confident that he had shamed her so she would not speak of it. And shamed she was. She has suffered in silence since, but even worse, my demon of a brother left his seed behind and it took root and poor Abigail is with child.

As yet, her mother does not know, and Abigail does not know for how much longer she can keep the truth from her as her stomach has already grown swollen. She begged me for help and I of course swore that I would help in whatever manner I could. I suggested we seek out Winnie's help. Abigail confided that she does not wish to carry the child to term, so perhaps Winnie will know of some way to assist? Abigail was reluctant to involve anyone else but did agree in the end that I could speak to Winnie.

I then told Abigail that if she did not wish to bring undue attention to herself, she would need to act as normally as possible. If anyone had seen the state she was in when she arrived, there would be no question something was amiss. Questions would be asked and conclusions drawn, and so she would need to have a mask firmly in place to dispel any doubts. She rallied, and I was able to present her to Mama an hour later as having dropped in for an unexpected visit. Mama was delighted to see Abigail and did not question it, and luckily, Jacob was in town with Father so she was not forced to see him. William offered to take her home after luncheon, but before she left I assured her I would speak to Winnie at the first possible opportunity. Watching her leave, I was shrouded in guilt for what *had been done to her at the hand of my own brother, but determined to make it right."*

They were all silent as Angie finished the entry.

"Well, fuck," Chip said, breaking the silence. "Is there any way to resurrect Jacob so I can kill him myself?"

"I'd be on board with that," Angie agreed darkly.

"Poor Abigail," Dawson said. "She must have been so scared and alone."

"Should I keep reading?" Angie asked.

"Yeah. Let's rip the band aid off," Chip said. "There's not much left to go, so we may as well get it finished tonight."

"Okay," she said, then started on the entry for the 7th of December.

"In a stroke of luck, Winnie and her parents had been invited over for dinner tonight. William is completely smitten with her and so it proved a little difficult to get her alone, but the opportunity did finally present itself when Father and Mr Johnson went to inspect the new well and requested William to accompany them.

I explained the situation to Winnie, leaving out the name of Abigail's attacker, and as I expected, she was sympathetic to her cause. Winnie is such a gentle soul and would rid the world of suffering if she had the chance. She immediately vowed to help and to keep Abigail's confidence, and then explained that there is a purgative she can mix for Abigail to take. Given that it has been close to three months, she did warn that the purgative may not be potent enough, but she warned me off any other treatment as they are dangerous and more often than not, deadly.

The Committee is meeting on Saturday afternoon to decorate the supper hall behind the church with Christmas decorations, and Winnie told me to make sure that Abigail attends and she shall give her the mixture there."

Angie paused and then looked at them both. "I know our health care system isn't perfect, but holy shit, I am so fucking grateful for it right now."

"I can't even imagine what that poor girl was going through," Chip murmured.

Angie took a deep, cathartic breath, before releasing it and continuing to read aloud.

"10th December. The members of the Church Committee were delighted to see Abigail today but it was most difficult for her to feign enthusiasm for the decorating with our clandestine agenda. When we stopped for morning tea, Winnie insisted on fetching a cup for Abigail. We sat as far apart from the group as was politely possible, and I could do naught but sit in stalwart support of my dearest friend as she drank a concoction that will, at best, cleanse her of the remnants of my horrid brother, and worst, kill her. Winnie explained it is a precise balance that must be struck when creating the oil of savin mixture, as too much can cause damage to the kidneys and liver. Abigail told her that she was more than willing to take the risk and downed her cup of tea in a rather unladylike swallow.

Now all we can do is wait."

Angie skimmed over the next couple of pages. "She doesn't say anything about Abigail over the next week or so, except to mention that she was absent from mass but Mrs Wiltshire didn't explain why. William and Winnie announced their engagement, Jacob was surly but nothing out of the ordinary, and Charlotte's mother was ill again so Charlotte was doing the lion's share of the household chores." She turned another page. "Oh, here we go.

20th December. I had begged Mama to invite Abigail and Mrs Wiltshire over for scones and tea to celebrate the festive season and it was arranged for today. Abigail was pale and wan when she arrived but I was not sure if that was due to the elixir that Winnie concocted having worked or not. She apologised for her absence from church and explained that she had been unwell. Mama sympathised, as she too had been struck down with an unseasonal flu and she assumed that Abigail had suffered the same, which she did not refute.

When I could speak to Abigail alone, she informed me that she did not believe the oil of savin had worked as she had not had her menses since. She appeared dejected, and said that she believes she can not keep her condition from her mother for much longer and that her future is now uncertain, especially with Thomas, for which she grieves."

"Oh, that poor, poor girl," Dawson said. Needing comfort, and beyond caring if Angie saw, he reached out and snagged Chip's hand in his own.

Chip gave him a gentle squeeze and then pulled their joined hands onto his lap. If Angie saw, she didn't comment.

"There's only three entries left," Angie said as she looked through the remainder of the diary, her voice strained.

Dawson understood how she felt. Charlotte was so diligent about writing every single day, so whatever had changed to stop her recording her thoughts must have been bad.

Angie continued.

"21st December. Mr and Mrs Wiltshire arrived unannounced this morning to speak urgently to my parents. Abigail was with them and she looked miserable. I could only assume that she had told them of what had occurred.

William was asked to sit with Abigail in the sunroom whilst our parents spoke in the loungeroom, and I was asked to fetch Jacob from the orchard. I admit that I was not at all polite in my summons of him. He was sullen and agitated as we made our way to the house, and when we arrived, it was pandemonium. Mr Wiltshire flew into a rage when he laid eyes on Jacob and struck him across the face, shouting about how he had disrespected his daughter and had brought shame upon her. When Jacob climbed to his feet, he found himself now facing Mama's wrath. She slapped him twice across the cheek and told him that he must do right by Abigail. It was then that William and Abigail arrived into the room, which was now most crowded with people and emotions. When Mr Wiltshire told Jacob that he was to wed Abigail, she became hysterical, crying that she would rather die than be tied to Jacob for the rest of her life. Her father accused her of being hysterical but I understood Abigail's feelings on the matter. Jacob is not at all husband material, unlike sweet Thomas, and they are surely condemning her to a lifetime of misery and abuse.

Father tried to calm the situation by assuring Abigail that Jacob would have more meetings with Father O'Reilly, to be led further along God's path, but Abigail could not be consoled. I am horrified on her behalf, and cannot fathom what it must be like to be told that you will be wed to the man who did such unspeakable acts to you. I did not think my parents, nor Abigail's, were so cruel, yet they are adamant that they will be wed immediately after Christmas.

William shared my dismay and tried to speak against the decision, but Father overrode his protests. Their decision has been made and although I should be overjoyed that my dearest friend in the world shall become my sister, instead I silently weep for her."

"Jesus fucking Christ," Chip muttered as Angie finished the entry.

"22nd December. Early this morning, I heard a horse approach the house, and when I ventured outside to greet our visitor, I found that it was none other than Abigail. She was relieved when she saw me and bade us speak in private. Father and William had escorted Jacob to the church for a meeting with Father O'Reilly, and Mama was still not feeling the best and was resting, so it was easy enough for us to sneak away into the cellar. It was there that Abigail shared with me her plan to escape being tied to my brother for the rest of her days. Her mother's sister, who is much younger than Mrs Wiltshire, lives in Toodyay.

By a cruel twist of fate, she has been unable to carry a child to term. Abigail believes that her aunt will be willing to take on the child and they can explain away her absence as going to stay with her aunt to assist her with her miraculous pregnancy. Due to the previous losses, it would come as no surprise to anyone that her aunt would refrain from going into town in order to protect the growing babe. She and her aunt could remain unseen on their farm until the birth of the child, and then Abigail could return to Brockman with none the wiser.

I could see the merit in her plan, and urged her to speak with her mother about it at once, before arrangements are made for a wedding that cannot be undone. She embraced me fiercely, as if this does eventuate, she will likely be sent off immediately with no chance of a farewell. I wished her luck, and if all goes well, I would see what I could do to convince Father and Mama to allow me to visit in the new year as we are aware of the true nature of the situation.

"I can't believe that poor girl was forced to come up with a plan to avoid marrying that fucker," Chip cried with righteous indignation. "This whole situation is completely fucked."

"It gets worse," Angie said sadly, looking down at the final entry in the diary.

"How the hell can it possibly get worse?" Chip demanded.

"*Abigail is dead,*" Angie read, and Chip's eyes welled with tears. "It's from the final entry, marked December 23rd.

My dearest Abigail is gone and I am crushed by my grief. William found her body in the dam in the south orchard early this morning, and the Brockman constables were called. They determined that she had killed herself, although no note has been found. My heart is broken for it is all my fault. I am to blame for all of this and my dearest Abigail was the one who paid the price. My most dear friend is gone and I cannot stop weeping for her."

Angie gently closed the diary. "That's it. That's the final entry."

CHAPTER 22

Chip

They were a solemn group when they gathered the following morning for breakfast. Chip had held Dawson close all night, but neither had been in the mood to do anything physical other than take comfort from being close to one another.

"Did you sleep okay?" Dawson asked Angie, as he filled a glass with water so he could take his anti-anxiety meds. He turned and leaned against the sink, his arms crossed, almost hugging himself.

"Not really," she said, slumping in the kitchen chair. "What about you guys?"

Chip shook his head and took the seat opposite her. "I couldn't stop thinking about what happened to Abigail."

"Same," Angie said. "Like, I know the local cops determined it was suicide but none of us believe that, do we?"

"Fuck no," Dawson said vehemently.

"No way," Chip agreed. "That fucker killed her, just like he killed Charlotte."

"What's our next step?" Dawson asked.

"I'll do a cleansing first thing this morning," Angie told them. "After Charlotte's little display last night, I'll also do some warding just in case."

"What does that all involve?" Chip asked, curious. He was still deeply sceptical of the entire process, but knew that since his house was well and truly haunted, he didn't have a leg to stand on.

"I'll do a smudging and use salt for the cleanse," Angie explained. "Then, there are some runes I've been shown to draw that help keep occupants safe from harmful spirits."

Chip frowned. "I thought you hadn't had any training?"

"Not officially," Angie told him. "But my aunt was very . . . distressed when she found out my parents had moved into a house inundated with ghosts. She was never comfortable with it, but when Mum fell pregnant with me, she felt like she had to do something. She did some research and found a lady who cleansed houses. She taught my aunt the runes, who in turn taught my mum, and then me when I was old enough."

"And they worked?" Dawson asked.

"I've only ever felt like I had to resort to using them a handful of times," Angie said. "But when I did use them, the spirits causing the troubles didn't seem able to harm me afterward."

"That's something at least," Dawson said. He pushed up off the counter and then added, "Let's have some breakfast so we can get this started. I swear, if she trashes our house *one* more time, I'm going to lose my shit."

After they'd eaten, they both watched as Angie fetched a canvas satchel bag from Dawson's room. She took out numerous items and laid them out neatly on the coffee table in the loungeroom. There were several thick fingers of dried plant material that had been tied together with string, which had a very distinct, earthy aroma. A large black-velvet pouch was next, and then several pieces of what looked to be the same sort of chalk you saw children using. Lastly, Angie pulled out a smaller velvet pouch that she bounced on her palm for a long moment, as if weighing it. The contents rattled together and Chip had the feeling they were stones of some kind. Eventually, she shook her head and returned it to the bag.

"What is all this stuff?" Dawson asked, watching her avidly.

"The smudge sticks are a mix of white sage and juniper," she said, pointing to the herb bundles. "The sage is a bit finicky to grow here, but it's worth persisting since it can be bloody expensive to find the good quality stuff locally. It's not native to Australia, and it's not exactly used in mainstream practices so there's not a huge demand for it. The juniper is native so that's much easier to get." She pointed to the large pouch. "That has my supply of black lava salt. Although any old salt will do in a pinch—pun totally intended—I've found this to be the most potent." She gave them a wry grin. "Apparently, it's also good for relieving gas and bloating and is a decent laxative, but I can't speak from personal experience."

Chip snorted but didn't interrupt.

"Finally, the chalk is to draw the runes. I do have some paint pens that I can use, but I only use them when it's really dicey and the spirits are unusually tricksey. The chalk will wash off but the paint pens are much more difficult to remove, and since your house is probably heritage listed, I don't really want to use anything permanent."

"The house isn't actually heritage listed, but I would prefer to try the chalk first," Dawson told her dryly. "Mum would freak out if she came to visit and saw runes painted onto the floor boards."

"What was in the other pouch?" Chip asked Angie.

"A selection of crystals that have protective properties, mostly black tourmaline," she explained. "I don't know how much use they'll be to us so I'll keep them for a 'just in case' situation." She rummaged in the satchel once more and pulled out a box of matches and a small bowl that looked to be made of shell. "Abalone," she told them, gesturing with the bowl.

"Does abalone have special properties too?" Dawson asked.

"Nah," Angie said, "I just think it's pretty and I use it to catch ash before it drops on the floor." She stood up. "Okay, let's get this started."

What followed was . . . anticlimactic, to say the least. Chip and Dawson followed along behind Angie as she wafted the pungent smoke from the smudge stick into all corners of the house. She then took a pinch of salt and left a tiny pile against a wall facing north, as well as ones facing east, south, and west. Above the salt, she drew a rune on the wall, as close to the skirting board as possible.

Chip didn't know what he'd been expecting, but he thought something more exciting would happen than one of the smoke detectors going off. He had half expected Charlotte to appear, enraged at the actions of "the witch" and flinging around furniture or making it rain blood again. She was nowhere to be seen, however. He'd also thought that Angie might say a spell or a prayer, or walk around chanting in a demonic language or something as she worked, but she didn't say anything except to ask them to move a small bookcase so she could get to the wall behind it. Maybe Charlotte had noted how very un-witchy it was and so that's why she hadn't shown?

Chip himself almost felt robbed. He'd suspended his disbelief that the whole thing was codswallop, and had been expecting something . . . mystical, but instead it had been relatively mundane. Where was the extravagance and showmanship? Where was the anger and resentment from their ghost? It wasn't that he *wanted* Charlotte to appear and destroy their kitchen again, but if she *did,* it would make it feel like the steps they'd taken were *real.* That they had *worked.*

"All done," Angie declared and began packing everything away into her satchel.

Chip caught Dawson's eye and noticed that he looked a little underwhelmed by the proceedings as well. He shrugged and Dawson smiled, and that was that.

"Okay, so we really need to find this diary," Angie announced. "If we have any hope of laying Charlotte's ghost to rest, we need to find out exactly what happened."

"We've searched this place top to bottom," Chip protested. "It's not here."

"And we've gone through all the stuff the museum has in storage," Dawson added. "I think we have to face the fact that we're probably not going to find it."

Angie hummed. "So we need to get the story some other way."

"But how?" Chip asked. "It's obvious no one considered her death suspicious at the time, since it was labelled as an accident in the paper. Charlotte's never talked to us so it's not like we can ask her."

"That's not strictly true," Angie told him. "She was pretty vocal last night when she was calling me a witch."

Chip frowned. "Okay, yeah, you're right, but that's the only time she's even spoken. That day we talked to her, it was almost like she *wanted* to speak but couldn't."

"So is something stopping her?" Dawson asked. "What could do that?"

"It might be something as simple as she doesn't have enough energy," Angie said, musing it over. "Projecting herself takes too much energy, so she doesn't have enough left to speak."

"But last night she was even more solid than usual," Chip said.

"And yet we've not seen a peep of her today," Angie noted. "Maybe because she's drained everything she had?"

"So how do we get her to talk then?" Dawson asked. "We can't just wait until she gets pissed off enough to start throwing her head around again and try to question her then."

"We can always provide the energy for her," Angie said. "Channel it to her so she uses that to speak instead of her own."

"I'm not going to like where this is going, am I?" Chip asked in a resigned manner.

Angie grimaced. "Probably not. And yes, I'm talking about a séance."

"I thought you said we wouldn't need a ouija board!" Dawson cried, looking at her in dismay.

She threw her hands up in surrender. "Because I didn't think it would come to that! It's not like we've been left with much choice."

"Urgh," Dawson huffed, and slumped down into a chair. "How is this even my life?"

"There, there," Angie said, patting him on the shoulder. "It could be worse."

Both Chip and Dawson stared at her, the question unspoken in the air between them.

"It could be a poltergeist," Angie said. "Now they're *nasty.*"

Chip found himself echoing Dawson's thoughts later that evening when he found himself sitting in the darkened loungeroom, candles glowing softly around the room, with an honest-to-god freaking *spirit board* in the middle of the coffee table. How was this even real?

Angie had spent the afternoon preparing herself for the séance. She'd gone for a walk around the property, even as dark clouds gathered and rain threatened, and then meditated to clear her mind. She hadn't told Chip or

Dawson to do anything of the sort and so they'd not done anything special. Dawson had scheduled some social media posts and then worked on his new song, and Chip had logged into his work emails to start clearing away the spam and nuisance messages, so when he got back to it, he wouldn't have such an avalanche of work to do.

They'd made toasted sandwiches for dinner, keeping it simple, before helping Angie set up as the skies opened and the rain began to pour down. They'd unplugged the television and made sure there were no electronic lights in the room. Their phones had been left in the bedrooms. Angie had placed the scrapbook on the coffee table, with the photo of Charlotte open to the room to encourage her spirit to answer their call. The candles around the edge of the room were plain white but the ones ringing the table were violet, as Angie said that colour helped to encourage communication. The rain continued to fall, pattering against the tin roof, and it was almost soothing.

"Are we ready to begin?" Angie asked them quietly.

They both nodded.

"Let us join hands," Angie instructed and reached out to both of them.

Chip had to stretch quite far to reach Angie's hand across the table with his right one, but Dawson was closer on his left. Angie had been concerned at first that they didn't have enough "sitters"—the people who joined the séance to provide energy for the spirits—but as they didn't really know anyone else in town that they could trust as yet, they decided to make do with just the three of them.

"Close your eyes and concentrate on our purpose here this evening," Angie said, her voice low and sonorous. "Our energy will grow within the circle as we all focus on the one we wish to speak to this evening—Charlotte Miller. Think of Charlotte. Think of the girl we have gotten to know from her writings. Think of your ancestor, Dawson."

Chip tried to banish the intrusive thoughts that kept popping into his head. The ones like, *"This is ridiculous,"* and *"What the ever loving fuck am I doing?."* Instead, he thought of Charlotte as she would have been when she was alive. A feisty girl on a farm who longed to do more than she was allowed. The girl who was quick to temper but even quicker to laugh. The girl who'd had her life cut short way too soon.

"We are reaching out tonight to Charlotte Miller, daughter of Tobias and Anne," Angie intoned. "If you are here, Charlotte, we ask that you please join us within the circle to give us counsel."

Chip wasn't sure if he was allowed to open his eyes yet so he peeked one open and peered around the room. He saw that Dawson was doing the same and fought down the urge to giggle like a silly primary school kid. Angie's eyes were open and she was casually looking around the room, so Chip took that as permission to open his eyes the entire way.

Nothing happened for a long moment, and then the door to the lounge-room flew open and banged against the wall, and a cold breeze filled the room. The candles flickered, but surprisingly, did not extinguish. The temperature plummeted and Chip was glad he'd thrown on a long-sleeved shirt beneath his hoodie. Was it sad he was getting so used to the signs that a ghost was in the room that he'd simply started to dress for the occasion instead of freaking out?

"Charlotte, we thank you for joining us tonight," Angie said respectfully. She then looked at Chip and Dawson. "Please place your fingers upon the planchette, but continue to be joined so we do not break the circle."

They all reached over the spirit board and managed to manoeuvre their joined hands so they were all touching the pointer. Immediately, Chip's shoulders felt the strain and he wriggled forward to ease the pressure. If Charlotte was feeling tight-lipped tonight, he'd be feeling it by the end.

"Can you confirm that you are Charlotte Miller?" Angie asked the spirit.

Deep down inside, Chip still expected nothing to happen. Even with experiencing a haunting first-hand and seeing the damage a ghost could do, he still held the deep-seated belief that the séance would be all smoke and mirrors. He knew it was a ridiculous notion to hold onto after everything they'd been through, but he'd never denied being a stubborn bastard. So when the planchette began to move smoothly towards the *Yes* box, he jerked backwards in surprise.

Angie's hand tightened on his and she said in a low, but stern whisper, "Do *not* break the circle."

He stared at the spirit board and swallowed loudly, trying to pull himself together.

"Charlotte, will you speak to us via your spiritual form?" Angie asked her.

The planchette moved across to the *No* box.

Angie frowned but didn't let the response deter her. They'd already discussed the fact that Charlotte may not have the energy to speak to them physically, and they might have to rely on the spirit board for answers. "Did you commence a diary for the year 1905?" Angie asked.

The planchette moved back to *Yes*.

"Do you know where the diary is?" Dawson asked.

Their fingers were guided back to *No*.

"Crap," Chip muttered.

"Did Jacob kill Abigail as well?" The question was almost whispered by Dawson.

A scream of rage pierced the air and the cold wind whipped into a frenzy, extinguishing the candles surrounding them. Only the violet candles on the table survived. The framed artwork on the wall that Carolyn had gotten for them as a housewarming present was flung across the room, the glass in the frame shattering as it collided with the wall.

"I guess that answers that," Dawson murmured.

"We need her to confirm it," Angie told them. "Charlotte," she said, raising her voice to be heard over the howling wind. "Did Jacob kill Abigail?"

The planchette was jerked roughly across the board but stopped before it reached the *Yes* box. It shook and shuddered as if invisible forces were fighting over it. Angie's eyes had narrowed and she instructed Chip and Dawson. "Let go of the planchette."

They attempted to remove their hands but it was as if they were glued to the wooden pointer. The planchette jerked again, moving over to the letters, touching briefly upon one before moving to another.

"Keep watch so we don't miss any words," Angie said in a terse voice.

They stared at the planchette, watching as it spelled out two words.

Too late.

"Too late?" Chip asked. "Too late for what?"

There was an explosive force from the centre of the board and all three of them were flung backwards, their hands ripped from each other's grip as they tumbled over painfully onto the floor. The spirit board rose high into the air even as the pressure in the room dropped, making their ears pop painfully.

And then a voice spoke. But it wasn't Charlotte's.

"My, my, what tales has my darling little sister been telling about me?"

CHAPTER 23

Dawson

Dawson gasped as a shadowy figure began to materialise in the centre of the room, hovering above the coffee table. Wisps of smoke-like material swirled together, taking form until a solid-looking ghost floated in the air, glaring down at them with a look of disdain. There was absolutely no mistaking him for anyone other than Jacob Miller. Even if he hadn't told them he was Charlotte's brother, the resemblance to Dawson was even more uncanny than when looking at a black and white photograph. They could have been twins.

A flicker in the corner of Dawson's eye caught his attention and he dared to glance away from Jacob. Charlotte was solidifying in the corner and she looked furious. Her mouth opened and closed as she shouted at Jacob—completely in silence. No matter how much she tried, she could not make a sound.

Jacob laughed, a cruel sound with little mirth. "What was that, sister dearest? Cat got your tongue?"

Charlotte darted forward but then her entire being flickered and she ended up back where she had begun. She tried again, but didn't make it halfway across the room before she returned to the spot she had materialised in. Her face twisted in anger and she silently snarled at her brother.

"What have you done to Charlotte?" Angie asked as she climbed to her feet. Her metallic silver hair was dishevelled, and a red mark was forming on her arm from where she'd struck the leg of the couch.

"My sister was always an unruly child," Jacob said with a sneer. "She needed to be put in her place in life and nothing appears different now in death."

"Release your hold on her!" Angie demanded, her voice strong with no hint of fear.

Jacob sneered at her. "No. She needs to learn her lesson."

"Are you hurting her?" Dawson demanded, drawing Jacob's attention to himself.

The way Jacob did a double take would have been comical if the situation hadn't been so dire. His eyes widened as he took in Dawson's appearance, and he leaned forward as if to get a better look. "Who would you be?" he asked, his voice losing the condescending tone and sounding almost polite.

"I'm Dawson Miller. You'd be Jacob?"

"Ah, you would be a nephew of mine? Descended from William, I presume."

"That's right."

"Shame," Jacob said, dismissively. "If you're one of *his,* I can't see that you'll have the disposition to be of any use to me."

"He's clearly not a complete fucking psychopath like you," Chip spat.

Dawson groaned as Jacob's attention turned to Chip. He sneered down at Chip. "Best close your mouth, boy, or you won't like the consequences of your insolence."

Dawson could see Chip bristling at being called *boy* by someone who hadn't been much older than him when he'd died, so he tried to shift the focus back to himself. "Why are you hurting Charlotte? What's the point?"

Jacob's eyes lingered on Chip for a long moment, clearly enjoying making Chip bristle, but thankfully, he then turned back to Dawson. "The point?" he asked. "Why must there be a point? Perhaps I simply enjoy bringing her pain?"

"You really are a monster," Dawson told him.

"What is it you want from us?" Angie asked.

"What do I want from you?" Jacob asked, placing a hand over his heart. "Oh, you poor simple human. I don't *want* anything from you. That implies you are worthy of my time. Will I take great satisfaction from your suffering? Without a doubt. But I don't *want* anything from you." His expression changed then, going from arrogant to downright deadly. "However, I *did* get what I *needed* from you."

Dawson had a sinking feeling that this wasn't good.

"And what would that be?" Angie asked, trying to keep the bravado in her voice but failing.

Jacob grinned, and it was all teeth. "The circle," he said gleefully. "Is broken."

And then he was gone.

As soon as Jacob's ghost disappeared, Charlotte's ghost was free of the invisible constraints. She darted forward to the centre of the room, her face a mask of fury. The coffee table flipped over, sending the ouija board and candles flying. The candles extinguished as they fell, plunging the room into darkness. Dawson heard someone crossing the room in the dark and then the lights flipped on, showing Chip standing by the switch. Charlotte was gone.

"Well, that went to shit," Angie muttered, rubbing at her eyes.

"How the hell did that even happen?" Chip demanded. "I thought it was safe!"

"Safe?" Angie asked, raising a brow. "What on earth made you think that a séance would be *safe*?"

Chip rolled his eyes. "You know what I mean! I thought the circle was to contain them and couldn't be easily broken."

"Yeah, normally they can't be," Angie admitted. "But it's not impossible if the ghost has the strength."

Chip looked like he was going to argue about that, so Dawson stepped in. "You clearly weren't expecting Jacob to appear at all," he remarked.

Angie shrugged. "You'd seen no sign of him up until this point, and I honestly didn't sense another strong spirit besides Charlotte. Being strong enough to break our circle? Let's just say that if Jacob had been close by since I got here, I would have felt him."

"What does that mean?" Chip asked.

"Either something we did called him here, or he was watching and waiting for his chance to appear."

Dawson frowned. "What would he be waiting for?"

"I'm not sure," Angie said. "Maybe he was just waiting for an opportunity he could take advantage of? Maybe he just likes to be close by to torture his sister?"

"So, I guess the million dollar question is," Chip said. "Can you sense him now?"

Angie's eyes got a faraway look to them as she concentrated. Eventually, she shook her head and said, "No, not right now. Charlotte is . . . around. Lingering in the background but not on the surface level. Otherwise, there's no one else."

Chip let out a long breath and ran a hand through his hair. "Okay, good, that's good. You'll let us know if that changes?"

"Of course," she assured him.

Chip gestured over his shoulder at the front window to where Angie had placed one of her runes earlier. "I don't mean to be rude, but did they actually *do* anything?"

Dawson winced. That definitely wouldn't have been how he would have phrased it, though he was curious to know the answer.

Angie's eyes narrowed. "Are any of us injured?" she asked pointedly.

"No, but—"

"But nothing," Angie barked, cutting him off. "The runes protect us from being physically harmed by dangerous spirits. We are not injured, ergo they worked. I know what I'm doing!"

"I didn't mean to imply that you didn't," Chip said, holding his hands up in a placating gesture. "You did just say though, that the circle can't usually be broken, but Jacob did just that. I was simply wondering if he was too strong for the runes."

There was a long beat of silence and then Angie's shoulders slumped. "Fuck, sorry. I didn't mean to get so defensive," she apologised. "You're right. I can't say for certain if the runes will be enough to keep Jacob at bay."

"So, we all need to be alert at all times," Dawson said. "If we see anything hinky, or something even feels off, then we tell each other straight away."

Both Angie and Chip nodded at this.

"So, what's the next step?" he asked.

"Tomorrow, I would like to go into town and get a large amount of salt," Angie told them. "I don't have enough on me for what I'm planning, and I think we need to create a safe haven that *we* can get into but a spirit can't."

"That makes sense," Dawson agreed. "We only have a little salt shaker in the kitchen. I'm guessing that won't be enough?"

She shook her head. "No. Maybe if I was just planning on doing one room but not for this."

"Are you going to salt the entire house?" Chip asked.

"Not the entire house," she replied. "But most of it. If I do the whole house, Charlotte won't be able to appear and I think we'll need her before this ends. I'm going to leave this room alone so we can communicate with her here, but I'll do the rest of the rooms and the hallway."

"That might piss her off," Dawson warned.

"I know, but I believe it's a risk we're going to have to take now that Jacob is on the scene," Angie said.

Dawson's jaw cracked open in a wide yawn and he realised just how tired he was. "Well, if there's nothing else we can do tonight, I think I'm gonna head to bed," he told them. "I'm buggered."

"I think an early night for all of us is a good idea," Chip agreed. He looked over at Angie. "Would you like the bathroom first?"

It took longer than Dawson had hoped to get horizontal. By the time they'd all taken turns in the bathroom, to shower and brush their teeth, he was almost asleep standing up. He fell into bed and let out a sigh of relief as his head sunk into the pillow. The rain had gentled now, but was still a steady thrum against the tin roof. "This one is much better than mine," he mumbled, patting the pillowcase. "I think I'll steal it once Angie's gone."

Chip slipped a hand over his waist and pulled him back against his chest. His breath was hot against Dawson's ear as he said, "Maybe I won't let you go back to your room. I kinda like having you in bed with me."

Dawson's skin broke out in goosebumps and he was suddenly a lot less tired than he'd been a moment before. Chip's warmth at his back and his words had Dawson's dick starting to pay attention. "Really?" he asked coyly. "What do you like best about me being in bed with you?"

Chip's hand as it trailed down Dawson's torso was still a little hesitant but he forged on, skating his fingers over the bulge in Dawson's pyjama bottoms. "Besides being able to hold you all night and listen to your little snores?" Chip asked.

"I do *not* snore!" Dawson protested, twisting his neck around to glare at Chip. Due to the lights being off, Chip wouldn't see it but he hoped he *felt* it.

Chip chuckled, and warm gusts of air puffed against Dawson's ear once again. *Fuck.* That had no right to be as hot as it was.

"You *totally* snore," Chip teased. "But it's kind of snuffly and cute."

"Hmph." Dawson was now pouting into the dark.

"Don't sulk," Chip admonished him.

"I'm not sulking." He totally was.

Chip huffed out another laugh and his hand continued to trace patterns on Dawson's stomach, dropping down every now and then to work over his erection. When it got to be too much and he needed more—so much more—Dawson rolled over and wrapped his arms around Chip's neck. "If you're not going to chase me back to my own room once Angie goes, I'm more than happy to stay here with you," he whispered.

"Yeah?" Chip asked quietly.

"Yeah," Dawson said, and he leaned forward and kissed him.

CHAPTER 24

Chip

Kissing Dawson wasn't something Chip ever thought he'd get tired of. It was addictive and he found himself chasing after his lips whenever Dawson pulled back. Most of the time, he found them and the kiss continued, but every now and then one of them would have moved a little too far in the dark and they'd bump noses or chins together. They laughed about it each time, and the next kiss would be stretched around a smile.

Dawson was still the more confident of the two of them when it came to sex, and he took charge, urging Chip to push down his sleep pants while he did the same. Once their cocks were free, he shuffled down the bed, taking his time to kiss over Chip's chest and hips before he came to a stop in front of his cock.

Chip's breath caught. He'd not expected Dawson to want to get up close and personal with his dick so soon. Dawson didn't hesitate, didn't *um* and *ah*, he just got straight to it, licking a stripe up Chip's cock from root to tip.

"Jesus fucking Christ," Chip swore, his whole body jerking at the sensation. He suddenly *had* to see, and he twisted slightly so he could reach the bedside lamp, more grateful now than he'd ever been for getting the touch lamp. Soft warm light illuminated their surroundings, and Dawson grinned up at him before he leaned in and licked over his frenulum and swirled his tongue around the tip.

"That's so hot," Chip muttered, unable to tear his eyes away.

"Tell me 'bout it," Dawson said, wrapping his fist around the base and slowly jerking Chip as he continued to explore with his tongue.

"Can't wait to try it on you," Chip said, fighting the urge to close his eyes so he could concentrate on nothing else but the way it felt. He wanted to commit every moment to memory though, so he forced his eyes to remain open, to watch each second of Dawson devouring him.

Dawson took his time, driving Chip wild with each and every long, languid swipe, kittenish lick, and sloppy suck. He never took Chip deep enough to gag and he was cautious of his teeth, and Chip was amazed at how good it felt. If Dawson was this good at it now, during his first attempt, how much better would it be once they'd had some practice? Chip was itching to reverse their positions and try it himself, but then Dawson dragged the flat of his tongue firmly across the head of his cock, ending the move with the tip sliding into his slit. "Holy fuck," he moaned.

"Shhh," Dawson cautioned, pulling back just a fraction. "Angie is just across the hall, remember?"

Chip winced and tried to remain quiet but it was harder than he thought. He ended up reaching up and biting down on the meaty part of his hand to keep from babbling about how fucking *good* it felt. His hips bucked of their own accord and Dawson had to pull back a few times to avoid being choked, but he'd return every time, licking and sucking like he was born for it.

When it was all too much and his balls were drawing up tight, Chip reached down and tugged on Dawson's hair in warning. Dawson pulled back and continued to pump him with his fist and Chip grunted his way through his orgasm. Dawson watched in fascination as Chip's stomach was covered in thick, creamy ropes of cum which quickly cooled in the night air.

"Fuck, that was awesome," Chip said as he fell back, boneless against the pillow.

Dawson pushed up onto his knees and then knee-walked up the bed. "Glad to hear it." As Chip reached for the tissues, he put a hand on his arm to stop him. "Don't bother cleaning up just yet," he said, and then began to jerk himself.

Chip's eyes widened as he watched Dawson work himself over above him. He couldn't seem to keep his eyes on Chip's face, his gaze constantly dropping down to the mess on his stomach. Finally, he reached out and scooped up some cum into his hand and used it to slick the way, the wet sound absolutely filthy in the quiet of the night. Both of them were breathing hard now and Chip's cock was valiantly trying to rise again.

The wind outside began to blow harder and the rain on the tin roof grew heavier. The contrast between the weather becoming wild outside and the safe, warm interior of the bedroom made the moment feel surreal. Was this what their future would be like? Would there be more nights like this?

There was a brief flash of lightning outside and the lamp flickered slightly before it steadied once more, and the dull roar of thunder greeted them shortly afterward. Dawson didn't falter as he jerked himself, and he made such a pretty picture with his hair golden in the lamp light, his face cast in shadows, and his eyes glowing.

Wait, what?

Why the fuck were his eyes glowing?

"Daw," Chip began, starting to push himself up.

Dawson's back bowed and his head tilted backwards and then he was coming, shooting his load over Chip's chest and throat. His body shook and shuddered and Chip watched warily, wondering what the fuck was going on. Then Dawson straightened and Chip finished pushing himself up to a sitting position so he could get a proper look at him.

It wasn't Dawson staring back at him.

"Well, well," Jacob drawled, one hand still wrapped around his cock. "It's been such a *long* time since I've felt such exquisite release."

Chip stared up in horror, trying to comprehend what the fuck was going on. What had happened to Dawson? Had Jacob possessed him? Taken over his body so he could use him as a puppet?

Fuck, fuck, *fuck*.

"What the fuck have you done to Dawson?" he snarled up at Jacob. "Get out of his body!"

Jacob bared his teeth in a vicious smile. "No." He then gave his semi-hard cock a few tugs, his eyes fluttering in desire. "I had forgotten what human pleasure felt like. I can see there will be some delicious benefits to having one again."

"Stop fucking touching him!" Chip roared, lunging forward.

"Uh, uh," Jacob chided, holding up a hand. "If you hurt me, you hurt your precious Dawson."

Chip hesitated, at a loss for what to do. It was true—there was nothing he could do physically to Jacob that he wouldn't also be doing to Dawson, and the thought of hurting him, even to save him, made Chip's stomach curdle. "Why are you doing this?" he asked, trying to buy some time to get his sluggish brain to work.

The look Jacob gave him was full of condescension. "Why? Because I can. And really, why *wouldn't* I?"

And just how the hell could Chip try and reason with that? Jacob didn't want anything, didn't *need* anything. He was playing with them because he was an evil fucker who enjoyed bringing misery to others. Even death hadn't changed that.

"Chip?" Angie called from across the hall. "Is everything okay?"

"Angie!" he cried, hope flaring in his chest. She must have heard him yell at Jacob and woken up. "Angie, help! Jacob has—" Chip was cut off as Jacob snarled and grabbed him by the throat. Immediately, his air was cut off and he struggled to breathe.

"Chip!" Angie yelled again, and he heard her bedroom door open and her footsteps as she crossed the hall.

Jacob pointed the hand not holding Chip by the throat towards the door, and whatever he did prevented Angie from opening it. She hammered on the wood, calling out. "Chip! Dawson! What's going on?"

Chip's vision was going fuzzy and his lungs were burning but he couldn't breathe, couldn't draw any air past the vice-like grip that Jacob had on his throat. He struggled weakly in his hold, unable to look away from Dawson's face even though it wasn't Dawson looking back at him from those familiar blue eyes. His hands scrambled uselessly at Jacob's wrist, and his lips, tingling and numb, formed Dawson's name even as everything started to go black.

Jacob's body jerked, a spasm shuddering through him, and the arm pointing at the door fell to the side. His eyes narrowed in annoyance, and he said, "There is no point fighting me, boy. I'm too strong for your weak constitution."

Chip didn't understand what Jacob was talking about. He wasn't fighting, he was too weak. Everything was going dark. He was dying.

Then the bedroom door crashed open.

Jacob looked over his shoulder at Angie and growled, then with a strength Chip knew Dawson did not possess, he flung Chip off the bed, sending him crashing into the wall by the window.

Chip's head spun as he lay in a crumpled heap, trying to get his bearings as he drew in one ragged breath after another. His nose was a few centimetres away from the skirting board and his eyes were having trouble focussing. He blinked, trying to get rid of the white dots that were still obscuring his vision. Slowly, his vision cleared and the east rune that Angie had drawn onto his wall came into focus. From across the room he could hear Angie commanding Jacob to leave Dawson's body but Chip knew it wouldn't work. Jacob was too strong. He'd taken possession of Dawson and mere words wouldn't make him leave.

His eyes fell to the small pile of black salt on the floorboards beneath the rune, miraculously untouched by Chip's abrupt arrival on that side of the room. He wondered . . . words might not work, but would salt?

He pushed himself up onto his knees and then pinched several of the larger crystals between his thumb and pointer finger. Would it be enough? The granules were much larger than those of everyday table salt but it was still a few scant crystals. He had to try. Dawson's life would depend on it.

Climbing to his feet, Chip looked over and saw that Angie had backed into the corner, with Jacob slowly advancing on her, taunting her with what he had planned for her. He was so caught up in outlining his horrendous plans that he didn't notice Chip advancing from behind.

Chip lunged at Jacob's back, wrapping his legs around his hips and looping his arms around his throat in a mockery of a piggyback ride. Jacob immediately began to jerk and buck, trying to dislodge him but Chip had thighs of fucking steel and he wouldn't be moved. Jacob's head turned to the side and he opened his mouth, likely to begin outlining to Chip in great detail all the terrible things he was going to do to him, but Chip didn't give him the chance. He seized the opportunity to shove his fingers into Jacob's mouth, dropping the salt crystals as far back as he could. Then he clamped his hand over Jacob's mouth, not allowing him to spit them out.

Jacob struggled against him but it was no use. As the salt dissolved on his tongue, his body was wracked with tremors. He stopped fighting Chip and clutched at his head, muffled screams coming from behind his closed lips.

Then his body arched and a pulse of energy exploded from him, dislodging Chip and making Angie crouch down to protect herself. Chip watched from the floor as black smoke poured from Dawson's mouth and nose, gathering above him. The door flew open and the smoke poured through it and Dawson's body collapsed into a heap on the floor.

CHAPTER 25

Dawson

Dawson groaned, trying to figure out why the hell everything hurt. What had happened? Where was he?

"Daw?" That was Chip's voice. "Baby, are you okay?"

Hands were on him, turning him over and he looked up and saw Chip's worried face gazing down at him. "Chip?" he croaked.

"Oh, thank fuck," Chip cried, and he pulled Dawson up onto his lap.

It took a few moments but Dawson slowly became aware of his surroundings. They were on the floor in the corner of Chip's bedroom, behind the door. They were naked. Oh, that's right—they'd been in bed together. So how did they get here?

"Dawson? You back with us?"

He froze. "Angie?" he asked. Turning his head, he saw her climb to her feet. She'd been pressed into the very corner of the room. "What's going on?" he whispered.

Angie walked over to the bed and returned with the sheet, draping it over them. "As happy as I am to discover that I was right about there being something going on between you two, I figure this isn't a conversation you'd want to have naked."

Dawson looked up at Chip, but the same panic he felt wasn't reflected in Chip's eyes. Instead, he looked relieved. His skin was flushed and red though, and on closer inspection, Dawson saw broken blood vessels in Chip's eyes. "What the fuck happened?" he demanded. "You're hurt!"

Chip shook his head. "I'm okay," he rasped, doing nothing to alleviate Dawson's growing panic.

"What happened?" he asked again.

Chip opened his mouth to speak and then cleared his throat. It sounded painful. Before he could try again, Angie said, "How about I go and put the kettle on while you guys get dressed. Some honey tea might be needed to soothe Chip's throat."

Chip nodded and Angie quietly left the room. Dawson went to speak but Chip just shook his head. "Please," he whispered, and all of Dawson's protests died. Chip sounded miserable.

They dressed quickly, and it took all of Dawson's willpower to keep quiet when he noticed the red marks on Chip's throat, and the drying cum on his stomach and chest that he did his best to clean up with tissues. How did the injuries to his throat happen? Why didn't he remember? How much time had he lost? He tried to be patient, knowing he'd have the answers soon, but it was difficult.

When they entered the kitchen, Angie was finishing making three cups of tea. She squeezed out the last tea bag and brought two cups over to the table. They sat down and Angie fetched her own cup before joining them.

"Please, I need to know what happened," Dawson begged them.

Chip sipped at his tea, wincing as he swallowed. "It was Jacob," he said, his voice still hoarse and raspy.

"What did he do?" Dawson demanded. There was a sick feeling in the pit of his stomach and he knew he wasn't going to like the answer.

Chip took a deep breath, and his eyes closed as if he were unable to look at Dawson while he told him. "He . . . possessed you? I guess that's what you'd call it? He took over your body."

A shudder went through Dawson and that sick feeling became more pronounced, making his stomach churn with bile. His chest was tight as his anxiety grew. "I don't remember that," he whispered. "I don't remember any of that. Why don't I remember?" He could hear the panic in his own voice and his breathing was becoming laboured.

Chip's eyes had snapped open at Dawson's panic and he reached out, taking his hand and squeezing it. "It's okay. He's gone, baby. He's gone."

"When? How?" Dawson managed to ask between gasps for air.

"Daw, baby, just breathe for me first. I'll tell you everything, but first of all, just take some deep breaths."

"No!" Dawson cried, rifling through his memories for the last thing he remembered. "I need to know what happened! Fuck, the last thing I remember was us . . . we were . . ." He broke off, unable to even look in Angie's direction. "Oh, God, did it happen during that?"

Chip's eyes were haunted as he gave a single nod.

"Oh, fuck," Dawson said, pushing his chair back and standing. "I'm gonna be sick." He rushed across to the bench and pulled the bin out of the cupboard under the sink, barely getting it under him in time before he was emptying the contents of his stomach. His skin was crawling and even as his stomach heaved, he clawed at his arms, trying to remove the sensation of ghostly hands on his body. He felt violated, and he wanted nothing more than to purge himself in fire.

A hand came to rest on his shoulder and he jumped, but calmed immediately when he saw it was Chip. He had a glass of water in one hand

and Dawson took it gratefully, rinsing his mouth and spitting into the sink before draining the rest of the glass. Once he was done, Chip wrapped an arm around his shoulder and pulled him against his chest. "I'm so sorry, baby," he murmured against his hair.

Realisation dawned on Dawson and he looked at Chip in horror. "Oh, no. No, no, no."

"What is it?" Chip asked, concern etched deeply into his features.

"If he took me over while we were doing that . . . Oh, Chip. You wouldn't have known."

Chip had gone still and then he shook his head. "Not until after, when he was finished."

The queasy feeling returned but Dawson fought it down. This wasn't just about him. Chip had suffered as well. "I'm so sorry," he cried, holding Chip tighter.

"It's okay," Chip murmured.

"It's not!" Dawson argued. "Nothing about this is okay, Chip!"

"I know," he said, and the painful rasp of his voice reminded Dawson there was still more to the story that he didn't know. "It's over now though, and we need to come up with a plan. I'll deal with everything else later."

We're both going to need therapy after this, Dawson thought to himself. He thought of the psychologist he had seen off and on over the years for his anxiety and wondered what she'd have to say about the situation. What *could* anyone say? It wasn't like being sexually assaulted by a ghost was in their wheelhouse.

One day at a time. They'd have to take it one day at a time. And at least they had each other.

"Are you still feeling sick?" Chip asked.

"I think I'm done barfing," Dawson told him. "Still queasy, but I think I can keep the water down now."

Chip tied off the bin bag and shoved the entire bin back under the sink to deal with later, then he led Dawson back over to the table. Dawson gave him a shaky smile, as Chip shuffled his chair over until he was right next to Dawson and threw an arm over his shoulder.

"Sorry 'bout that," Dawson told Angie, who was watching them with sympathetic eyes.

"Don't you dare apologise," she said fiercely. "I can't even imagine how you're feeling right now. It's me who should be sorry."

Dawson frowned. "Why?"

"Because nothing I've done has been enough to stop any of this. I thought the circle would protect us during the séance but Jacob was too powerful. My runes were supposed to stop you from getting hurt from a spirit and Jacob circumvented that by possessing Dawson's physical body. I feel like I've just made the situation so much worse."

"This isn't your fault," Dawson assured her. "I swear, Angie. No one is to blame here, apart from Jacob."

"I just wish I'd been able to do more." She was looking at the table in defeat.

"If you hadn't been here, who knows what would have happened," Dawson told her.

"We wouldn't have known about the salt," Chip agreed. "That got rid of him."

Dawson frowned. "How?" He shook his head. "Wait, that's the end, I want to hear what happened from the beginning. Are you feeling okay to tell me? Can you speak that much?"

"I'll try," Chip said, and took another sip of tea. Then he began to speak.

Dawson listened, horrified, as Chip told them what had happened. He didn't spare any details, speaking in a matter-of-fact voice that hid all signs of emotion, even as he spoke of how Jacob had taken advantage of him.

Dawson knew that Chip would bottle it all up to deal with later, so all he could do was hold his hand and offer his silent support until they could *both* work through their trauma.

When Chip got to the part about Jacob strangling him, Dawson felt the anger inside him rise, overpowering his anxiety until he was shaking from rage, not panic. Jacob had tried to *kill* Chip. He probably would have succeeded if it wasn't for Angie breaking down Chip's bedroom door.

"How did you get in?" Chip asked Angie, breaking off from his story. "He seemed to be able to prevent you from getting in at first."

"I shoved some black salt crystals under the door, creating a break in his power," she said. "I didn't know if it would work, but I had to try. I was throwing myself at the door, kicking it, doing anything to get in. I think I might have splintered the wood." She looked sheepish. "Sorry about that."

"Better a new door than a coffin," Chip told her.

"True," she agreed.

"It seems like that salt is worth its weight in gold," Chip noted. "Its what I used on Jacob. I shoved some in his mouth and it seemed to banish him. We should probably get more of it."

"I doubt our local IGA carries it," Dawson said.

"I got mine online," Angie told them. "We can place an order later."

Chip was looking thoughtful. "I think some of it might have been Dawson as well."

"What do you mean?" Angie asked.

"Just something Jacob said. He was strangling me, but then he kind of jolted and said something like '*Stop trying to fight me*'. I'm pretty sure he wasn't speaking to me." He looked at Dawson. "I think *you* were fighting him."

"I don't remember any of that," Dawson admitted.

"It made all the difference," Chip told him. "It distracted him enough to let up on whatever he was doing to the door so Angie could get in."

"Well, I'm glad. What do we do now?" Dawson asked. "I have to admit, I'm not really looking forward to going back to bed."

"Tonight, we stay together," Angie told them. "Between your table salt and the rest of my supplies, we'll be able to salt your bedroom. We'll camp out there tonight until we can get hold of what we need to do the rest of the house tomorrow. Hopefully, we'll all manage to get some sleep."

It was a nice sentiment but one that none of them managed. They piled onto Dawson's bed—Angie on one side, Dawson in the middle, and Chip wrapped around him. It was weird being back in his own bed. He'd grown used to Chip's bed since they'd been here, and despite everything that had happened tonight, he wished it was safe enough for him and Chip to return there. To cuddle up and take comfort in one another. To close their eyes against the world and heal their wounds.

But that would have to wait.

Dawson had had visions of them emptying the shelves of the IGA of every container of salt they carried, and then being judged harshly by the older lady who manned the check out. He'd been surprised, therefore, when Angie had directed them to the hardware store and led them to the pool supplies aisle.

"Pool salt is still salt," she told them as she hefted a twenty kilo bag of it into a trolley. "We'll grab a few, just to be sure."

So they headed to the check out with four bags of pool salt and no one in town thinking them odd. After loading up the boot of Chip's car, they climbed in, with Angie insisting that she was fine to sit in the back. Dawson let his head roll back against the headrest and tried to keep his gritty eyes open. He was absolutely exhausted, both physically and emotionally, and he simply wanted this damn ghost issue to be over with. "I need coffee," he muttered, rubbing at his eyes and letting a yawn free.

"Fuck, yes," Angie agreed.

"We'll stop by the bakery after we've dropped these boxes back," Chip said. He was wearing a jacket which was zipped all the way closed and also had a scarf wound around his neck. Luckily the day was cold and overcast, with dark clouds gathering, as overnight his throat had bloomed with dark blue and purple bruises, making the scarf a necessity to avoid unwanted questions. It had been shocking to see, and his raspy voice was another reminder of the attack by Jacob. Dawson looked down at his hands, the very hands that had closed around Chip's throat, and shuddered, trying not to think about how close Chip had come to death. Tried not to think of the other horrible things that had occurred.

They'd decided to return the boxes to the Historical Society before they got caught up in a ghostly tantrum and were destroyed. Janet may have appeared to be a kindly older woman but Dawson had no doubt that she would rip them a new one if they allowed the donations of their family history to be damaged whilst in their care. That wasn't a risk either of them were willing to take.

The historical precinct was packed and they struggled to find a park. Chip circled the car park twice and then saw a family leaving the museum. He clicked on his indicator and waited for them to get into their car and leave, despite several cars pulling up behind him, their drivers annoyed at the wait.

They headed inside to the front counter and waited until one of the volunteers was free to help them.

"G'day," an older gent greeted them. His name badge identified him as Arthur. "Three tickets?"

"Oh, um, we're not here to actually visit the museum," Chip told him. "We were wondering if Janet was working today? She let us take home some boxes full of items our family had donated, and we've finished with them and wanted to return them."

Arthur smiled at them. "Oh! You'd be the Miller boys. Yes, she told me all about that. She's just running a tour at the moment, but if you're just dropping them back I can help you with that. Where are you parked?"

Chip explained where exactly they were parked and how many boxes there were.

"Alright. Let me grab a trolley and we can load them up. It won't take all of us though, so why don't you two have a look around the museum while you wait?" Arthur suggested to Dawson and Angie. "No charge. You'll find the old Roads Board building most fascinating—everything we have on display from the Millers is in there."

Dawson looked at Chip. "Do you mind?"

"'Course not, man," Chip said. "As Arthur said, we got this."

Dawson and Angie followed the signs and headed back outside, crossing the car park to the old stone building at the front of the precinct. The wooden door creaked as they opened it and an old-fashioned bell tied to the door jingled. To Dawson's surprise, it was quiet inside. "I guess people don't bother venturing out here much," he said as they looked around the dusty entrance hall.

"It's a bit weird, having all this stuff on display away from the actual museum," Angie remarked.

The building was quite small, with a room off either side of the hall. One had a large wooden table in the centre, and there were pictures and copies of meeting minutes from the previous century displayed on the walls. "Looks like this is all the Shire history," Dawson said, before they crossed back over the hall and into the other room.

This room was set up like an old-fashioned living room, and Dawson immediately recognised the photos on the walls as being his long-dead relatives. The space was cluttered, with bric-a-brac covering every available surface. A headless mannequin in one corner was dressed in the everyday garb of a woman living on a farm in the late 1800s, and there was a porcelain doll with a chipped face lying in a rattan pram next to an old sofa. Bookcases and buffets lined the walls, filled with books, photo frames, figurines, and crockery.

They browsed the space, making the occasional comment here and there, but essentially killing time until Chip was finished helping Arthur bring in the boxes. The small bell jingled again and was joined by the sounds of voices as the door opened and people entered the space. A moment later, a couple peered into the room, then upon seeing Dawson and Angie, crossed the entry hall to explore the other room first.

"Holy shit," Angie said with a gasp, drawing Dawson's attention back from the couple.

"What's up?" he asked, crossing to where she was standing in front of one of the heavy wooden buffets.

"That's one of Charlotte's diaries!" Angie whispered excitedly, pointing at a book on the other side of the glass.

Dawson peered through the slightly grimy glass and immediately identified the notebook as the same as the other diaries. "Do you think it's the one we're missing?" he asked.

Angie was searching for the display information, and when she found the wooden placard, she skimmed down the listed items. "Item 10: Diary belonging to Charlotte Miller, 1905." She looked up at him. "1905 is the year we need, isn't it?"

"It is," he said. "Do you think they'll let us take—what the hell are you doing?"

Angie was already pulling open the cabinet and reaching inside for the diary. Dawson's head swivelled as he looked for an alarm siren or a flashing light, anything to indicate that the museum staff were being alerted that someone was breaking into the display.

But there was nothing.

"Angie!" he hissed. "We can't just take it! What if we're caught?"

She tucked the diary into her bag and closed the buffet door. "Dawson, look at this place. None of these displays are locked, there's no cameras, and no alarms. There's a layer of dust an inch thick over everything so I doubt the staff even come in here often. No one is even going to notice the diary is missing. We can take it to read and then return it once we're done and no one will know any difference."

The idea of stealing something from the museum, even a piece of his own family's history, was abhorrent to Dawson. But before he could protest further, the couple from before wandered into the room, seemingly disinterested in the dry and dusty history of the Brockman Shire that was in the other room. Angie made for the door and he gave them a polite smile as he passed them by, following her out of the Roads Board building.

Chip and Arthur were standing out the front of the museum, chatting, and they made their way over to them. Dawson hoped his guilt wasn't obvious on his face.

"Please give Janet our thanks once again when you see her," Chip was saying as they reached them. "We won't take up any more of your time today. I can see how busy you are."

"Sunday's our busiest day," Arthur agreed. "You lot take care now. I hope you'll get a chance to come and have a proper look at the display soon."

"We certainly will," Chip promised, then ushered Dawson and Angie towards the car.

"So, wanna know what we found?" Angie asked as they were in and belting up.

"Stole," Dawson corrected her. "What we *stole*."

Chip looked at them with a raised brow. "Have you two been on a crime spree and didn't invite me?"

"Yes." Dawson replied even as Angie said, "No."

Dawson turned in his seat to glare at her. "We totally stole something from the museum, which in case you didn't know, is a *crime*."

"You're so dramatic," Angie said, rolling her eyes. "They let you take the other stuff no problem, so they would have let you take this. We just saved a bit of time by skipping the part where you told them."

"Are you gonna tell me what it is or are we going to play Twenty Questions?" Chip drawled.

"It's the missing diary!" Angie cried, pulling it out of her bag and holding it aloft in triumph.

"Put that away!" Dawson hissed, his eyes sweeping the car park, waiting for Arthur to realise what they'd done and come chasing after them.

"Oh, for the love of all that's fucking holy," Angie muttered, putting the diary in her lap. "Don't give up your day job for a life of crime. You suck at it."

"Well, *excuse me* for not being a criminal!"

"It's not exactly the crown jewels!"

"The value of the item isn't the point!"

"Are you two finished?" Chip asked, interrupting their bickering. "Because if you are, how about we head to the bakery for our much needed caffeine fix, and then get this mystery sorted once and for all?"

Both Dawson and Angie grumbled a little bit, but the lure of coffee—and more importantly, solving the mystery—was too strong, and they grudgingly agreed.

Angie perked up when they walked into the bakery and found that Lucy was working. It was much too busy for her to stop and chat with them but that didn't stop the two of them eye-fucking one another as the trio waited for their drinks.

"You really clicked with her, huh?" Chip asked Angie as they waited.

"Yeah. We've been texting a bit and have agreed to meet up again before I head back home. I took the whole week off work so I may as well make the most of the annual leave."

"Do you think it'll go anywhere or just be something casual?" Dawson asked.

Angie pursed her lips as she thought. "Honestly? I hope so. I know a drunken hook-up at a pub isn't the way most long-term romances start, but she's really sweet and we have a lot in common." She smirked. "Plus, our chemistry is off the charts. Obviously, it's too soon to say if it'll work or not yet, and it's not like we've had any conversations about long-term plans, but I'd like to try."

"Good for you," Dawson told her.

Their drinks were ready, and after a final wave to Lucy they headed back to the car.

"So, what's your story?" Angie asked them as they started for home. "How long have you guys been together?"

"Oh, um, about two days," Dawson admitted.

"Two days?" Angie shrieked at them, leaning as far forward as she could in her seatbelt to give them both an incredulous look. "Are you freaking kidding me? You've only been together for two days?"

Dawson ran a hand through his curls. "Uh, yeah. Well, I guess technically later today makes it three days."

"I thought you'd been a couple for years!" Angie told them, still shocked. "You always just had that spark in your videos."

"Well, I was kinda straight until very recently," Dawson admitted.

She went to speak but then shook her head. "Okay, we really don't have time to delve into this now, I know that, but as soon as this ghost situation is dealt with, you guys are telling me *everything*. Got it?"

Chip grinned over his shoulder at Angie even as he reached out and squeezed Dawson's knee. "Got it," he agreed.

CHAPTER 26

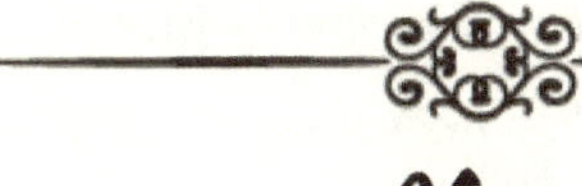

Chip

As soon as they got home, Chip and Dawson grabbed a bag of salt each and followed Angie's instructions to create a salt circle in each room, except for the loungeroom. The line had to be kept thick and unbroken, and they had to go over certain sections where the salt hadn't poured cleanly.

Angie also gave them a piece of black tourmaline each to wear around their necks, though she wasn't sure how effective it would be against a spirit as strong as Jacob. They all agreed that it was better to be safe than sorry and she once again apologised. "I really should have given them to you the moment I arrived."

"It's okay," Dawson assured her. "We all make mistakes."

Chip tried not to think of eyes glowing in the dimly lit bedroom and Jacob's expression as he hovered above him on the bed, his release covering Chip's body. Could that have been prevented? Would the tourmaline have stopped Jacob from possessing Dawson and hijacking such an intimate moment? Dawson's guilt over the situation was palpable and so Chip didn't want to voice just how much the whole situation had affected him. But it had. He had been on edge already due to Charlotte targeting Dawson, but now he was twitchy and jumping at every shadow, terrified that Jacob would appear at any moment.

Could that have all been avoided if Angie had simply given them the tourmaline at the start, instead of waiting?

He didn't blame her, not really, but there was a tiny part of him who resented her caution. He knew it was probably just misplaced anger—he couldn't take it out on Jacob and so he was directing it at her instead, but he couldn't help how he felt.

They gathered in the kitchen, stepping carefully over the salt that ringed the room, and sat around the table.

Dawson was clasping his takeaway coffee cup in both hands and he gestured with his chin to Angie. "Wanna do the honours?" he asked.

"Sure." She cracked open the diary.

"Sunday, 1st January, 1905. It is a new year, and yet I find no joy in committing to paper the recordings of my daily life as I once did. It has been nine days since my dearest Abigail was found in our dam in the orchard. Nine days since this world lost a little of its light. Nine days since my brother walked free of her murder. For murder it surely was. I do not know the details as yet, but I know it in my heart that Jacob was the cause of dear Abigail's death. I have not had much success in questioning Mrs Wiltshire about whether Abigail indeed discussed with her to go to Toodyay, but the responses to the few questions I have managed all indicate that she did. In fact, a comment made at the funeral by Mrs Wiltshire to her sister, after her sister lamented that she had not gotten the chance to fully know her niece, reiterates my theory. Abigail had found a

way to circumvent a marriage to Jacob. I knew Abigail almost as well as I know myself and therefore I am certain that with a plan in place and her mother in agreement, she would not have resorted to taking her own life.

I shall continue to search for the evidence I require in order to confront Jacob and bring about his downfall. He may be my brother but he is only my brother in blood, not in my heart. Jacob is dead to me. As dead as my beloved Abigail."

"She was a smart cookie, wasn't she?" Dawson remarked when Angie finished the entry.

"She fucking *knew* that bastard was to blame," Angie agreed.

"Sadly, that's probably why Jacob killed her," Chip said.

It was a sobering thought.

Angie read through the next few entries, but mostly it was all to do with the plans for William and Winifred's wedding. They had originally planned on a May wedding, but had decided to bring it forward as they felt that a happy celebration would be welcome after such a tragedy just before Christmas. Charlotte wrote that she had to pretend to be excited about being part of the wedding planning, but her heart simply wasn't in it. There was nothing else of note until the 10th of January.

"I have so far been unsuccessful in finding an opportunity to search through Jacob's belongings, as he locks all of his valuables inside a chest that he keeps beside his bed. Today, I was asked to fetch him for supper and William said that he was in their room. I was quiet as I walked to the end of the hall, quite deliberately, so I could perchance take a moment to spy on him unseen. Luck was on my side as when I got to the doorway of the room that he shares with

William, Jacob was sitting on his bed with his chest open beside him. I saw that he was holding something but it was small and I could not see what it was. As I leaned forward to see better, he noticed I was there, and he quickly hid the item away in the chest and got very angry towards me, shouting about respecting his privacy and accusing me of spying. I denied his accusation, however true it was, and insisted I was simply coming to find him to call him to supper. Mama took my side and accused Jacob of being dramatic, which led to him raising his voice at Mama and earning a cuff to his ear from Father. Supper was a very sullen affair afterward.

I simply must get into that chest of his to see what he is hiding. Where does he hide the key?"

Angie looked up at them. "This is some real Nancy Drew shit right here."

"Do you think Charlotte raised her concerns with the cops?" Dawson mused. "I can't see her staying silent when they ruled it a suicide if she had suspicions about Jacob."

"Maybe it was too soon and too shocking for her to contemplate at that stage?" Angie suggested.

"Or maybe they were all keeping quiet about her being pregnant so they wouldn't shame her in death?" Chip added sadly.

"I think the cops might have already known," Angie said. "I honestly think that's the reason *why* they thought it was a suicide. You know, since back then it was *so* scandalous to be pregnant out of wedlock."

"Yeah, probably," Chip conceded. "It's still all so fucked though."

"On that, we can agree," she said, and then skimmed through the pages to find the next relevant entry. There weren't many left—they were all aware that Charlotte had died on the 16th.

"Friday, 13th January. Today, disaster struck. I had thought I was being so clever, waiting for Jacob to leave to help Father with the bore. I snuck into his room and searched through his belongings for the key to his chest. Halfway through, Jacob returned and caught me! He was most furious and raised a hand to me, slapping me across the face. It was at this moment that William came in and when he saw what Jacob had done, he took him outside and gave him a thrashing. Jacob was shouting the entire time, saying that I deserved it and more but William did not listen. I managed to sneak away but Jacob has been keeping a close watch of me every moment since and I fear he has deduced that I suspect him of this heinous crime."

"I usually don't condone any sort of violence," Dawson said. "But I'm kinda glad William beat the crap out of Jacob."

"Same," Chip and Angie agreed in unison.

They were silent for a moment, a quiet sense of sad anticipation in the air. Would the last of the diary entries finally give them the answers they sought? Charlotte had seemed insistent that the diary was important, but was it the final answer or simply part of it?

Angie didn't keep them waiting.

"Saturday, 14th January. Mama let slip today that Jacob will be once again meeting with Father O'Reilly tomorrow, but unlike the previous occasions, it will be both before and after mass. His violent tendencies appear to be escalating

and Mama said that if he cannot learn to control his temper, they may be forced to send him away for help beyond what Father O'Reilly can provide.

Knowing he will be away from the house for that length of time, today I began to complain of feeling unwell, and I heated a wet cloth on the stove so I could press it to my cheeks to mimic the flush of a fever. I am confident that tomorrow I will be able to beg off going to mass and remain behind, which will give me the time I need to search through Jacob's chest. I have secreted away from Father's workshop a pair of heavy bolt cutters, and although the broken lock will be proof of my actions, I feel that the proof I shall surely find within will be shocking enough to absolve me of my own guilt."

They were all on tenterhooks and no one spoke as Angie immediately turned to the final diary entry that Charlotte had written in her short life.

"Sunday, 15th January. It is only midday and yet I write this now for I fear I shall not get the chance tonight.

My plan worked. I feigned a convincing malaise and was excused from mass to remain at home and rest. It was most obvious that Jacob was suspicious, but his hesitation to leave was brushed off by my parents as he had counsel with Father O'Reilly to attend.

As soon as the buggy disappeared from view of the house, I hurried to Jacob's room. The bolt cutters made short work of the lock and I admit that I did hesitate on the precipice of discovery. Would the shards of the broken lock repair the shards of my broken heart? Or would they shatter it beyond repair? But I knew I must take action, for my dearest Abigail, and for myself. Jacob must be stopped, and as no one else seems willing to do so, the responsibility has fallen to me.

Within the chest, I found hidden away a silver locket, oval and engraved with a heart, and I recognised it immediately as being the one that Abigail's parents gifted her on her sixteenth birthday. She was rarely without it and Mrs Wiltshire has been most upset that she has been unable to locate it. I also found a letter, written in Abigail's hand, addressed to me. It was a farewell, as her mother had agreed to her plan to go to her aunt in Toodyay and she was to leave immediately. From what I can tell, she must have snuck out from the house before the sun had even risen so she could deliver me the letter before they left for their journey. Between the letter and the locket, I believe the evidence will suffice to bring an investigation upon my brother and his involvement in Abigail's death.

I had planned to bring this to Father's immediate attention upon their arrival home, but alas, fate does not smile upon me today. Our immediate neighbour, Mr Jessop, has just been to bring me word that Mama had taken a turn for the worse at mass and Father and William are riding to Moora to seek urgent medical care for her, after Dr Harrison informed them that the means and knowledge to help Mama were beyond him. He said that Jacob would be home shortly from the church and we are welcome to sup with him and Mrs Jessop tonight. I *graciously accepted his invitation, as I do not wish to be alone with Jacob. In fact, the mere thought of it terrifies me. I do not know if Jacob will immediately notice the broken lock on his chest, or if I shall be safe until our parents and William return. I can only do my best and pray that I am able to distract him until it is safe to reveal my accusations."*

Angie softly closed the diary. "That's it. That was Charlotte's final entry."

They sat in silence for a long moment, absorbing the information they now had. Chip realised that he had subconsciously hoped the missing diary entries would tie everything up in a neat little bow, and that simply reading them and acknowledging what had happened to Charlotte would be enough to help her move on. Of course, that wasn't the case. It was never going to be. She didn't get a chance to nip home and write a final entry before she bled out after being decapitated. The final piece of the puzzle was still missing.

"So what do we do now?" Chip asked, feeling at a loss.

"I don't know," Angie admitted, chewing on a hangnail.

"I think I do," Dawson said, and Chip looked over to see that he was staring out the kitchen door and across the hall.

Twisting in his seat, he saw Charlotte standing in the doorway of the loungeroom, with her head held high and hope in her eyes.

CHAPTER 27

Dawson

"We need to speak to Charlotte," Dawson said, sounding as confident as he felt. He wasn't sure why he suddenly felt so sure, but he just *knew* that Charlotte would lead them to the answer.

"But she can't speak to us," Chip protested.

Dawson was already rising from the table. "I just have a feeling that she's not going to have to." He knew he was being vague and confusing but he simply couldn't shake the certainty that now that they'd come this far, Charlotte could somehow share the rest of the story.

He was relieved when Chip and Angie got up and followed him.

"What happened to you, Charlotte?" Dawson asked as they came to a stop in the hallway.

Charlotte didn't speak, but she raised her hand and pointed towards the front door.

"You want to show us?" he asked her.

She nodded and gestured again to the door but she didn't move.

It was the salt. Without even thinking, Dawson stepped forward and broke the salt line that crossed the doorway to the loungeroom, isolating it from the rest of the house. Angie made a small sound of protest but it was too late—Charlotte was moving from the loungeroom, towards the front door. Dawson beat her to it and scuffed the salt line there as well, then he opened the door and politely gestured her through.

Charlotte smiled at him and her face lit up. It was a far cry from the terrifying mask her decapitated head had assumed when it had rolled from the linen cupboard all that time ago.

They followed Charlotte outside and away from the house. She was still easy enough to see as the sky was even darker now with storm clouds, but she was the only one not affected by the chill wind that was whipping around them. The odd fat raindrop fell onto their faces and the sky felt heavy and full, threatening to open at any moment.

"I think we're going to get wet," Chip said, echoing Dawson's thoughts.

It was soon clear that Charlotte was leading them to the sole remaining orchard on the property. The dam there was the very one Abigail had drowned in. It was surprising—as soon as they'd gone outside, he'd fully expected that she would lead them to the paddock where she had died herself. They didn't know exactly where that was though. Was it still part of their property? Or did it now belong to a neighbour? Or perhaps that wasn't the place that was most important to Charlotte and it was actually the location of Abigail's death that mattered the most to her?

Dawson supposed they'd find out soon enough.

From the distance came the rumbling of thunder and the drops of rain became heavier. Dawson flipped up the hood on his hoodie and noticed the others were doing the same. By the time they had entered the old orchard, it was raining in earnest as the storm grew closer.

Charlotte didn't look back, just led them steadily along the alley between the rows of ancient orange trees. The trees had long ago stopped flowering regularly but the rain brought out the smell of citrus in their leaves, and if it wasn't for the current circumstances, it would have been pleasant.

The old trees gave way and then the dam was in view, but Charlotte didn't stop. Maybe Dawson had it wrong after all? She skirted around the side and they followed, slipping and skidding on the slick clay. Dawson had explored as far as the dam but he hadn't been beyond it. "What's past here?" he murmured to Chip.

"Nothing really, just bush," Chip replied, his eyes darting around to take in as much of their surroundings as he could.

They didn't go much further, only about twenty metres into the bush. It wasn't too thick, mostly a canopy of jarrah and marri trees with a few grass trees dotted about and other smaller shrubs. Dawson was glad they were a little too far north for parrot bush to be common as he had never once traversed through parrot bush terrain without leaving behind most of his skin.

Back towards the house a kookaburra sang out and the distant sound made Dawson realise just how quiet it was nearby. Normally, there would be numerous birds all trilling and adding their songs to the chorus, from the warbling cry of a magpie to the two-toned call of the twenty-eights, along with the screeches of the carnabys and pink and greys. Over the sound of the rain, Dawson could hear none of the usual wildlife. It was eerie and they came to a stop next to the weeping trunk of a marri tree, the gum making the tree look like it was bleeding.

"This was once a cleared paddock."

They all jolted at the new voice. It was Charlotte.

"How are you able to speak?" Angie asked her.

Charlotte gave her a wan smile. The rain did not seem to touch her and her skin and clothes were dry, even as the three of them were being steadily soaked to the bone. She may have looked solid and real, but she wasn't really here. "In the house . . . the energy there, it was enough for me to appear but not speak. I'm not entirely sure, but I believe my brother was exerting some influence over me, preventing me from conversing with you. He comes and goes, and is not always here like me. There was once, some time ago, a woman that I could speak to as Jacob was gone then, but I do not think she believed I was real." Her brow furrowed. "Time is . . . different here. I do not know how long ago this was."

"What was her name?" Dawson asked.

"Elizabeth," Charlotte told them.

"That was my grandmother," he explained.

"She was kind," Charlotte said. "She always spoke to me but it was more in a manner that made me think she was talking to herself."

Dawson felt a pang of sadness for his grandmother. He knew she had suffered from mental health issues all her life, and he wondered how much of that was actually because she was attuned to the spirit world and could see things that others couldn't, and how much was a legitimate disorder.

"Can you tell us what happened the day you died?" Chip asked her, and Dawson winced a little at how blunt the question sounded. Chip must have heard the harshness himself as he blanched and gave Charlotte an apologetic smile. "Sorry. It's just, we read the rest of your diary and we know that you'd found Abigail's locket and the letter she wrote to you amongst Jacob's things. Will you tell us what happened?"

Her eyes grew distant but she nodded. "I knew that things would go badly," she whispered. "As soon as Mr Jessop told me that my parents and William had gone to Moora and left me alone with Jacob, I just *knew* I would likely suffer the same fate as Abigail. I managed to avoid being alone with him for the afternoon and evening after he returned from meeting with Father O'Reilly. I went immediately to our neighbour's so I could help Mrs Jessop with making supper. Jacob came over as the sun was setting and he put on such a show." Her jaw tightened at the memory. "He was friendly and charming and was so nice to me, and they were completely won over by him. He'd always been able to fool most people."

"But not always," Dawson said quietly. "Your family saw through it, and so did Abigail."

Charlotte nodded. "I suppose it was too much of a chore to keep that mask in place constantly. When he let his walls down, we saw the real him." She swallowed hard, and Dawson wondered if she was even aware that she retained the same mannerisms in death as she'd had in life. He shivered, but he wasn't sure if it was from the cold or simply from the situation. "The real Jacob was a cruel, selfish man, yet to the majority of the world he was a good man, perhaps a little lost, but good nonetheless." She shrugged. "Apologies, I digress. After supper was done, Mr Jessop walked us home and as he lingered to speak to Jacob, I took the opportunity to escape to my room. I barricaded myself inside by pushing my dresser in front of the door, fearful that if he was able to gain access during the night, I surely would not wake come dawn."

"I bet that went down well," Angie muttered, only just audible over the pouring rain.

"If you mean that Jacob was angry, then yes, he was. I kept watch out of the window and saw Mr Jessop returning to his farm, and not five minutes later Jacob was pounding on the door, demanding entry. He was shouting at me, saying that he knew I had gone into his room and accessed his chest. I refused to come out, no matter what obscenities he shouted at me, and he kept up his vigil of my bedroom door the entire night."

"He tried to get in the *entire* night?" Chip asked, shocked.

"Indeed," she confirmed. "It was a sleepless night for us both, but Jacob had reasoned that as I did not have access to food or water, I would surely have to emerge at some point. The terminable night finally turned into the light of day and still I remained in my room. Once the sun had risen fully, I could no longer hear Jacob on the other side of my door but I did not wish to risk leaving in case he was still there, waiting in ambush. Alas, I was so focused on listening for him inside the house that I did not keep watch upon the window."

Angie gasped, completely caught up in the story. "Oh no!"

"He crept around the house and suddenly he struck the window with a large rock, shattering the glass. He could not immediately enter through the window as there were sharp shards still in the pane, and he had to smash them away lest he injure himself. I do not know where my strength came from but I was able to shove the dresser away from the door much faster than I had positioned it there, and as Jacob was climbing in through the window, I was running out my bedroom door. He chased me through the house and I ran out the rear door and towards the outbuildings. I managed to escape him for some time, hiding amongst the piles of chopped firewood, and he continued on, towards the orchard."

Dawson's heart broke for Charlotte as she told her tale. It appeared that she had come so close to escape, but of course, the story had already been written and the final chapter had come to be already, and nothing they could say or do would rewrite her ending. All they could do was relive it with her and then help her move on.

"Once I was sure that Jacob was gone, I moved as quietly as I could to the stable. My intent was to take a horse and ride as hard for town as I could. I suspected Jacob would expect me to head for the Jessop's farm and I did not wish to place them in danger if they rendered me aid. I had the horse almost saddled when Jacob burst into the stables. I mounted quickly but the horse was skittish as Jacob was blocking the entrance and he was showing no fear of the beast. It reared, almost throwing me, and I came half off the saddle. As I scrambled to right myself, Jacob mounted another horse, not bothering to saddle up, and before I even knew what was happening, he was chasing me out of the stables and towards the orchard."

"Oh," Dawson said quietly, as understanding dawned on him. "This here was once the paddock where the sheep were."

Charlotte nodded, and swiped away a tear. Dawson watched as the ghostly drop merged with the rain as it fell from her face. "Yes. I fled through the orchard and around the dam, but Jacob did not relent. My horse was terrified as he drove his own animal at its flanks, and when it saw the fence it did not slow, it simply jumped over the obstacle." Tears were now streaming down her face. "I was a good rider but not that good. As the horse hit the ground on the other side of the fence, I slipped, and my foot caught in the stirrup. I was hanging half upside down, unable to wrench myself free. Father and William had trained the horses extensively, and so my mount came to a halt. I was struggling to right myself when Jacob appeared at my side." She sniffed. "I was so stupid. Some small part of me, deep inside, clutched at the hope that he would help me." She gave a bitter laugh. "But of course he didn't. No, he unwound the lead rope from the saddle and he wound it around my throat. I tried to fight him but I was tangled and turned around and I did not have the strength."

They all stared at her, and Dawson almost wanted to tell her to stop, that he didn't want to hear the rest. *Couldn't* hear the rest. But Charlotte had been the one to experience it firsthand and so the least they could do was bear witness as she recounted her story.

"Jacob looked me right in the eye," Charlotte continued. "He smiled at me and it was such a cruel smile. He said, *'Give my regards to Abigail,'* and then he slapped my horse's rump and it started running. I remember feeling the rope tighten as we crossed the paddock and that is the last thing I remember." She paused, and they respectfully remained silent. "It is odd. I do not remember dying and I should not *know* the exact manner of my death, yet I do. That gruesome knowledge appears to be engraved upon my very soul." She looked down at the ground. "My blood soaked into the earth beneath our very feet."

"Oh, Charlotte," Chip whispered. "I'm so sorry."

She gave him a tremulous smile. "Thank you. I do not know what came next, only that the truth of Jacob's involvement was never revealed. It has prevented me from moving on, tying me to this place, unable to rest."

"You're right," Angie said. "He convinced everyone that you were both feeding the sheep when your horse spooked. He told everyone he tried to save you, but it was too late."

"He was lauded as a hero," Dawson added bitterly. "He murdered you and yet they all praised him for trying to save you."

"Now, now," came the last voice that Dawson ever wanted to hear again. "Charlotte fell from her horse," Jacob drawled, stepping out from behind a tree, looking as solid as Charlotte did. "It was surely not *my* fault that she did not have the skills to remain seated in her saddle." His whole face transformed as he laughed, sounding rather maniacal. "It was the most glorious sight!" he cried. "Her hot blood rained down before her head came free and her life drained away. I wanted to roll in the puddle like a dog and cover myself in the scent of her blood, but I was too cautious." His eyes grew wild. "But perhaps once I have sent you all beyond the veil, I shall indulge myself, and it shall be *your* blood that I bathe in."

CHAPTER 28

Chip

They didn't have time to react before Jacob was upon them. Moving faster than they could see, he lunged at Angie and flung her backward. She hit a nearby tree with a sickening *crack* and she fell to the ground, unmoving. Dawson cried out as Jacob turned to him next, knocking his legs from under him and straddling him.

"Well, well, my little doppelgänger—shall we have some fun once again?"

Chip darted forward, yelling at Jacob, but he flung his hand out, sending Chip reeling backwards by an invisible force. He leaned down over Dawson, eyes alight with glee, and then he turned to mist and sank downwards.

And then stopped.

The mist solidified back into Jacob and his face was a mask of fury. "What is this?" he snarled.

"They are protected," Charlotte told him smugly, striding forwards.

"Your pathetic protections will not keep me out," Jacob threatened.

"They're not *mine*," Charlotte said. "Can you not feel the power of the gemstone?"

Jacob reached down and tried to swipe at the front of Dawson's hoodie but his fingers couldn't quite seem to grasp the fabric. Chip realised that he owed Angie an apology as the tourmaline appeared to be making it impossible for Jacob to possess Dawson. It may not have saved him before as she'd not given it to them then, but she had more than made up for that now.

"Leave them alone!" Charlotte snapped, and reached for Jacob.

Jacob was off Dawson in a second and then he was reaching for Charlotte. No, he was reaching *into* her. His hand sank through her chest, despite how solid she appeared at present, and her eyes went wide and her mouth opened in a silent scream. Then Jacob tensed his arm and *twisted*, and then blood was bubbling out of Charlotte's mouth as she began to convulse.

Chip had no idea if it was even possible for Jacob to kill Charlotte again, or if whatever he was doing would simply incapacitate her ghost, but right now that wasn't his priority. He hurried over to Dawson and dragged him to his feet and away from the two ghosts. "Let me grab Angie and let's get the fuck out of here," he told him.

Dawson looked pale but otherwise unharmed and he gave a shaky nod.

Chip turned towards Angie and froze as he saw Jacob rip his hand from Charlotte's chest, holding what appeared to be her heart in his hand. How the fuck did a ghost even have a heart? How was this possible?

Jacob gave him no time to ponder this before he was on Chip, knocking into him so he fell painfully to the ground, all the air in his lungs leaving him at once. Jacob leaned over him, triumph in his eyes. "Your precious gem may keep you safe from *me* but can it keep you safe from nature?"

Chip had no idea what he was talking about, and he had no chance to even ponder it before Jacob was grasping one of his ankles and taking off at inhuman speed. Chip was dragged over the sodden ground, rocks and sticks tearing at his clothes and skin. He scrabbled for purchase, trying to find a hold on anything he could use to stop Jacob, but it was no use. Jacob had a supernatural strength to him, even if he was simply a ghost, and no matter how much Chip struggled and fought, he couldn't gain any traction against him.

The leaves and grass turned to slick clay as they neared the dam and Chip fought even harder, using all of his strength to avoid what he knew was coming. The tourmaline kept him safe from being possessed by Jacob but it wouldn't stop him from drowning.

Lightning lit up the sky overhead, and a mighty boom of thunder followed almost immediately afterward as the storm raged above them. The rain was coming down heavier now, obscuring Chip's view. He couldn't see Dawson, he couldn't see the trees, only the rain streaming down from above. He cried out, wishing he could see Dawson just once more before the end. He'd not gotten the chance to really tell him how much he loved him, how happy Dawson had made him. He wanted just one moment more.

There were no more moments.

Chip felt the angle of the ground shift and he was accelerating as he moved downwards, both being pulled by Jacob and slipping on the clay banks of the dam at the same time. He was already chilled from the rain and the storm but nothing prepared him for the icy water as he was plunged into the dam.

His entire body seemed to lock up as he was entirely submerged, but the iron-like grip Jacob had on his ankle did not abate. He was still being pulled along in his wake, deeper and deeper into the dam. The murky light from above grew dimmer and dimmer even as his chest grew tighter and tighter. He fought the urge to gasp in a breath, knowing he would inhale nothing but death.

Fighting to find a reserve of strength, Chip kicked out, trying to dislodge Jacob. He twisted and turned but his struggles grew weaker and weaker. His lungs burned, burned, burned, and he needed air. He needed to breathe. His panic grew and he wondered why everyone always said that drowning was peaceful. This wasn't peaceful. This was terrifying. He needed to get out, to kick towards the surface, to break free of this watery grave and to gulp down lungfuls of sweet, sweet oxygen. Instead, he was pulled even further under the chilly water.

He couldn't do it anymore. His body was going to override his brain and he was going to suck in a breath. It didn't matter that he *knew* it would kill him. He wasn't going to be given a choice. Spots danced before his eyes and he stilled, all fight seeping from him. This was it. This was the end.

I love you, Dawson.

The ghostly grip around his ankle was suddenly gone but it didn't matter. It was too late.

I love you, Dawson.

Chip's hip bumped against something and he dimly realised that it was the bottom of the dam. His arm was aching—a dull, throbbing pain from where his skin had been dragged over a sharp rock. He was likely still bleeding, but what did it matter? He was going to drown well before he bled to death.

I love you, Dawson.

Goodbye.

He reached out, trying to find the bottom, one last desperate attempt to push himself towards the surface. His fingers brushed against something hard in the mud and closed around the object reflexively. His eyes were growing heavy and they began to close.

A face suddenly appeared before him but it wasn't Jacob and it wasn't Charlotte. It was a teenage girl and he immediately knew it was Abigail. She smiled at him and then she was grasping him around the waist and they were shooting up through the water, so fast that if he'd had oxygen to spare, Chip would have been dizzy.

They breached the surface of the water and Chip gasped in a breath, half choking on the rain and dam water. The pressure around his waist was gone and so was Abigail. He didn't know where she'd gone, and he couldn't find the energy to spare a thought for the mystery as he could hardly tread water to stay afloat. If he didn't make it to the edge and climb out, he would drown again, and he doubted he'd be rescued a second time.

"Chip!"

Through the pouring rain, Chip could make out Dawson standing on the edge of the dam and he began slowly swimming in that direction. He didn't have the breath to spare to call out, he just hoped that Dawson would see him. He made slow progress, and if it wasn't for Dawson finally spotting him and calling out encouragement, he may have given up entirely. His whole body ached, but nothing more so than his lungs and with each laboured stroke, his chest burned.

Finally, Chip got his feet beneath him and he staggered towards the edge. He craned his neck as he looked at the steep slope of the dam wall and he almost let out a sob. He was so tired he didn't know how he was going to climb out. Dawson was waiting for him though, calling out to him. "Just a little further! I can almost reach you."

He had to try. They couldn't risk Dawson coming down to him, otherwise they might both get stuck in the water, so he pushed up, digging his hands into the soft clay to find some sort of grip and began to climb, one agonising inch at a time.

Only to be yanked back down by a hand wrapping around his ankle again.

"No!" he cried as he slid back down, splashing into the water that he'd just escaped.

"Chip!" Dawson screamed.

Chip kicked out with all his might and to his surprise, he made contact. He heard Jacob grunt and the grip on his ankle loosened. He didn't hesitate, just threw himself forward and scrambled away.

"I'm not done with you!" Jacob shouted, and he lunged forward and grabbed Chip around the waist.

"I don't think so," said a female voice.

Chip twisted his head around and saw Abigail standing waist deep in the water. There was a flicker of light and then Charlotte was beside her. She was staring at her friend with longing in her eyes.

"Charlotte?" Abigail whispered, reaching for her as if she didn't think she were really there.

"I've been unable to reach you," Charlotte told her. "But I'm here now." She looked at her brother with disdain in her eyes. "Let's finish this."

Abigail smiled and reached out her hand, which Charlotte took. "Yes, let's." She turned back to Jacob and her expression was deadly, matching her voice. "You've come into my territory, Jacob. Blood and vengeance have nourished me and I shall have my revenge."

"You caused so much pain and misery," Charlotte told him. "This ends now, brother. No more."

"You cannot stop me!" Jacob said, letting go of Chip to face the larger threat.

"I believe you'll actually find that we can," Abigail said. She looked at Chip. "I believe you have something of mine," she said, gesturing at his hand. "If I may have it back?"

Chip looked down dumbly at his fist and found that it was still clenched around the item he'd brought back with him from the bottom of the dam. He saw then that it was a silver chain with a locket still attached. Jacob must have thrown it into the dam to hide the evidence all those years ago. With one last reserve of energy, he tossed it towards Abigail, who deftly caught it.

And then she and Charlotte stepped apart and converged on Jacob.

"Chip!" Dawson cried, sounding much closer than before. Chip turned back around and saw a hand hovering just in front of his face. Dawson was on his stomach, reaching for him, and Angie was on the edge of the dam, holding on to his feet. "Come on, we've got you," Dawson said.

Chip reached out and locked his hand around Dawson's wrist, and between Dawson and Angie pulling and Chip clawing at the clay, they managed to get him up, out of the water and over the lip of the dam.

The three of them collapsed into a heap, and Chip breathed deeply, the rain on his face feeling fresh and warm compared to the water of the dam. He turned to look down the steep slope and saw that Abigail and Charlotte had reached Jacob. He screamed and lunged at them, but Charlotte twisted away and then spun back, managing to pin his arms to his side. Abigail slung the necklace around his neck, and it immediately seemed to tighten, looping around Jacob's throat like a noose. Then both Charlotte and Abigail grasped Jacob's upper arms and they plunged down into the water, disappearing from sight.

"Is that it?" Dawson asked, when the final ripples from their submersion had calmed. "Is it over?"

"Fuck, I hope so," Chip said. His arm was stinging and he reached over to rub at the spot just below his elbow. His fingers came away slick with blood. "Huh."

"What is it?" Dawson asked, concerned.

"I'm still bleeding." Oh. "Um, so I think I know what Abigail meant by the 'blood and vengeance' bit ," he said. "I think that's what gave her that boost of power."

"You know what?" Dawson said. "I'm not even surprised that blood gives ghosts power boosts. Nothing fucking surprises me anymore." He sighed. "Can we go home now?"

"That sounds so good," Chip agreed. "Let's do that."

"Dibs on the first shower," Angie called.

"Urgh, no fair," Chip complained but he secretly didn't mind. He was relieved to see Angie up and about, since she'd gone down hard.

They climbed painfully to their feet and used each other as props as they started to slowly make their way back towards the house. They couldn't help but check behind them, wary that Jacob would reappear at any moment. They'd made it around the dam and in amongst the orchard when two figures appeared in front of them.

Charlotte and Abigail.

"Is he gone?" Dawson asked them.

Charlotte nodded. "My brother has been banished. He'll no longer be able to cause anyone pain, ever again."

"And you?" he asked. "Can you rest now?"

Charlotte turned to Abigail and they shared a smile. She reached out a hand and Abigail took it in hers. "I hope so."

"You're not sure?" Chip asked.

Charlotte sighed. "I know it is silly, but I selfishly wish that the real circumstances of my death were known. Everyone believed Jacob to be a hero and I'm not sure if I will ever truly rest with that untruth in the history books."

"So if the truth was revealed, you could be at peace?" Dawson asked.

"Yes," she said simply.

"Well, that's an easy fix," he said, and he pulled out his phone from his back pocket. It was scratched and there was a crack in the screen but it was intact. "Within minutes, hundreds of thousands of people will know the truth and you can finally rest." He opened the Vewz app and hit *Go Live.* "Hey everyone," he said to the camera. "Sorry I've not been online much the past few days, but I'm going to make it up to you. I have got the craziest story to tell you all about my great-great-*great*-aunt, Charlotte Miller."

EPILOGUE

Six months later

Chip

The sun was bright and hot but Chip turned his cap around so it faced backwards. He'd probably have to listen to a lecture from Dawson later about sun safety, but right now he wanted his vision completely unobscured. It was the start of the twentieth over and the visiting team needed eight runs to win, but the Brockman Bobtails only needed one wicket to take the match and the season.

Chip hadn't expected them to make the final of the T20 cup but the team had worked hard, played harder, and had also gotten lucky a time or two. They'd finished at the top of the table so they had the pleasure of hosting the final, and it appeared like the entire town had turned up to watch. Angie was up for the weekend and was sitting with Lucy on a picnic rug under the trees opposite the pavilion. Janet and the team had closed the museum early so they could watch the game. Chip had also caught sight of Ellen, and a few of the other weekday staff from the bakery who were sitting with Joyce—the stern-faced, judgmental cashier from IGA—and others from town that they'd gotten to know over the past several months. Then there were the numerous fans of Dawson's who had made the trip out to cheer him on once word got out on Vewz that their team made the final.

Dawson was preparing to bowl the final over, and he and Blake were standing at his mark, talking. Blake nodded and then called out to their team, adjusting the field. They'd gone for an in-out field, since they needed to cover boundaries but also cut off as many singles as possible. Eight runs off one over only needed a couple of balls to go for two runs and the rest could be singles, and it would be game over. Blake clapped Dawson on the shoulder and hurried back to his position at cover. Chip was in the slips, as Dawson had a bit of an off-swing and maybe they'd get lucky with a nick.

The crowd began to clap and cheer, stamping their feet and building into a frenzy as Dawson commenced his run up. Chip wondered if this was what it felt like for the professional players who could easily fill Optus Stadium with fifty thousand fans. The energy was making his skin buzz in the very best of ways.

Dawson's first ball was a yorker and it went through to the keeper, and the crowd cheered the dot ball. The second ball was struck well by the batter but was fielded by Noah at gully, and they kept it to a single. By the time Dawson was running up to deliver his third ball of the over, the crowd were losing their minds, and Chip grinned. Dawson had earned some "real-life" fans here in Brockman, who were competing with his online fans for who could be the loudest.

There was the distinct sound of the cherry hitting wood and Chip moved instinctively as he tracked the ball. He threw himself to the left, the ball smacking into his hand, and he hit the ground and rolled, the catch secure. He rolled to his knees and held the ball aloft in triumph as his teammates ran towards him, cheering. Their keeper, Jake, reached him first and pulled him into a rough hug, thumping him on the back, and then Raj was there, jumping half on top of him and screaming in excitement. Chip was grinning but he hardly registered his other teammates as it was then that Dawson collided with him, knocking him back a step.

Chip's arms circled Dawson and held him close even as they jumped up and down to celebrate.

"Fucking oath, boys!" Blake yelled as he joined them, hugging them both. Then their other teammates got in on the hug, and Chip found himself at the centre of it, crushed against Dawson and grinning madly.

"Nice catch," Dawson whispered against Chip's ear, which sent a wave of goosebumps down his back.

He resisted the urge to kiss him then and there. They'd not exactly made a secret of the fact they were together, but they certainly didn't flaunt it. It hadn't just been Angie and Ellen from the bakery who had taken a blasé attitude towards them being a couple. It had been refreshing, though Chip had honestly expected more disgust and judgement—not that they *hadn't* been on the receiving end of that. There had been a handful of people who had made remarks or verbally abused them, but surprisingly, the vast majority of people had been accepting. Even their parents.

When they'd decided they could no longer hide their relationship from them, they'd sat Carolyn and Harry down one night when they were up for a visit and explained the situation. They'd expected resistance, but instead, Harry had opened his wallet and handed over fifty bucks to Carolyn. "You boys couldn't have waited another year?" he grumbled. "That was my lotto money for the month."

"Suck shit," Carolyn sang happily as she pocketed the note. "We are stopping at Spotlight on the way home and I'm buying some yarn."

"You already *have* yarn at home!"

"But not the latest colours that are coming out for autumn," she said. "Besides, there's a sale."

Harry rolled his eyes. "There's *always* a sale."

Neither Chip nor Dawson had known what to say. Their parents were always razzing one another so it wasn't like their behaviour was out of the ordinary, but to discover that they'd not only apparently *known* but had placed *bets* on when they'd get together was hard to comprehend.

"You're not mad?" Dawson asked.

"Sweetie," Carolyn said, reaching over and taking his hand. "Harry, Nat, and I used to joke all the time that we wouldn't be surprised if you two got together when you were older. You were inseparable from the moment you met and you always seemed closer than best friends."

"Really?" Chip asked. "I mean, I knew Mum knew how I felt, but I didn't realise you guys did."

Dawson looked over at Chip in shock. "Wait—your *mum* knew? But she died when you were seven!"

He smiled sadly. "I told her the week before she died that I was going to marry you when I grew up."

Dawson's eyes watered and he stood so he could lean over the table and hug him. "You've really liked me since then? All this time?"

"Daw, I've *loved* you all this time."

"Oh, fuck, I'm gonna cry," Carolyn said, sniffing and pulling out a tissue from her pocket. "You boys are just too precious."

Chip had already told Dawson that he loved him by then so it wasn't like it was the first time, but it *was* the first time he'd told him in front of other people. Somehow it had made it a little more real. The fact their parents were so accepting? That just made it all the sweeter.

So no, they didn't hide their relationship, but they also didn't make a habit of indulging in public displays of affection either. The haters in town had simmered down but it wouldn't take much to rile them up again, and that was trouble neither of them were interested in. They'd grown to love living in Brockman and wanted to stay for years to come, so they would do what was needed to keep the peace.

The team finally broke apart and moved amongst the other team to shake hands and to thank them. They were from a neighbouring town and were on friendly terms with the team, and as Chip was shaking their keeper's hand, saying, "Cheers, mate. GG." Blake was already inviting them all to the club for drinks, and Ken was lamenting with one of their bowlers about the aches and pains gentlemen of a certain age felt after a game.

Angie and Lucy shouted and cheered as they ran onto the field to congratulate them, Janet gave them both a motherly hug, and Chip felt the bone deep happiness inside, of finally being home.

Dawson

It was late by the time they got home, having joined the team at the club for drinks. Chip had told the boys they'd only stay for one drink, always conscious of Dawson's limits for socialising, but Dawson had found that his social anxiety wasn't too bad and so one drink had turned into four. It was only when the adrenaline of the win was wearing off that he started to feel overwhelmed, and they bid their friends goodbye and headed towards home.

The closer they got to home, the more Dawson realised he was actually feeling horny for once. His anti-anxiety medication meant that he didn't feel up for sex often and they were only intimate once every week or two. It had taken them a while to even get to that point. Chip had struggled in the beginning, after what Jacob had done, and they'd both had some therapy sessions with a psychologist in Perth who did consults over Zoom, individually and as a couple. It had taken some time, and they'd not shared *everything* with her—they'd not mentioned that Jacob was a ghost who had possessed Dawson *or* that they were stepbrothers. Withholding that information may have unintentionally made her job harder, but neither had felt comfortable sharing the entire story, and it was either share half the story, or skip the therapy altogether. They'd *both* needed to work through the ramifications of the assault and so they'd gone with the lesser of two evils.

Therapy had helped them heal emotionally, but the physical side effects of Dawson's medication weren't going to change anytime soon. They still cuddled, and he loved helping Chip get off, but he rarely reached completion himself. When the urge struck, and he *knew* that his body was going to be on board, like now, he made the most of it. As soon as they were through the door, Dawson turned and shoved Chip against the wall, stepping up close.

Chip grinned and brushed their noses together. "Hi there," he murmured.

"Hello," Dawson said in a breathy voice and then captured his lips in a soft kiss.

"I'm all sweaty," Chip muttered. "Wanna wait till we've showered?"

Dawson shook his head. "Nope. Don't wanna wait. Just want you." He stepped back and took Chip's hand and then led him down the hall to their bedroom.

They'd moved all of Dawson's gear into Chip's bedroom the day after Angie had left, neither of them seeing much point in them having separate rooms. Chip had been the one to suggest turning the spare bedroom into a recording studio of sorts, so Dawson would have a place where he could make quality recordings of his songs and edit the videos to post to his socials. His music was starting to gain more traction online and his following had grown even more. Last week, an exec from one of the biggest recording studios in the country had started following his page, which had been enough to make him jump up and down and scream for a minute or two. It made the hard work of soundproofing a room in their historic little cottage worth it.

Chip backed him towards the bed, and they quickly stripped off their clothes, dropping them on the floor to deal with later. "How do you want me?" Chip asked him, between kisses.

Dawson thought about it for a moment. "Can I fuck your thighs?" he asked.

Chip grinned. "Fuck yes."

Their physical relationship had progressed slowly as they'd learned what they both liked. Very early on, they'd come to the conclusion that penetrative sex held no interest for either of them. Dawson had done some research online—as he was known to do—and had figured out that they weren't tops, or bottoms, but sides. He liked the term, and Chip would tease, saying that Dawson was his "side piece," but that was okay because Chip was his. Perhaps it wasn't a typical relationship between two men, but then again, what *was* typical? No two relationships were the same and given that they were stepbrothers, Chip was demi, and Dawson had a low libido thanks to his meds, it wasn't like they had a hope in hell of *ever* being considered typical. They were happy though, and that was what counted.

Chip grabbed the lube and then fell onto the bed and squeezed out a dollop of lube onto his hand. He gestured Dawson forward and he knee-walked across the mattress until he was within reach. He groaned as Chip took him in his slick hand, and Dawson couldn't help but pump his cock into Chip's fist a few times. "Feels so good," he said, eyes falling closed in bliss.

"It'll feel even better soon," Chip said, and let go of Dawson's dick to wipe the remaining lube between his thighs.

Dawson leaned down and kissed Chip, even as he nudged the head of his cock against the taut muscles in Chip's legs. He loved this so much. Chip had some seriously amazing thighs and sliding his cock between them, feeling the powerful muscles clamp around him, was one of Dawson's favourite things. He pushed forward and groaned as he felt the contrast between the smoother skin on the inside of Chip's thighs and the rasp of the hair on the outside.

It didn't take long to set a rhythm and soon he was rocking his hips, pushing his cock in and out of the tight, warm space between Chip's legs. His cock would brush against Chip's balls every now and then and even press against his perineum, which would elicit a gasp or a moan. They shared messy kisses, tasting the salty sweat on the other's skin, and soon Chip was reaching down between them to take himself in hand, jacking himself in time to Dawson's thrusts.

Chip came first, as was usual. Dawson took a lot longer, and sometimes couldn't even finish, but tonight he climbed the precipice and was able to fall over the edge. He cried out as he came, spilling himself between Chip's legs, before slumping down on top of him.

"Oomph," Chip groaned.

"Shut it," Dawson mumbled against his chest. "I'm not that heavy."

"Yeah you are," Chip teased, but he wound his arms around his back and held him tight, not allowing him to move.

Neither moved for a long while, both content to snuggle, but eventually Chip nudged him off. "My legs are going to be permanently glued together if I don't get in the shower soon."

"You'd make a cute penguin," Dawson said around a yawn. "Waddling everywhere you went."

"I think you'd cry if you lost the ability to push your cock between my legs," Chip said. "But if that ever *does* happen, I'd waddle outside and find you the nicest rock I could."

"Awww, you're the perfect penguin boyfriend," Dawson cooed.

They laughed as they climbed out of bed and, still naked, headed for the shower. They'd clean up and then maybe make a cup of tea, have a snack, and then wile away the rest of the night together. Neither of them had to be up early tomorrow so they didn't have to go to bed just yet. Chip would probably read, and Dawson would probably film him reading and make it into a video to post on Vewz, sharing with the world their version of domestic bliss.

Dawson had never expected his life would take such a turn when he and Chip moved into Grandpa Miller's old farmhouse, but he was eternally grateful that it had. Even if things *did* still occasionally go bump in the night—that just seemed to be part and parcel of owning a haunted house.

The end.

About the author

Addison Acres has a big smile and a gentle temperament which leads many to believe that she is sweet and innocent. Given that she loves to write raunchy stories, many with a hefty dash of kink and taboo, this is patently untrue.

Addision lives in the Wheatbelt of Western Australia, swears like a pirate, and is a profound supporter of the Oxford comma.

Come join her Facebook group, Addison's Addicts, or check out her websitehttps://addisonacresauthor.mailerpage.io/. You can also subscribe to her newsletter for freebies, news, and her general ramblings.

Also by Addison Acres

<u>The Tally Marks Series</u>
Festival of Fun
Friday Night Fun
Midnight Fun
Festive Fun in the Sun (Coming soon)
<u>Standalone Titles</u>
The Accidental Summoning
By The Light Of The Full Moon
<u>Free Short Stories</u>
Familiar (The Accidental Summoning 1.5)